Deadly Degree

An Amanda Winters Mystery

by

Carmen Will

Copyright © 2018 by Carmen Will

For information, email Cozy Cat Press, cozycatpress@aol.com or visit our website at: www.cozycatpress.com

COZY CAT
PRESS

ISBN: 978-1-946063-59-5

Printed in the United States of America

10 9 8 7 6 5 4 3 2 1

Dedication

For Paul, David, and Andy: The three of you have always been my inspiration. Believe it or not, I write for you as much as I write for me.

For Leah, John, and Danny: You've each been blessed with unparalleled levels of creativity and sensitivity that lift the spirits of all those around you. I'm so very proud to be your Grammy.

For Wayne . . . always.

Prologue

Everyone who knew Sherry Davenport said she was born to be a model: five feet, eight inches tall, 114 pounds, well-defined cheekbones, thick black hair that fell in a perfect cascade to her shoulders…she had it all. Sherry did, in fact, give modeling a try, but she quickly became bored with the endless hours of sitting, standing, and posing, not to mention all the inane directives tossed at her by photographers: *Sherry, sweetie, glance over your left shoulder and look coy. Sherry, honey, purse your lips and look seductive. Sherry, darling, put your hands on your hips and look defiant.*

But the only thing Sherry wanted to do was read. She read everything she could get her hands on: newspapers, magazines, blogs on current events and the culinary arts, novels, biographies—she even managed to pack in a bit of reading during film reloads at photo shoots. After an uncomfortable situation involving a lovestruck agent who couldn't take no for an answer, Sherry decided she'd had enough. A good lawyer got her out of a three-year contract, and she terminated her relationship with the Haskell-Neeley Agency in Los Angeles. Within a week, she enrolled in the English program at St. Priscilla's University, a private institution nestled on a five-acre greensward that bridged Phoenix and Chandler, Arizona. Sherry never looked back, first completing her bachelor's degree in English literature, then a master's in comparative literature, and finally a doctorate in educational philosophy. She considered it her good fortune that the dwindling number of novitiates entering the order of the Sisters of the Blessed Redeemer was compelling the diocese to recruit professionals from the laity. Sherry was hired to replace Sister Clara Runkel, who'd retired after overseeing St. Priscilla's English Department for fifty years. This year marked Sherry's third as chair of the university's English Department. In her view, the special bond she enjoyed with her colleagues and students was the most rewarding part of her job. She loved them, and they loved her right back. Or so she believed.

That August Monday morning (Sherry's last), the temperature had reached 88 degrees by six a.m. As usual, Sherry had been the first to arrive at the English Department's suite of faculty and staff offices. She adjusted the thermostat to crank up the air-conditioning, turned on the overhead lights, opened the blinds to let in some natural light, and flipped Mr. Coffee's on-switch. After taking a moment to savor the delectable aroma of Colombian Supremo, she inspected the office that Amanda Winters would be using for the next six weeks and smiled with satisfaction. Everything was in order: The computer and printer were wired, the phone had been connected, and the cream roses she'd arranged in a vase to welcome Amanda looked lovely, their fragrance sweet but not overpowering. The wingback chair Sherry had borrowed for Amanda's Aunt Sally was positioned in a corner near the window and looked comfortable and inviting.

With a heavy sigh, Sherry pulled the door shut, poured coffee into her mug, and went to the office that served as her private retreat. Her first order of business would not be pleasant. She turned on her computer and noted the clock: seven a.m. The staff wouldn't be in for another hour, which would give her some quiet time to decide how to handle the disturbing situation that she'd recently become privy to. She hoped she was wrong. She hoped that the whole mess was just a horrible mistake, her misinterpretation of a completely benign set of circumstances. She shuddered at the thought of what lay in store for her—and for St. Priscilla's—if she was right.

After taking care of a few emails, Sherry put together a list of the files she'd need from the basement archive; some of the files contained information that would confirm her findings. Sister Fred, St. Priscilla's beloved president, would be heartbroken to hear the allegations that Sherry would be bringing to her today.

Sherry took the elevator down two floors to the basement. The corridors, used mainly by Security and Maintenance staff, were dimly lit as usual, and she passed no one on her way to the archive, referred to by employees as "the Tomb" because of its heavy iron door and gloomy interior. She set about collecting the files she needed, some of them belonging to recent graduates who'd requested copies of official transcripts, the rest belonging to alumni who'd last set foot on campus years, or even decades, earlier.

Sherry had gathered the last of the folders when she heard the sound of footsteps behind her. "I guess I'm not the only one to get an early start on things today." Attempting to convey a cheerful mood, she turned to see who'd entered the room. Her lighthearted façade vanished when she saw the person standing just inside the doorway, staring at her with what could only be described as malevolence. "Well, this is a surprise...." She managed a weak smile, but the tremor in her voice betrayed her unease. When Sherry saw the second figure—knife in hand—enter the room and move toward her, she clutched the folders close to her body as if they might serve as a shield. "What are you doing?!"

The heavy door closed with a shudder. While one figure watched, the other continued toward her steadily and silently. Numb with shock, Sherry could focus only on the knife, which was now so close to her throat that she could almost feel the edge of its blade.

Chapter One

"I didn't kill her, I tell you! I didn't do it!" The little
man pulled a handkerchief from his pocket and dabbed
beads of sweat from his brow. "In any case, you have
no proof!"

Perry Mason, eyes smoldering, hands in pockets,
sauntered up to the witness stand. "Ah, Mr. Dalrymple,
but you're quite wrong. I do indeed have proof."

This was the pivotal moment. My heart quickened as
I leaned forward to get a closer look at Perry going in
for the kill. Unlike today's popular crime series, Perry
didn't need a decomposing corpse or a sophisticated
computer program to nail the bad guy. Back in the day,
a cigarette butt left behind in an ashtray or a lipstick
smudge on a martini glass was sufficient.

I was nursing my morning coffee and had passed on
the local news in favor of some classic TV when a
high-pitched ping echoed through the hallway to alert
me that I'd received an email. I hit "pause" on the
remote and made my way to the guest room that served
as the office where I worked part-time as a freelance
copy editor. Sixteen years ago, I was diagnosed with
"cluster C," a personality disorder consisting of various
phobias and what I like to call "quirks." The disorder
prevents me from driving a car for more than a few
familiar blocks or working in a typical office setting—
meaning one that I have to share with other people. A
remote job is the best option for me and any potential
colleagues who might have a problem working next to
someone who could, without warning, hyperventilate,

collapse during a bout of vertigo, and occasionally lose consciousness.

At my desk, I pulled up my email account: DetectiveAmandaWinters@gmail.com. I'm not actually a bona fide detective, but my ancillary role with the Maricopa County Sheriff's Department gives me a certain license to blow my own horn a little without being too obvious. The new message was a reminder from the library about a book that was due by the end of the week. I'd somehow missed an earlier ping signaling the arrival of an email from my good friend Sherry Davenport, chair of the English Department at St. Priscilla's, one of the oldest and most respected private universities in Arizona's East Valley. During her graduate studies, Sherry had completed a practicum at the local high school where I'd taught English until my panic attacks became so disruptive that the school board "advised" me to find employment elsewhere. Before St. Priscilla's entire enrollment process had gone online, I'd helped out the English Department during registration sessions each semester. It was during these registrations and St. Priscilla's special events that Sherry and I had developed a close friendship. Unlike a few of my one-time friends, she never lost patience with the unpredictable symptoms of my panic disorder or let them negatively impact our relationship.

In her email, Sherry thanked me again for accepting her job offer. An odd "P.S." that she'd tacked onto the end of the message said, "I hope you won't regret it—things may be about to get pretty uncomfortable around here." I'd have to ask her what she meant by that. Sherry's email also confirmed that I was to start my temp assignment that day. For the next six weeks, I'd be meeting with the English Department's graduate students in a small private office in Raslin Hall to help them polish their master's theses. I sighed and pressed my eyes shut. Because of my cluster C, the only way I'd been able to accept Sherry's offer was to get her to agree to my bringing along an "anchor" who could drive me to and from the university each day and help me navigate the campus and its people, thereby reducing my anxiety and its associated risk of panic attacks.

Aunt Sally, my late dad's 72-year-old baby sister, would be that anchor. At first, she resisted: "Really, Amanda? What am I—a service dog?!"

I was relieved when she'd reluctantly given in. I'd finally regained her trust: A year had passed since I'd managed to get the two of us trapped in an abandoned copper mine with only a bottle of water and a stale, pretty-much flattened cheese Danish to sustain us. Technically, that hadn't been my fault—the rockslide that had blocked the entrance had been orchestrated by a cold-blooded killer.

Of course, in exchange for Aunt Sally's help with my new job, I had to promise to treat her to six weeks of lunches in the university commons, whose aesthetics were so pleasing and whose offerings were so mouth-watering that many believed it was St. Priscilla's biggest draw for potential students.

"What am I supposed to do all afternoon while you're working with those knucklehead students?" she'd asked.

"I wish you wouldn't call them that, Aunt Sally. They're good students who just need a little help, like we all do sometimes."

"I don't know, Amanda—this gig sounds like a real yawner to me."

"You can bring a book, work on your sudoku puzzles…and I'll bring my laptop and headphones so you can watch movies if you want. It's just four hours a day—one to five p.m. And you don't have to be at my side the whole time. I'm not completely helpless."

"I guess I'll do it. I don't have any better offers right now."

"Thanks," I said, wishing that my pesky anxiety disorder would magically disappear so I could live like a normal human being.

I'd arranged for Aunt Sally to pick me up each day at 11 a.m., which would give us plenty of time to make our way through the student lunch lines and nab a small table in the commons well before my first student's arrival. (Long tables full of strangers tend to kill my appetite.)

As I sent off an email to Carole Ann Trebley, the English Department's secretary, to ask if she'd assigned us a particular space in the faculty lot, the phone rang. Not being a fan of incoming calls thanks to my avoidant personality disorder (another gift courtesy of cluster C), I broke out in a cold sweat and stared at the phone with dread. Someone, of course, was calling with bad news. I breathed a sigh of relief when I saw "StPriscU" on the screen. It must be Sherry, calling to make sure I hadn't changed my mind about the assignment.

"Hey, Sherry, I'm ready, willing, and ab—"

"Amanda, you—you're home!" It was Carole Ann, her voice uncharacteristically shrill.

I opened my eyes and peered at the monitor in front of me, where a tiny, round icon continued to rotate sluggishly, indicating that my email to Carole Ann was stuck somewhere in transit. I needed a more reliable Internet provider, but I was determined to explore five options before making a decision, and I still had two to go. "Wow, Carole Ann, you're good. You didn't even get my email yet. How did you—"

"Amanda, stop—Sherry's dead!"

See?! This is why I have major problems with answering the phone. Carole Ann's words entered my brain one by one, but they failed to link together to form a meaningful sentence. Sherry couldn't be dead. She was only 38 years old, not to mention the healthiest person I've ever known, a vegan yoga enthusiast who spent her lunch hours working out in the faculty gym.

"Not possible," I said numbly. "I just got an email from her." I was pretty sure dead people couldn't send emails. At least I didn't think technology had come that far. I checked the time Sherry's message had been sent: 7:10 a.m. It was now almost 9:30.

"It's quite possible, Amanda. She was murdered." I heard Carole Ann put down the phone and blow her nose loudly. When she picked up again, she said, "Sherry was always the first one in the office every morning and the last one to leave—and look where it got her...."

"H-how?" I asked.

"Eddie from Security noticed blood on the floor just outside the Tomb. He found her inside. She was already dead. Amanda—her carotid artery was severed."

There was an extended period of silence as my mind attempted to process that horrible image. The Tomb was the basement archive that housed all kinds of university records and documents: alumni transcripts, old grade sheets handwritten in faded blue ink, green-lined cards painstakingly typed on Underwood typewriters, bankers' boxes stuffed with microfiche records, and decades' worth of musty catalogs. There were even Gimbels' shopping bags full of manila folders that thrifty nuns, it was rumored, had hand-washed and hung on clotheslines to dry in the sun for reuse long before recycling had come into vogue.

It had taken nearly sixty years, but the Tomb had finally lived up to its name. I pressed my eyes closed…masked them with my hand, but the image remained. "W-who?!"

"W-who?!" Carole Ann repeated.

We sounded like a couple of panic-stricken owls. "Who did it? Who killed her?!"

"They don't know. They don't know anything yet."

"Are the police there?"

"The sheriff's office, the Phoenix and Chandler police and fire departments, investigators from the medical examiner's office—they're all here. They said they need to talk to all of us. Amanda, everything's been canceled for the day, so you don't have to come in."

"Yes, I do." For what reason, I had no idea. "I'll be there as soon as I can."

I replaced the receiver, and the phone immediately rang again. That would be Carole Ann, laughing at my incredible naiveté. *Sherry Davenport murdered. Ha! You fell for it!*

"Not funny!"

"Sweetheart? You okay?!"

I'd recognize that voice anywhere. It belonged to Terry, my husband of 26 years. "I thought this might be Carole Ann Trebley from St. Priscilla's. She called me a few seconds ago with some horrible news, and I was hoping it was just a very bad joke."

"What horrible news?" As an associate news producer with a local TV station, Terry was used to horrible news. But this news was even more horrible than usual because it had a familiar face.

"Sherry Davenport was murdered this morning. They found her in the basement archive with her throat cut."

"Oh my God, no! Was it one of the students?!"

I slipped into sandals and pulled a comb through my hair. "Carole Ann says they don't know anything yet.

I'm hoping to learn something when I get there. I need to get hold of Aunt Sally to tell her what happened and to see if she can pick me up early…the original plan called for her to be here at 11."

"I know how you must feel, but I wish you wouldn't go anywhere near St. Priscilla's right now."

I knew the sad narrative that Terry was likely replaying in his mind. Our godson, Nathan Reynolds, had been murdered a year ago, and we still hadn't recovered from that tragedy. I doubt that we ever will.

"I'll be all right, Terry. Carole Ann says the place is swarming with all sorts of official types. I promise to check in with you later."

"Don't forget."

"I won't. So why did you call me, anyway?"

"No special reason…just wanted to say I love you."

"I happen to think that's a pretty special reason. I love you, too."

When kids take flight and leave parents untended, one of two things happen: You drift apart as a couple, no longer having anything in common, or you cling to each other for dear life, finding new things to talk about, discovering each other all over again. Terry and I had chosen the latter. The romance that had been the basis of our courtship and marriage, but had languished as we turned our attention to raising our son Jeff, had returned with full force. I closed my eyes and imagined his arms around me now.

Terry's voice was tentative. "Are you sure you want to go through this again? Maybe I should come home…."

"Thanks, but we both know I can't have you leaving work and running to my side every time—" I didn't know how to finish the sentence…*every time someone I love is murdered?*

Among my cluster C symptoms, chronic panic disorder, social anxiety, and agoraphobia are the most disruptive. I'm now able to leave the house as long as I'm with a trusted companion (the aforementioned anchor). Working at home and limiting my driving to within a few miles of my house have given me the illusion that I have some control over my environment, although lately, some small part of me has been chastising myself for simply giving in. Therapy hasn't proven effective for me, and I opt not to take medication. Left to my own devices, I'm able to think clearly most of the time, and I'm usually able to stay awake until ten p.m.

I was able to connect with Aunt Sally via her cell phone and explained the change of plans.

"What is this, Amanda—did you join the murder-of-the-year club or something?" My silence prompted her to add, "I'm sorry, hon. I know she was a good friend."

Arnold, Aunt Sally's classic Cadillac convertible, pulled into the drive 15 minutes later. She took one look at me and said, "I hope those aren't your work clothes."

"I won't be working today, Aunt Sally. You'll have to forgive me—I couldn't find anything suitable to wear to a murder."

She shook her head. "At least change that T-shirt. It's got some kind of stain on it that looks like Florida."

I ran into the bedroom, whipped off the T-shirt, and threw on a clean one before hurrying back out into the living room. "There. Are you satisfied now?"

Aunt Sally looked me up and down. "Not really, but if it's the best you can do—"

I grabbed her arm and nudged her out through the front door. "Right now, it's the best I can do."

The route to St. Priscilla's from Sun Lakes zigzagged through narrow streets and crowded avenues.

Since I don't do well with traffic, I'd asked Aunt Sally to avoid the I-10 freeway and 101 loop. As I gazed out the passenger window, I saw everything through a surreal fog, as if I were in a dream. I was well-acquainted with the many houses and strip malls we passed, but now they appeared as strange as the notion that someone could murder Sherry Davenport, an idea my mind had not yet been able to process.

As we drove through St. Priscilla's park-like grounds and pulled into a space near Raslin Hall, reality took over. I marveled that nothing had changed with respect to the campus proper. Other than the fact that the north parking lot was crowded with emergency vehicles and very few students were on the walking paths, everything looked the same. There were the familiar red-brick buildings: the Edward Anderson Theater, the Colton-Smith Art Gallery, the Elizabeth Rafferty College of Nursing, Thatcher House, which contained the student dorm rooms, and Raslin Hall, the large I-shaped administration building. All the buildings were surrounded by courtyards dotted with benches and fountains, and connected via flagstone paths lined with Mexican fan palms.

The room where Sherry's body had been found was located in the basement of Raslin's south wing, opposite the main parking lot. As we walked toward the building, I noted where all the doors and emergency exits were located. Assuming the killer had accessed Raslin via the front doors, he or she would have had to walk the length of the first floor to the south elevator or stairs, or take the north elevator down to the basement and walk past the Maintenance and security offices. Someone in the right place at the right time would have seen something. A stranger roaming through the corridors would have been noticed.

I checked my face in the side mirror of a parked pickup and gasped in horror. My eyes were bloodshot and swollen, and my face had taken on a weird reddish hue that wasn't at all attractive. I hadn't applied make-up—or showered—that morning. I looked down at my feet to make sure my sandals matched. They looked pretty much the same, except one was black and the other brown—I figured that given the circumstances, no one would notice. With Aunt Sally trailing behind me, I hurried up a short flight of concrete steps and peered through one of two heavy glass doors before pulling it open. The main reception area was deserted, its large, crescent-shaped desk unstaffed by the full-time attendant, Lynn Goodman, or even the requisite student worker. I told Aunt Sally to stay put at the desk.

"I'll be back in a little while. I just want to try and find out what happened."

"I'll tell you what happened: Someone just murdered your friend in the basement of this building. Amanda, I hate to dwell on this point, but your life is beginning to look like reruns of *Murder She Wrote*. Don't be surprised if people start to avoid you." She examined me critically, her eyes taking me in head to foot. "And don't even get me started on the subject of personal hygiene."

I exhaled and counted to ten. "Please, Aunt Sally. Just wait here for me. I want to see if I can get some details. I'll be all right as long as I can see you from the mezzanine." I started up the stairs, then turned back to add, "And don't touch anything."

Raslin Hall's third and fourth floors accommodated classrooms for the College of Arts and Sciences, while the Admissions Office, commons, and library comprised one half of the first floor; several meeting rooms, a solarium, and Sister Fred's administrative suite took up the other half. Academic departments

were located in the second floor's east wing, and the
west wing housed the Academic Advising, Financial
Aid, Registrar's, and Business offices. A large
mezzanine overlooked the first-floor reception area and
featured stairways at each end that gave access to the
floors above and below it.

People were gathered in clusters along the
mezzanine's balustrade. Standing in a close huddle with
Tony Loduca, Sherry's assistant chair, and a few people
I didn't recognize, was Roy Staatz, deputy commander
of the District 1 Maricopa County Sheriff's Office. I'd
met Roy during his investigation of my godson's
murder. He and Nathan's mother, my best friend Dinah
Reynolds, have been dating for several months, so I've
gotten to know him quite well. Roy doesn't only have
good taste in women, he also has good judgment when
it comes to hiring them. After I'd helped him with
Nathan's murder investigation, he arranged for me to
work as a consultant on District 1 cases. A bonus is that
the sheriff's outpost where Roy is stationed is within
both my walking and tolerable driving ranges.

Roy acknowledged my presence with a curious
frown before returning to his conversation with Loduca.
At the balustrade, Carole Ann stood posed like a
mannequin, her arms crossed in front of her, hands to
elbows. When I noticed her body begin to sway, I
hurried over and put an arm around her waist. "You
okay?"

She brushed aside a fall of curly brown bangs and
aimed a tearful gaze at me. "No, I'm not okay. Amanda,
what are we going to do?"

"We're going to take a few days to mourn our loss.
And when we return on Thursday, we'll take things a
day at a time, continue to do what we do every day—
teach our students, go to meetings, the usual." The
voice boomed from a broad-shouldered woman in a

lightweight burgundy tweed suit and sensible black pumps. A sturdy woman of 64 whose steel-gray pageboy resembled a WWII Wehrmacht helmet, President Frederica Abner—Sister Fred, as she was known to students and employees alike—made a point of knowing everyone at the university and everyone's business to boot. No one questioned her wisdom or her authority...ever. Today, her normally clear eyes were red and puffy: Despite her brave front, she'd done a fair amount of crying during the past few hours.

She examined my disheveled appearance with overt disapproval. Not good. Sister Fred still hadn't forgiven me for being a Protestant, let alone an unkempt Protestant with a panic disorder. "Amanda, I presume no one told you that your services wouldn't be required today?"

I placed one foot behind the other in an attempt to hide my mismatched shoes. "I need to be here, Sister Fred. Sherry was a good friend."

"Well, since you do have a quasi-official role with the Sheriff's department these days, I suppose you can stay. However, if it comes to my attention that your presence is interfering with the investigation currently underway, I won't hesitate to ask you to leave."

The reputation I'd earned for getting in Roy's way now and then during my godson's murder investigation had apparently reached St. Priscilla's. Before I could think of an appropriate response, Sister Fred dismissed me with a pat of her hair and turned to Carole Ann. "You look a bit pale, dear. Unless Detective Staatz needs anything more from you, I want you to take the rest of the day off and go home. We're closing down the campus for a few days, in any case. There's no need to have students and staff mucking about a crime scene. Beginning Thursday...business as usual."

Carole Ann looked to me as if seeking confirmation before responding. "Well, if you're sure...."

"I'm quite sure." Sister Fred raised a hand to summon Roy, who'd moved on to question a woman who looked to be about nine months pregnant, someone whose name I couldn't remember. The mother-to-be, who worked in the Advising Office, held a protective hand atop her prominent belly and cast a tearful glance at Sister Fred, who was now waving her hand wildly to capture Roy's attention. "Excuse me, Officer...."

Roy turned his attention from the pregnant woman and approached Sister Fred. "It's Detective Roy Staatz, ma'am."

"Detective Staatz is a deputy commander with the Maricopa County Sheriff's Department," I added. Although Roy elected to use the designation of "detective" for practical reasons, I saw no reason to keep his impressive new title a secret.

Sister Fred extended a hand to Roy. "I'm Sister Frederica Abner, president of St. Priscilla's. Please let me know if you require assistance of any kind." She pulled a white handkerchief from her sleeve and used it to dab her forehead before continuing. "Are you familiar with the namesake of this university, Detective?"

Roy peered at her over the top of his John Lennon glasses. "Ma'am?"

"Priscilla was a noble martyr of the Church. She was a wife and mother whose husband was put to death for one reason and one reason alone: His wife happened to be a Christian. Despite Priscilla's tragic loss, however, she remained true to her faith. Saint Peter himself was a frequent guest at Priscilla's house in Rome."

"That's all very fascinating, ma'am—Sister—but..."

"Yes, well, I believe that anyone with an interest in what goes on here should have a clear understanding of the university's legacy. Now, may my staff leave as soon as you've finished questioning them?" She flicked some invisible lint from her lapel. "We've already canceled the day's classes and all staff meetings."

"Yes, of course. We'll need complete contact information in case we have further questions."

Sister Fred shooed Carole Ann toward the stairs. "Go on home, dear. You heard the man."

I gave Carole Ann a reassuring hug. "I'll see you Thursday."

"Really? I mean, considering what happened, everyone would understand if you want to back out of the temp job."

"No. I gave my word to Sherry, and I'm going to keep it. I'm afraid you'll have to get used to seeing me around here for a while."

Carole Ann made her way down the stairs to the front entrance as if she were sleepwalking. At the balustrade, I followed her progress and, from the corner of my eye, noticed that Aunt Sally was intently rummaging through the contents of one of the reception desk's drawers. I considered throwing a pen over the railing to get her attention so I could tell her to stop, but then figured no harm was being done—she appeared to be only looking, not taking. When I turned back to look for Roy, I saw that he'd escaped Sister Fred and was proceeding with his questioning of the staff. Tony Loduca and Ian Malcolm, director of Financial Aid, were engaged in quiet conversation at the mezzanine wall opposite the balustrade, where several framed paintings by the university's art students were on display.

I decided to take a peek at the office where I'd be working. Other than the entire department being empty at this normally busy hour, one would never guess that the day had gone horribly wrong—that a young woman had just been murdered two floors below. Carole Ann's desk, its surface uncluttered as always, was positioned to welcome students as they walked through the door into the suite. Beyond Carole Ann's desk was the door to Sherry's office. I turned a corner and moved along a narrow hallway. All the doors to the English faculty offices were open, the work spaces significantly more modest than Sherry's. They were cozy and served their purpose, however, affording privacy to meet with students and a quiet place to eat lunch if the occupants didn't feel like tramping down to the commons or across the street to the Perk-Up Café. I opened the door at the end of the hallway, and as soon as I saw the flowers on the desk and the wingback chair in the corner, I knew that this was to be my office. It was just like Sherry to go out of her way to make me and Aunt Sally feel welcome and comfortable. I closed my eyes in an attempt to stem a new rush of tears and tried not to think of what her final moments on this earth had been like. Abruptly, the room started to spin, and my arms and legs turned to rubber.

As I fought off the first wave of what promised to be a full-fledged panic attack, a shadow darkened the doorway to the office, and a soft voice said, "Amanda?"

I pivoted to face the door and saw a tall brunette standing there.

"Sherry," I said, just before everything went black.

Chapter Two

When I came to, I was seated in the wingback chair, which was now in a reclining position in a corner of the office. Roy Staatz was standing over me, his face a mask of worry. "Are you all right?"

I found the side control handle and pulled the chair to a sitting position. "I think so. I—I thought I saw Sherry."

"You saw me, Amanda." My best friend Dinah Reynolds appeared from behind Roy and knelt in front of the chair. "Panic attack?"

I shook my head. "I felt one starting, but it never had a chance to develop. I think I just fainted from plain old shock. Dinah, you really do look like Sherry. Your hair, the shape of your face…."

Dinah gave me a sad smile. "I'll take that as a very generous compliment." She glanced up at Roy, then back at me, her eyes reflecting concern. "I heard what happened, and I knew you were supposed to start your temp job today. When I couldn't reach you, I called Aunt Sally on her cell, and she told me that the two of you were here. I know how close you and Sherry were. Amanda, I'm so sorry."

"Where *is* Aunt Sally?" I tried to rise from the chair and, when the room started to spin, sat back down. "I have to find her—"

"She's fine," said Roy. "I sent her to the commons with Deputy Spanner."

Dinah handed me a bottle of water. "Here, drink."

"Thanks." After a few minutes, I rose to my feet. "I'm good now."

"Just rest here for a bit," said Dinah.

"No—I'm fine...really." I made a move toward the door, and she caught my arm. "You don't want to go out there right now. They're getting ready to transport Sherry's body to the medical examiner's office."

I pulled my arm free. "It's all right."

We went out to the hallway and down the stairs to the first floor. Three attendants were in the process of lifting the gurney holding Sherry's body into the back of an ambulance. She appeared even more slender in death, her form a narrow oblong mound beneath a black vinyl sheet.

Suddenly, I wanted to see the murder scene—had to see it. I needed to do whatever I could to learn the circumstances surrounding Sherry's death. I owed her that much. "Dinah, come with me to the commons? I want to see if Aunt Sally's ready to drive me home."

"Sure." She turned to Roy. "See you tonight for dinner?"

"You bet. Remember, you're cooking." I loved that my best friend had found someone. Someone who could help her recover from the loss of her son.

She smiled. "Oh, don't worry—I won't forget." Taking my arm, she said, "Let's go see how Deputy Spanner is getting along with Aunt Sally."

"Uh-huh." But as soon as Roy was out of sight, I steered Dinah into the hallway leading to an enclosed stairway.

"Where are you going? The commons is on this floor."

"I know, but I want to go down to the basement first."

"I don't think Roy would approve."

I opened the door to the stairway and turned to look at her over my shoulder. "He won't know unless you tell him. And you won't have to lie, because why would he even think to ask?"

"All right. But if he *does* ask, I'm not going to lie."

We took the stairs down to the basement and passed two uniformed police officers from the Chandler Police Department who were engaged in an animated discussion about the Cardinals' upcoming season. I fully expected them to stop us, but they were so focused on their conversation that they didn't even glance our way. The door to the Tomb stood wide open, and Dinah and I linked arms as we approached it slowly. From working the registrations, I knew that no one was overly keen about having to look for a student record in the windowless room: The fluorescent ceiling lights flickered and sometimes fizzled out for unknown reasons despite the Maintenance Department's best efforts. Even worse, the Tomb featured a thick, vault-style door that was known to swing shut, seemingly at its whim, to trap some hapless employee inside. The door had been propped open with an old iron anvil, a doorstop that was rarely used because it was simply too heavy for most people to move.

We stopped dead in our tracks, both of us gasping as we caught sight of the blood. There was lots of it, a dark expanse of wetness that reflected an eerie purple hue in the harsh light. The killer hadn't been playing around. Judging by the blood's proximity to the door, Sherry had either just entered the room or was getting ready to leave it when she'd met her killer.

A number of manila folders, their contents spilling out onto the concrete floor, lay just beyond the pool of blood. There was also a lined sheet of note paper on which someone had printed a list of names and numbers. I broke free of Dinah and, giving the blood a wide berth, walked over to where the files, speckled with red, were fanned out like a grisly hand of poker.

"Amanda, I don't think you should touch anything."

"I'm just looking," I said, then immediately stooped to retrieve the small sheet of paper, which I quickly crumpled and stuffed into my pocket. I bent closer to get a good look at the folders when I saw something glinting on the floor beneath the edge of one of the file cabinets. A stern voice echoed from the hallway just as I was closing my fingers around the small object: a ring.

"Excuse me, ladies, but you can't be in here." Apparently the officers in the hall had noticed us after all. One of them was the approximate age of my son Jeff. Hands on hips in an authoritative stance, he now stood in the doorway. "This is a crime scene, and Forensics hasn't been here yet. I'll have to ask both of you to leave right now."

Dinah tossed me a glance that said *I told you so.*

"Sorry, Officer." I looked to Dinah for support, but she'd dropped back against the wall in an apparent attempt to make herself invisible. "The door was open. I'm—I was a friend of the victim."

The young officer directed his eyes at the pool of blood, then back at me. Without another word he raised an arm, urging Dinah and me out into the hallway. We made our way through the basement's main corridor, past Security and Maintenance, and took the elevator back to the first floor. "I hope he doesn't report us to Roy," said Dinah.

"How can he?" I dropped the ring into my purse. "He didn't even ask for our names."

We found Aunt Sally sitting at the reception desk, flipping through a magazine she'd found. "Are you ready to go?" she asked. "Because I sure am...everyone around here is a gloomy Gus. This place is about as lively as a funeral home."

I started to scold her but thought better of it. This wasn't the time to get into an argument over the importance of sensitivity. "I'll be just another minute. I want to see if Roy's free."

Dinah and I took the stairs up to the mezzanine, where I learned that Tony Loduca had been looking for me. A 28-year-old computer geek, Tony had been in his position as Sherry's assistant chair for only a few weeks. It was clear to most everyone that, while adept at technology, he might be a bit over his head when it came to other functions expected of an assistant chair: communicating with faculty and staff, for instance.

"Amanda, I understand that you're going to go ahead and start your temp position Thursday?"

"That's right."

He reached out and touched my arm. "Thanks for hanging in there with us. I'm sure this must be difficult for you."

"Murder is difficult for everyone, don't you think?" said Dinah.

He glanced at her with a flash of annoyance. "Of course," he said, then took off abruptly toward the English Department.

Dinah raised her eyebrows. "Touchy, isn't he?"

I believed that Dinah's comment had been uncalled for, but since I knew that the memory of her son's murder had prompted it, I cut her some slack. "Could be he's already feeling the pressure of being in charge."

"I suppose." Dinah shrugged and checked the time on her phone. "Anyway, I have to get going. I'm scheduled for an open house this afternoon." She gave me a hug and stepped back to study my face. "Are you going to be all right?"

"Yes—but maybe not for a while."

After Dinah left, I used my cell to leave a message for Terry. I needed the comfort of hearing his voice. Because of my avoidant personality disorder, I'd never wanted a cell phone. Terry, however, had recently convinced me that placing calls to others is a harmless activity that even I could safely participate in and surprised me with a smartphone for my last birthday. I pulled the slip of paper I'd found from the pocket of my shorts and went to a quiet corner where I could examine the list of student names and ID numbers. Most of the numbers were old, some decades old, based on their juxtaposition to other numbers on the list. Sherry must have gone down to the Tomb to pull these files. But why? I knew that individual colleges occasionally received requests for copies of transcripts and sometimes retrieved the files for the Registrar's Office, but I couldn't figure out why the English Department would need that many old, inactive student files at one time. Faculty and staff generally worked with current files, and those were kept inside the department.

Roy looked to be finishing up a conversation with Laverne Hutchins, the Business Office's head cashier. As I made my way toward them, a wave of vertigo hit me like a bolt of lightning, and I grabbed the balustrade railing to steady myself. This particular kind of attack, a response to my agoraphobia, frequently strikes whenever I happen to find myself alone in open spaces and without an anchor person in sight. My dizziness subsided when I looked over the railing to home in on Aunt Sally, who'd discovered the recreational benefits of a desk chair that could swivel 360 degrees.

Roy was at my side within seconds. "Amanda, are you all right?"

"Maybe everyone I know should save their breath and make a recording of that phrase." I smiled weakly. "I'm fine."

"Do you have a few minutes?"

"I was about to ask you the same thing."

We took seats on one of the long, leather-upholstered benches opposite the balustrade. Roy cleared his throat and turned on his iPad. "I realize that you're not a full-time employee here, but you were a friend of the victim…so I have a few questions for you. First—how long did you know Ms. Davenport?"

"She'd want you to call her Sherry," I said with a half-smile. "She wasn't the formal type. We met when the two of us worked at Reagan High School while I was teaching English and she was doing a practicum. But we really got to know each other during registrations here at St. Priscilla's."

He frowned in confusion and said, "When I was in college, we registered for classes in the gym. There were long lines…crowds. Is that how they do it here?"

I nodded. "They do it exactly like that. The only difference is that now students can register online. But they still have to show up at registration to have the department chairs sign off on their schedules."

"How did you get through it when you worked registration—you know, with your cluster C?"

I shrugged. "I managed."

"It must have been difficult. Large open spaces, high ceilings, crowds.…"

Roy was well-acquainted with my disorder, including the agoraphobia part of it, a condition that also happened to plague his mother.

"I never had to set foot in the gym. Sherry let me review registration forms in the English Department, and the students would take them to the gym for signatures. It's all pretty computerized now—the university hasn't needed my help for the past few years."

Roy settled back on the bench and pulled a pack of Juicy Fruit from his pocket, rolled a stick, and popped it into his mouth. "Tell me about Sherry."

"She was vivacious, beautiful, smart...."

"Boyfriends?"

"She dated some, but the last time we spoke she complained that she was at the age where the only available men were rejects or—no offense, Roy—divorcés with overly close ties to their mothers."

Roy smiled. "No offense taken. But she never mentioned anyone serious?"

I shook my head. "She once told me that back in her modeling days, she'd dated one of the agency reps for a few months. She broke it off, and...let's just say the guy didn't take it well. But that was way before she worked at St. Priscilla's."

Roy made a note in his iPad and shrugged. "Some people have very long memories—and hold very long grudges. Do you have a name?"

I searched my memory and came up with a first name. "Travis something, I think."

Roy made a note and continued. "What about work? Did Sherry have any problems with students or employees?"

"Not that she ever said. She loved her job, and she never had a bad word to say about anyone."

It occurred to me, then, that if I wanted to examine the blood-spattered files I'd seen on the Tomb floor, I'd have to ask Roy about their disposition. And, of course, I couldn't do that, because then he'd know I'd been snooping around an active crime scene. I decided to put that question on hold and instead asked, "Roy, is it true...about the way she died?" I was desperate for it not to be true. Death by a blade to the throat could never be quick—or painless—enough.

Roy nodded. "Can you think of anyone who would want to do something like that to her?" He tossed out the question while typing something on his iPad, then stopped and studied my face.

I briefly considered my answer, dismissing the idea that anyone who knew Sherry would have reason to kill her. "Sherry had lots of friends, but enemies? Never in a million years."

"Well, Amanda, it looks like she had at least one."

Chapter Three

That night Terry grilled steaks for dinner after settling me on the patio with a glass of wine.

"Mmm," I said. "Kendall Jackson Merlot—2009?"

"Yes, indeed. I wanted you to have something you love."

"Well, I have you. But this is one terrific bonus."

He walked over to the gas grill and lifted the lid. Minutes later, a wonderful sizzling caused me to salivate like one of Pavlov's dogs hearing the bell. Meat fork in hand, Terry turned to me and said, "It's been a rough day. You should turn in early and get a good night's sleep."

"I can't believe this is happening again." I sipped the wine and let the sweet cherry notes play on my tongue.

"Murder, you mean?"

"Yes, that's exactly what I mean. Terry, most people don't come face-to-face with one homicide, let alone multiples. It's kind of like lightning…you wouldn't expect it to strike a person more than once." Remembering Aunt Sally's *Murder, She Wrote* comment, I continued, "Two people that were close to us have been murdered in just over a year. Don't you find that odd?"

Terry sliced a New York strip in half and loaded our plates with the steak, crisp sliced potatoes, and mushrooms. As he settled into the chair next to me, he said, "It's more than odd—it's downright alarming. I really wish you wouldn't go back to St. Priscilla's

Thursday—not unless Staatz has arrested Sherry's murderer by then."

"Those students need to finish their theses in order to graduate, and I'm going to help them do it." I took another sip of wine. "Besides, the campus is on major security watch right now. I'll probably be safer there than I would be anyplace else."

Terry took his good-natured time enjoying some food and wine before speaking, and I knew that he was using the time to measure his words carefully. "You said yourself that there was no reason for anyone to want to hurt Sherry. If her murder was a random act, don't you have to assume the killer is some crazed lunatic who could strike again?"

I shuddered at the prospect of some maniac clutching a knife and lurking in a dark corner of St. Priscilla's basement, waiting for his next victim. "As you well know, darling, I don't assume anything when it comes to murder."

***

I spent Tuesday and Wednesday cleaning up a couple of editing projects I'd been avoiding. Both were articles for academic journals—one on obesity in rats, and the other on the spending habits of teenagers in China. Needless to say, I was happy when Thursday came along.

Aunt Sally and I walked into Raslin Hall at noon and immediately headed for the commons to enjoy our first lunch there. I marveled at the twenty-foot-long salad bar, its glass protector spotless and reflecting a scattering of tiny white circles from the Italian pendant lights suspended above it. Being among the first in line, we were rewarded with a wide array of fresh fruits and vegetables before moving on to the hot entrée station. Despite the wonderful aromas that permeated the cafeteria, however, the collective mood remained somber, a holdover from Monday.

After lunch we took the elevator up to the English Department. In my office, I settled Aunt Sally into her cozy corner with a sudoku and went back out to the reception area to have a quick chat with Carole Ann. A handful of faculty members, some I knew and some I didn't, greeted us with nods or half-waves as they passed through to their offices. Sherry's murder had brought a black cloud to the department, but everyone knew that Sherry herself would be the first person to say that all should continue as usual for the sake of the students.

"I guess I'll go to lunch," Carole Ann said, her thin face drawn, her eyes red and puffy behind tortoise-shell glasses. "Your first appointment's in 15 minutes. Do you have everything you need?"

"I think so—I'll have to check. Were you able to get any sleep the past few nights?"

"Some. You?"

"Some."

Carole Ann pulled her purse from her bottom desk drawer. "Sister Fred has declared a mandatory buddy system. No one can be alone anywhere on campus until further notice. Today I'm having lunch with Laverne from the Business Office."

"Laverne's always been willing to cash a personal check for me if there's a line at the ATM," I said. "I like that in a person."

Carole Ann chuckled and rolled her eyes. "Laverne's okay as long as she's not moaning and groaning about her husband's shortcomings."

I leaned in closer. "Shortcomings? What shortcomings?"

"Uh…never mind. I shouldn't have brought it up. When I get back, give me a list of any supplies you need."

"Thanks. I will." I stepped into the hallway and watched as she and Laverne made their way down the stairs to the first floor. A quick retreat to the familiarity of the suite was necessary, however, when noisy groups of students emerged from the stairways and elevator and bustled their way toward the Business Office to take care of fiscal concerns during their lunch period.

I returned to my office to find Aunt Sally seated at my desk with her hands poised above the computer keyboard. She was cracking her knuckles as if limbering up to play "Moonlight Sonata."

"I haven't used a computer since 1986," she said. "Funny…it's just like riding a bike—although I don't remember the keys being so danged small."

"Aunt Sally! I have my first appointment's records pulled up—confidential records!"

"Oh, calm down…I didn't see anything. Besides, I couldn't make out all that academic mumbo-jumbo. I just wanted to do some research."

"If you didn't see anything, how do you know about 'all that academic mumbo-jumbo' on the screen? And just what kind of research do you need to do?!" I circled around the desk to stand behind her and looked at the display. My mouth fell open. It wasn't porn, but one more click could have been big trouble. "'Sexy Single Seniors'?! Aunt Sally, are you trying to get me fired?!"

She brushed me off with a wave of her hand. "Come on, Amanda. Who could get fired from a temporary job?!" She paused and thoughtfully studied the ceiling. "Come to think of it…*you* probably could. Anyway, how would anyone know what we've got pulled up on this computer?"

"*You*, Aunt Sally—what *you've* got pulled up on this computer! And *anyone* would know because in this day and age, workplace computers are monitored to prevent this sort of thing."

She looked around the small room. "Are you saying this place is bugged?"

I was about to further explain some of the idiosyncrasies of a twenty-first-century office, when there was a light tapping on the door.

"Hello? Are you Mrs. Winters?" A young woman in jeans and a St. Priscilla's T-shirt tentatively stepped into the room.

I literally jumped to hit the "clear" key while simultaneously pushing Aunt Sally toward her chair.

"Yes, and you must be Kim Vong. This is my Aunt Sally. Do you mind if she stays in the office while we work?"

"Oh no...not at all. My mom has to watch my grandma during the day sometimes, too."

"Geez, Louise," said Aunt Sally, "do you ever have that one backwards." She gave Kim the once-over. "Are you Chinese?"

Kim frowned in bemusement. "I'm American. My grandparents are from Vietnam—"

Before Aunt Sally could ask which side they'd been on during the war, I pulled a chair up next to mine at the desk. "Have a seat, Kim, and we'll get started. "I have the thesis you emailed me on the screen."

But to my horror, what was on the screen was not Kim's thesis but a large photo of an eighty-year old man wearing nothing but a leopard-skin Speedo. The man, arms stretched out above him with his hands supporting his head, was lounging on a deck chair.

"Ugh, that's gross!" exclaimed Kim, narrowing her eyes to stare at the bizarre picture on the screen. "What are you into, anyway, Mrs. Winters?"

I glared at Aunt Sally, whose head was buried in her sudoku book, and turned the screen out of Kim's view with a jerk that would have sent the monitor flying if I hadn't grabbed onto it in the nick of time. "Oh, this?!" My voice came out in a squawk. "It's the craziest thing! Just some weird computer glitch, I'm guessing. I'll get your thesis back in a minute. In the meantime, why don't you open the APA style manual and find the chapter on citations?"

Despite its precarious beginning, my first student appointment went well. I logged out of the system and left Aunt Sally to watch a movie on my tablet, then ducked out to see if Carole Ann had returned from lunch. I thought I'd better cue her in on the computer fiasco just in case Kim decided to file a formal complaint. The last thing I needed was a sexual harassment grievance on my record.

"How'd it go?" asked Carole Ann. "Kim was just leaving as I was coming in."

"Really? Did she seem okay to you?"

"She seemed fine. Why?"

I explained what happened, and Carole Ann broke into laughter. "Oh my gosh, Amanda. Don't worry about it. I'm sure Kim's seen a lot worse than some old guy in swimming trunks!"

Grateful for Carole Ann's vote of confidence, I perched on the edge of her desk, and she spent a few minutes updating me on the university's staff and policy changes. "Detective Staatz has reinforced our Security with squad patrols, but remember the buddy system. Word is that Sister Fred has already suspended three students she caught walking alone on campus."

"You won't get any resistance from me there." I pointed toward my office. "My buddy is quite handy. Did you hear anything more about the investigation?"

Carole Ann shook her head. "No. And you'll probably hear something before I do, you being so close to Detective Staatz and all."

Staatz! I'd forgotten all about the ring, which was still buried in the purse I'd used the day I found it. And I still hadn't made a copy of the list of student names and ID numbers I'd found. It would be an understatement to say that Roy was going to be upset about the fact that I'd held onto what might be important evidence for three days. I promised myself to get the ring and the list to him as soon as possible, no matter the consequences.

The rest of the afternoon passed without incident. Tony poked his head into my office to thank me for coming in "despite everything that had happened." Sister Fred also checked in to make sure that all was running smoothly, and Carole Ann was kept busy rescheduling all the students whose appointments had been canceled Monday. I took a look at my next appointment: 2:00 p.m., Roberta Matthews, a re-entry. Roberta had left her graduate program 15 years earlier and was now coming back to complete her thesis and to finish up her degree.

Carole Ann had told me that information was being uploaded into the university's new information system by staff in the Registrar's Office during rare downtimes. The course data entry had been completed, but student records were being entered working backward from the current year. With the beginning of the new semester, data entry had been put on hold after completing the academic year 2007–2008, which meant that my re-entry student's data were not yet in the system: I'd need to find Roberta's original paper records. I went back to the reception area to ask Carole Ann if she'd retrieved the file. "I'd like to see how far Roberta got with her program before she left."

"Oh, my gosh," she said, flustered. "What with all that's happened, I completely forgot to pull her records. I'll grab a buddy and go get the file right now."

"No, that's okay—I can get it. I'll take Aunt Sally along with me to the Tomb."

"Will you know where to look?"

"Yep…I used to help Sherry pull re-entry files for registrations, so as long as things haven't been moved around too much, I'm good to go."

"You'll need the key." Carole Ann removed it from a hook screwed into the side of her desk and handed it to me. "Be sure to prop the door open while you're inside. Last month Dave Merriweather from the Math Department got locked in for nearly an hour."

"I'll be careful." I hesitated before asking, "Did they get the room—I mean, is the room…."

Carole Ann nodded. "Sister Fred had a professional cleaning service in as soon as the forensics team was done; Detective Staatz cleared it."

I returned to my office to find Aunt Sally stretched flat on her back on the floor, the toes of her black loafers pointed outward like angel wings. Her eyes, magnified to an alarming size through her thick eyeglass lenses, were opened wide in a vacant stare.

Chapter Four

"Aunt Sally!" I rushed over to her, fell to my knees, and checked her throat for a pulse.

Her eyelids fluttered wildly as she struggled to a sitting position. "What the heck do you think you're doing?!"

"Are you trying to give me a heart attack?! What are you doing on the floor?!"

"Oh, lighten up, Amanda! I do five sit-ups every afternoon after lunch. It helps my digestion, especially when I've had food like that slop I ate in the commons today. I hope the kitchen's been inspected recently. I wouldn't want to get botulism and have to sue the place. Sister Fred has enough problems right now."

"Slop?! Aunt Sally, they serve only the best food here, and the kitchen's run by a gourmet chef."

"I don't give a hoot if Gordon Ramsey himself runs it. The food's lousy! We're going to have to renegotiate where to have lunch for the next six weeks."

I gritted my teeth and jotted my re-entry student's name and ID number on a sticky note. "Aunt Sally, I can't afford to pay for off-campus lunches for six weeks."

She thought about that for a minute. "Okay, then I guess we'll go Dutch. But I won't be happy about it."

I told Aunt Sally about having to go to the Tomb.

Her eyes threatened to pop out of their sockets. "Wait a minute—you want me to go to the room where your friend was just murdered?"

"Sister Fred has had the room thoroughly cleaned, and Detective Staatz has given it the all-clear. It'll be fine." I held the door open for Aunt Sally to follow me into the hallway. "We're going to be in there for only a minute or two."

In the basement, we made our way along the dark corridor. I glanced into the security office and saw Director Ralph Michaels, feet up on his desk, enjoying a sandwich with great gusto while watching a small TV that had been wedged in among a line of surveillance monitors. I could make out the ESPN logo in the lower right-hand corner of the screen that was currently holding his attention.

"Hey, Ralph!"

With nary a glance at us, he nodded and flapped his sandwich in our direction.

"We're just going to get a file."

He turned toward us with a nod, waved his sandwich again, and took a huge bite before turning his attention back to whatever was apparently more interesting than anything coming through on the security monitors.

"See?" I took Aunt Sally's arm and guided her down the hallway toward the Tomb. "If it wasn't safe down here, I'm almost positive Ralph would have stopped eating long enough to warn us."

I instructed her to stand guard at the door while I looked for the file. "Just stay right there, and don't let the door swing shut."

I had my cell phone in my purse, but why tempt fate? Though claustrophobia was not in my cluster C repertoire, I didn't relish the idea of being trapped inside the Tomb. I made an effort to avert my eyes from the section of floor where Sherry's body had been found, but curiosity won out, and I looked at the spot head-on. It was clean but, given the lack of air flow in the windowless room, still damp from what I figured must have been a good strong mix of water and cleaning solution. Staying close to the wall, I circled around to the back of the room to the other side of a long bank of filing cabinets. Within minutes, I located a manila folder with Roberta Matthew's name and student ID number on the tab. "Got it!"

Not having budged from her post at the door, Aunt Sally was staring down at the semi-dried spot on the floor, which had assumed the indeterminate shape of a person. "That's where she...."

I nodded, nudged her through the door into the hallway, and let the heavy door swing shut behind us, waiting for the distinct click of the lock. We made slow progress to the elevator, with Aunt Sally sliding her left foot along the floor in an attempt to dislodge an overlooked remnant of yellow crime scene tape from the bottom of her shoe. The elevator door opened, and the university's bursar, Mike Kraemer, stepped out and held the doors to allow us entry. "Ladies." His eyes brightened with recognition. "Amanda, good to see you!"

I returned his smile as we entered the elevator. "Good to see you, too, Mike." But I observed that since the last time I'd seen him, his face, handsome in the classic sense with craggy features and a nose that was just short of patrician, had hardened with an apprehension that tightened his mouth and made him look older than his forty-some years.

"What are you doing here?" He quickly dropped his head and shook it as if to undo his words. "Sorry. That didn't come out quite right."

"No problem. Sherry asked me to help out in the English Department for a while, before...."

His eyes clouded with sadness. "I thought Sister Fred would close down the campus for at least the entire week."

"No kidding," said Aunt Sally. "The Tomb floor's not even dry yet, and the kids are back in class already. God forbid St. Priscilla's would lose a buck by showing some respect for the dead."

I quickly pushed the elevator button. Twice. "This is my Aunt Sally—she'll, uh, be assisting me while I'm working here. See you later, Mike."

He raised a hand in a half-wave. "See you later, Amanda."

Just before the elevator doors closed, I saw that Mike was headed directly for the Tomb. I had to wonder why, since only academic records were stored there. Financial records, the ones that would be of interest to Mike, who was responsible for St. Priscilla's cash receivables and payables, were housed on the second floor in a large, secure file room connecting the Business Office and Financial Aid suites. I didn't even think Mike's staff had a key to the Tomb: As far as I knew, other than the one kept in a locked master panel in Security, only the Registrar's Office and each of the department secretaries had keys.

Back in the English Department, I returned the Tomb key to its hook on Carole Ann's desk. I had three more student appointments that afternoon and, by the end of the day, was feeling quite relieved: Not a single panic attack had reared its ugly head. Other than the embarrassing incident with Aunt Sally's tasteless computer site, all had gone like clockwork. We were getting ready to leave for home when the phone on Carole Ann's desk started to beep. Carole Ann had already left for the day and must have forgotten to log out of the phone system. I hesitated for a moment—I knew I was probably going to regret it, but I picked up the receiver anyway. After all, who would be calling me with bad news on Carole Ann's phone?

Aunt Sally threw her hands up in the air. "Make it quick, Amanda. My friend Thelma and I are going to the club tonight to check out some of the new cheesecake. And I'm not talking about the dessert menu."

I shushed her, cleared my throat, and said, "St. Priscilla's University. May I help you?"

"Hi…listen, this is Jennifer Baranski. I need to talk to someone about a mix-up. I have a tuition bill here for my sister, but…."

"Oh, I think you want the Business Office."

"No one's answering there." The caller's voice had abruptly changed from a normal tone to one that was creepily soft and placid.

I knew what was coming next and braced myself for the attack.

It came without delay. "You people are trying to rip off my mom, and I want you to know right now that there's no way she's going to pay for classes my sister never took! I'll report you to the Better Business Bureau!"

"Jennifer, was it?" Refusing to respond to the caller's anger, I said with forced composure, "I'm sure this is an easy fix. If you give me your number, I'll personally follow up and have someone in the Business Office call you tomorrow."

"Who is this, anyway?"

Tone almost back to normal, situation hopefully defused.

"I'm Amanda Winters—in the English Department. I'm sorry that no one answered in the Business Office, but pretty much everyone locks up promptly at five o'clock, and it's just past that. Unanswered calls bounce to the next logged-in phone in the chain. In fact, this phone should already have been logged off for the night."

"Lucky for me it wasn't, because this is really important."

Jennifer spelled her last name and gave me her phone number. I tore a sheet off Carole Ann's memo pad and jotted down the information. "You said your mother was charged for classes that your sister didn't take…are you talking about the current semester?"

"Yeah. My mother's being charged for 12 credits. But Sam—Samantha—isn't taking any classes this semester."

"Are you sure about that?"

"Positive—we buried my sister a few months ago. She finished her freshman year just before she got sick, but that was paid in full."

"I'm so sorry, Jennifer. And Samantha's name is on the statement?"

"Uh-huh. Now that I'm looking at it, the current tuition and fees come to $10,750, and it says here that some kind of financial aid was taken off of that. Still, there's a balance of almost $5,000."

"Things have been a bit hectic around here lately, Jennifer. I'm thinking that an ID number may have been entered incorrectly. It happens sometimes."

"Thanks. My mom's been through enough, you know? I don't want her to have to worry about this on top of everything else."

"You have my word. Someone will get back to you as soon as possible."

For the umpteenth time in my life, I tried to imagine the despair of losing a child. I thought of Nathan's murder and felt a rush of sadness, remembering Dinah's attempted suicide in the wake of her tragic loss. I'd lost my godson, and I'd nearly lost my best friend, too. In no way could my brain—or my heart—ever accept even the possibility of losing my son Jeff. He lives in an apartment near ASU's Tempe campus, but I know that after his graduation in December, far-off places will likely lure him away from us. Right now, Terry gets to see Jeff a lot more than I do because he's completing an internship at the station where Terry works.

I gave my office phone number to Jennifer so she'd have a direct contact and made a mental note to take her message to Mike Kraemer the next day. As a bursar, Mike was an astute business person, but he had a heart of gold when it came to students. He'd do whatever he could to resolve this issue quickly.

As soon as Aunt Sally dropped me off at home, I retrieved the purse I'd used the past Monday and dumped its contents out onto the desk in my office. The ring I'd found on the Tomb floor was set with a large onyx stone etched with a gold scorpion. It was actually a lovely piece, although I didn't know many people who'd want to wear scorpion jewelry. I used my printer to make a copy of the list I'd found and vowed to get both items to Roy the very next day.

I changed into shorts and a tank top before joining Terry outside on the patio, where he was busy grilling hamburgers and corn on the cob. While sipping port wine over ice, I closed my eyes for a few minutes and enjoyed the intense warmth of the setting sun on my cheeks. The rest of me was cool and comfortable: Terry had recently purchased a small swamp cooler that allowed us to use our patio even during the 100-plus-degree days of August. I watched as my favorite personal chef, a cold bottle of Stella Artois beer in one hand, used the other to delicately probe the burgers with a meat thermometer.

"And we're done!" he said with a broad grin.

I can't imagine life without Terry. He's the perfect blend of William Powell, circa 1936, and Elmo: classy sophistication combined with the cheerful disposition of a Muppet. He has a cute, button nose, and although his hairline is starting to recede a bit, he looks ten years younger than his 49 years. My features are unmistakably Germanic, my bone structure not well-defined or dainty. Still, I've been told that I have an interesting face. Terry frequently tells me that I'm beautiful, and whenever he does I'm reminded of *The Enchanted Cottage*, that wonderful old movie: Inside the cottage, the war-ravaged Robert Young and an uncharacteristically homely Dorothy McGuire see each other as perfect. True love engenders some powerful magic.

As Terry and I were getting ready for bed, I discovered that I'd left my wallet at the office. "I took it out of my purse when Aunt Sally asked to borrow a dollar for the snack machine. I'm pretty sure I set it down on Carole Ann's desk when I answered her phone."

"Well, it'll still be there tomorrow—just call Carole Ann in the morning and ask her to set it aside for you."

"If we don't go get it now, I'd lie awake all night worrying about it—my driver's license is in there, my credit cards, my social security card—"

Terry groaned. "How many times do I have to tell you not to carry around your social security card? Have you ever heard of something called identity theft?"

"I know, I know," I said, stepping into my shoes. "If we leave now, I can call Security and have someone bring my wallet down to the main entrance. It won't take long."

Terry climbed back into the pants he'd just thrown off. "I guess I have no choice but to drive you if I hope to get any sleep tonight."

It was after 11 p.m. when we pulled in front of Raslin Hall. I had Security's number on my cell. Eddie Gruber, the third-shift guard who'd found Sherry's body, answered my call. "Not to worry, Mrs. Winters. Give me about ten minutes."

"Thanks so much," I said, as Eddie appeared at the door and handed me my wallet. Behind him loomed the reception area and the hallway beyond, its nighttime auxiliary lighting insufficient to permeate the thick darkness. "I wouldn't want to work nights around here right now."

"Aw, I'm not worried," said Eddie, scratching the beginnings of a white beard. "That Detective Staatz has his squads patrolling the campus pretty regular." Eddie waited at the door until he saw that I was back in the car, then waved good-bye before disappearing into the gloomy interior of the building.

"Someone must be working late." Terry started the car and nodded toward a red pickup truck parked along a stand of Arizona pine edging the parking lot.

"That looks like Brent Redmond's truck. It's odd that he's here so late." Brent was assistant registrar and coordinator of St. Priscilla's thriving online program. I'd gotten to know him pretty well over the past few years, and I would never have tagged him as an overachiever. A blue Volkswagen Beetle pulled past us and parked next to the pickup. Brent got out of the car's passenger seat and gave a slight wave to the driver, a slender woman with shoulder-length hair that shone platinum in the glow of the car's interior lights, before getting behind the wheel of his truck.

"Hmmm," I said. "That driver looks pretty young. And she's definitely not his wife Betsy…remember, we met her at last year's Christmas party? Do you suppose Brent's carrying on with one of the students?"

Terry shot a warning glance at me. "Don't go jumping to conclusions, Amanda. It's probably nothing."

"Right—it's probably nothing."

On the way home, however, I couldn't help but wonder: What was Brent doing on campus at that hour, and who was he doing it with?

Chapter Five

The next morning, I was drawn to the kitchen by the inviting clatter of pots and pans on the stove. Terry had just dropped a couple of eggs into hot water for poaching, and bacon was beginning a soft sizzle in the frying pan.

"Breakfast will be ready in just a minute." He pressed a mug of freshly brewed coffee into my hands. "You look tired."

"Bad dreams."

"Staatz called while you were in the shower. He wanted to know what we were doing on campus last night. One of his patrols took down our license plate number."

Having stationed myself at the stove, I nudged a strip of bacon with a fork and flipped it over. "Well, if they'd wanted to know what we were doing there, why didn't they just stop and ask us? Didn't you tell Roy we were just there to pick up my wallet?"

"I did, but he still wants both of us to come into the outpost this morning—says he has a few more questions for you." He shook his head as he filled two plates with bacon and carefully placed the eggs on two perfectly browned pieces of toast. "I had to call the station to let Marge know I won't be in until noon. I told you we shouldn't have trekked over to the university last night. There was no reason you couldn't have waited till this afternoon to get that wallet."

I shrugged and sipped my coffee. "I'm sure everything will be fine. Our visit to the campus was perfectly justifiable. And I have a couple of things I need to give Roy, anyway."

Terry raised what remained of his eyebrows (old grill mishap) and pointed his spatula at me. "What couple of things, Amanda?"

I put on my most innocent face, which, at the best of times, never looks all that innocent. "Just a ring with a scorpion etched into its stone and a list of student names and numbers."

"And where did you get them—this ring and this list?"

I gulped. I never could lie to Terry. "I found them on the floor of the Tomb."

"When?"

"The day Sherry was murdered."

He pressed his eyes closed and groaned. "Please tell me you haven't been withholding evidence from Staatz."

I took the plates over to the kitchen table. "Okay. I won't tell you that."

"Remember the last time?" He held up his hand and pinched his thumb and second finger together. "You were this close to being charged with obstruction of justice. More than once, as a matter of fact."

"What I found probably has nothing to do with Sherry's murder. Some clumsy nun could have dropped that ring back in the eighties."

"Try telling that to Staatz. He's going to have a conniption fit."

"Do you want to walk or drive?" I asked.

"Drive," said Terry. "It's not even ten o'clock, and it's already 98 degrees out there."

At the District 1 outpost, the desk attendant, Deputy Mateo Sanchez, welcomed us with a grin. "Amanda, hi! Does Roy have you on a case?"

"I'm not sure yet. He asked Terry and me to drop by this morning for a chat." When I spied someone familiar seated in a far corner of the room, I exclaimed, "Cory Matuck!"

Cory, a linebacker with St. Priscilla's Desert Hawks, had just started a work-study assignment in the Registrar's Office. He sat in a straight-backed chair facing one of the desks, across from a uniformed woman who looked young enough to be one of his classmates. "Hey, Mrs. Winters."

"Cory, what—"

The young woman, whom I'd never met, looked up from her computer. "Excuse me, ma'am. May I help you?"

"We're here to see Roy," I said.

She raised her eyebrows.

Mateo came to our rescue. "Caroline, this is Amanda Winters. She works with Roy sometimes." He turned to us and said, "Deputy Steele is helping us out for a while." He nodded apologetically. "Roy says he'll be with you in just a minute."

"No problem." Terry pulled me toward a row of chairs along the far wall. "We'll just have a seat over here."

I studied Cory's face as Deputy Steele continued to question him, but its expression didn't give me the slightest hint about the nature of his visit. If Roy had wanted to interrogate Cory about Sherry's murder, why would he leave the questioning to a deputy instead of handling it himself?

Roy emerged from a doorway at the back of the room. His shoulder-length brown hair was flowing loose and wavy today. He looked more like the front man for a seventies rock band than a deputy commander with the sheriff's department. I once asked Dinah if the long hair bothered her, and she said, "Not at all. Now, a beard—a beard I wouldn't be able to handle."

"Hey, Amanda...Terry. Thanks for coming in." Roy led us into his office, a small room at the end of a short hallway. He cleared stacks of paperwork from two chairs opposite his desk and motioned for us to sit. "Can I get you some coffee?"

The air in the room was bitter with the unmistakable odor of a brew that had long passed its flavor peak. "No, thanks...I'll pass. But I would like to know what Cory Matuck's doing here."

Roy folded his hands and rested them on the desk in front of him. "How do you know him?"

"I met Cory in the Registrar's Office yesterday, and my first impression was that he's a nice guy. He's on the football team. He can't possibly have anything to do with Sherry's murder...."

"His being here has nothing to do with the murder. The dorm room across from his got burglarized over the weekend, and I'm just bringing in some of the students to see if they saw or heard anything."

"So...when did Deputy Steele start working here?"

Roy narrowed his eyes at me. "Amanda—I'm pretty sure I'm the one who's supposed to be asking the questions right now." He straightened his glasses and turned on his iPad.

I glanced sideways at Terry, who'd chosen to ignore the mild rebuff Roy had aimed at me.

Roy cleared his throat. "But since you did ask, we're borrowing Steele from the Apache Junction substation for a few months, while Ben Phillips is out on medical leave." Roy stared down at his iPad in silence until his notes appeared on the screen. "Okay, then. What were you two doing at St. Priscilla's after 11 p.m. last night?"

"As I believe Terry mentioned to you on the phone this morning, we were getting ready for bed when I realized I'd left my wallet on Carole Ann's Trebley's desk. My driver's license and credit cards were in it, so I had to go back to the office to get it."

"You couldn't have waited to get your wallet today?"

I looked to Terry for support, but he'd suddenly become deeply absorbed in a sad-looking bonsai tree on the credenza behind Roy's desk. "No, I couldn't."

Roy nodded thoughtfully.

I thought it would put me in a good light if I offered a bit more information. "We stopped there just long enough to get the wallet. We didn't go inside—Terry didn't even get out of the car. Eddie Gruber will corroborate that."

"Eddie Gruber? The security guard who found Sherry's body?"

"He's a third-shift regular, and he was on duty last night. Roy, I honestly didn't think that going to St. Priscilla's to pick up my wallet would be an issue."

"It isn't, really. It's just that until I make some major progress with this investigation, I'm keeping close tabs on any unusual comings and goings."

"In that case, I'd like to mention that someone—a young woman—dropped Brent Redmond off in the parking lot last night just as we were leaving."

"Dear God in heaven," said Terry quietly.

I placed a hand on his. "Are you okay, dear?"

He slid down into his chair a little. "I'm fine, Amanda," and muttered again under his breath, "just fine."

Roy flipped back several pages in his iPad. "Brent Redmond, the assistant registrar?"

I nodded and strained forward in my seat in a vain attempt to make out some of Roy's notes. It's a shame that I never mastered the art of reading upside down.

"I'll talk to him. But my deputy didn't mention seeing anyone else last night—just the two of you."

"Well, unless your deputy drove past Raslin at precisely the right time, he wouldn't necessarily have seen Brent. He was there for only a minute."

"And how long were you there?"

I looked at Terry, who said, "No more than ten minutes."

Roy snapped his iPad shut, rose from the chair, and placed his hands in his pockets. Terry followed his cue and got up from his chair, while I remained seated. I didn't think Roy was done with me yet. And I was right.

"I'll follow up with Gruber," said Roy. "Amanda, when did you last talk to Sherry?"

"A few weeks ago—it was a Wednesday, I think. That's when she called to offer me the temporary assignment."

"Did she seem troubled or distracted?"

"Not that I could tell. Did she have reason to be?"

"The night before her murder, she called Mike Kraemer at home and asked to meet with him the next day. Kraemer said she sounded—" He retrieved his iPad from the desk and swiped back a few pages "—distressed."

I tried, without success, to picture Sherry in any kind of agitated state. She'd always been the picture of serenity. During the last registration I'd worked, some accrediting agency reps had shown up unexpectedly to audit the English Department's files, and she'd remained perfectly calm while the rest of her staff scurried around like ants in a rainstorm.

"I never saw her agitated or angry, Roy. Never, in all the years I've known her." I rummaged in my purse and retrieved the ring I'd found on the floor of the Tomb and the list of student names and ID numbers. "By the way," I said casually, "I forgot to give you these the other day."

Roy cocked his head and leveled a stern gaze at me. "I was wondering when you were going to bring up your little foray into my crime scene. You stepped way over the line when you entered that room before the forensics team cleared it. Even worse, you coerced another person to act as your accomplice."

So Dinah had really meant it when she said she wouldn't lie to Roy. Since I felt the same way about Terry, I really couldn't blame her. Still, I was somewhat disappointed with the betrayal. "Accomplice? Roy, that's going a bit far—"

He took the ring into the palm of his hand and examined it. I noticed the color drain from his face. "You found this in the basement archive? Where Sherry was murdered?"

"On the floor. I've never seen a ring like that before, have you?"

"As a matter of fact, I have. This is the signature ring of a gang that calls themselves the Scorpions. Everyone who runs with them has a ring just like this one."

"Scorpions? I've never heard of them—the gang, I mean."

"They're an offshoot of the King Cobras."

I nodded slowly. "I've heard of the Cobras."

"Yeah, I'm not surprised. They've been active in the Phoenix area for over thirty years."

"So how did that ring end up in the Tomb, Roy? Only a handful of university employees have access to that room, and I'm quite sure that none of them moonlight as gangbangers."

He shook his head. "That's a good question." He reached for the piece of paper I still held in my hand. "And what's this?"

"It's just a list of students, mostly inactive students—it may not even have anything to do with Sherry's murder—anyone could have dropped it. If you give me a list of the ID numbers from the files that were scattered on the Tomb floor the day of the murder, I could compare them with this list and—"

He held up a hand to silence me. "I'll think about it." After he took a moment to study the list, he said, "I can tell you this right now. There are 24 student IDs on this list, but only eight folders were recovered from the archive floor." He gave me a quizzical look. "So what happened to the other 16?"

"Sherry obviously didn't get the chance to pull them."

"Right." Roy folded his arms and sat on the edge of his desk. "Still, when you get a chance, check the archive for those 16 files and let me know what you find. I take it you kept a copy of the list?"

I nodded. "Anything else?"

"How well do you know Tony Loduca?"

I shrugged. "Not very well. Sherry recently hired him to manage the technical end of things in the English Department. Why?"

"No reason in particular. Did he and Sherry get along?"

"I'm going to tell you the same thing I told you yesterday. Sherry got along with everyone."

"Carole Ann Trebley applied for the assistant chair position. It must have been rough on her when Loduca got it. I assume the promotion would have meant a significant salary increase." Roy studied the blank screen on his iPad when he asked, "Did you have any conversations with her about that?"

I was starting to hyperventilate. *Focus, Amanda*. It was true that Carole Ann had been crushed to learn about Sherry's decision. After all, Carole Ann had ten years of experience in the English Department compared with Tony's three. Although she'd confided in me that she'd been scoping out other opportunities for the past few months, I knew that her loyalty to Sherry, not to mention her love for St. Priscilla's, would persuade her to stay put.

"Of course she was disappointed," I said after taking a deep breath. "Anyone would have been. If you're suggesting that Carole Ann murdered Sherry because she didn't get the assistant chair position...." I began to sputter. "That's the most ridiculous thing I've ever heard."

"You couldn't have heard it, Amanda, because I didn't say it. I have to ask these questions, explore every possible avenue. You understand?"

"Yes, I do. And with all respect, here's something *you* need to understand. Carole Ann is one of the gentlest, most forgiving people I know."

"Amanda," said Terry, "Roy's just doing his job. I'm sure he isn't accusing Carole Ann—"

"I hope not. Roy, it's true that Carole Ann wasn't happy about Sherry's decision, but she accepted it. Tony has the technical expertise to integrate the English Department's applications with the university's CRM functionality. That was the reason he got the job, plain and simple. And Carole Ann knows that."

Roy had been making copious notes but stopped and gave me a questioning look. "CRM...?"

"Customer relationship management—the system that contains all the university's information: student and employee demographics, academic histories, program and course data, financial information. The

CRM houses and manages everything needed to run the university."

Roy stood to signal that our meeting was over. He walked over to the door, opened it, and smiled as he ushered us out. "Thanks for coming in." He leaned casually against the door jamb. "I know that you both need to get to work. But Amanda, please call me if you see or hear anything suspicious on campus, and stay alert. I still don't have a handle on this murder."

"I'll be careful."

"And let me know if you find those files."

"I will. Am I officially consulting on this case, Roy?"

"Do you want to be?"

"Yes, most definitely."

"Then consider yourself official."

On the way to the front door, we walked past Deputy Steele's desk, where Cory continued to be questioned. I attempted to get his attention, but his head was bent low, his eyes directed at his feet.

In the car, Terry dialed Jeff only to get his voice-mail message. When he hung up, I said, "Why didn't you leave a message?"

"I left one for him this morning. I'll probably see him at work later, anyway."

"Something's wrong," I said. "I can feel it." I pictured Jeff in his orange Rav4, the door on the driver's side crushed in, his body slumped over the wheel. One of the most unfortunate symptoms of my cluster C is the random sensation that something terrible has just happened, or is about to happen. Every now and then, thankfully not often, the sensation turns out to be valid.

"Nothing's wrong, Amanda. I'll be sure to have him call you tonight."

My fears about something horrible happening to Jeff had significantly increased since our godson's murder. I missed my son terribly since he'd gone out on his own, and that heartache had evolved into a physical pain. "He hardly ever calls anymore. It's because of the new girlfriend, isn't it?"

Terry glanced sideways at me. "Probably—and that's perfectly normal."

As we pulled into the driveway, I asked, "Don't you think it's odd that Roy would have Cory Matuck come in for questioning about a theft that took place in a dorm room that isn't even his?"

Terry shrugged. "I don't know. These days, 'odd' seems to be the new normal."

***

As Arnold pulled into the St. Priscilla's parking lot that afternoon, I tried to make amends with Aunt Sally for not having time to stop off-campus for lunch. "Here," I said, and handed her a ten dollar bill. "Take this and go get yourself something to eat. Just drop me off at the front entrance. I'm perfectly capable of walking up to the office alone."

"Good luck with that." She waved the ten at me. "I'm driving to the McDonald's over on Hamilton Street, and I'm keeping the change!"

A few of the English professors, their moods only slightly more jovial than the day before, were beginning to shuffle in from lunch. I supposed they were happy that their classes hadn't been postponed for more than a few days. Rumors had been circulating that Sister Fred was considering putting all courses on hold until Sherry's murder case was closed. I was determined to present an emotionally stable appearance to my new colleagues, which meant that I'd have to get out there and mingle. With sweaty hands and trembling voice, I visited each of the instructor's offices to greet the few I knew and to introduce myself to those I'd never met. By the time I returned to my office, my heart was pounding so hard I had to press both hands to my chest until the palpitations subsided. Social anxiety is no walk in the park.

I tried to tell myself that all was well on campus, but images of Sherry's murder continued to intrude on my thoughts. Aside from taking a friend and colleague, the crime had cast a pall over what would otherwise have been the perfect work environment for someone with cluster C. I once took a job at a call center where hundreds of people were crammed into tiny cubicles. The cacophony that filled the room—voices clamoring, computers beeping, and phones buzzing—was more than I could handle. I'd spent much of my first day on the job, which was also my last, cowering in a ladies room stall. In comparison, St. Priscilla's University—demented killer notwithstanding—was like relaxing on a white sand beach.

Carole Ann stopped in at my office. "I just learned that Sherry's parents are flying her body back home to Michigan for the funeral."

"I guess that means none of us will be able to go," I said sadly, suddenly hit by the realization that I would never see my dear friend again, at least not in this world.

Midafternoon, I was rummaging through a desk drawer in search of a half-eaten bag of M&Ms I'd tucked away and discovered the memo slip with the information from Jennifer Baranski's phone call. I'd completely forgotten about it.

Aunt Sally had nodded off in her chair shortly after returning from lunch, and I didn't want her to wake up to an empty office. I shook her shoulder gently to rouse her and told her that I had to go to the Business Office but wouldn't need her to tag along.

"Are you sure you won't get lost or spaz out?" she said, her eyelids fluttering open. "I can come with you if you want. Remember the buddy system."

"Thanks anyway, but that won't be necessary. I'm not going cross-campus—just down the hall. If my next appointment shows up before I get back, have him wait out in the reception area." I paused in the doorway. "And stay away from my computer."

Mike wasn't in the office, so I talked to Laverne Hutchins, the petite head cashier. Laverne came to work every day dressed in stylish vintage clothing, and her blonde hair was always done up in a perfect French twist. I explained that Jennifer was adamant about her sister not being registered for the current semester. "Is it possible that she signed up for classes, and her schedule was never deleted?"

"Could be," said Laverne. "I'll see what I can find out."

I handed her the message slip. "Here's Jennifer's phone number." At the door, I hesitated. "One more thing—if you call and the mom answers, I would just leave a call-back message for Jennifer. Mrs. Baranski is pretty upset."

"Considering the circumstances, I don't blame her." Laverne placed the slip near the phone on her desk. "I'm so glad you brought this to my attention—mistakes like this should never happen."

Chapter Six

The weekend passed in a blur, but at least it was a nice, normal blur that took my mind off murder for a short while. Saturday morning I spent the afternoon cleaning the kitchen until it was spotless and then decided to make a double batch of spaghetti and meatballs, which required me to clean the kitchen all over again. That evening, Terry and I cuddled up on the sofa with popcorn and watched *Alien: The Director's Cut* for the third time. (There will be a fourth.) It was a perfect Saturday evening.

Sunday morning after church Terry made omelets, and I sliced some of the banana bread I'd taken from the freezer the night before.

"I'm so thankful to be married to a man who's both handsome and talented in the kitchen."

"Don't forget intelligent," Terry said, and smiled. "I like to think of myself as a triple threat."

I waited for the caffeine to bring my brain to a fully awake state before raising the problem that had been gnawing at me all day. "You know, I'm still trying to figure out who that girl was with Brent Redmond the other night."

Terry held up a cautionary hand. "As disgusting as the thought of a 45-year-old man carrying on with a coed is—and I feel obligated to point this out to you—it's none of our business."

"The way I look at it, any out of the ordinary behavior at St. Priscilla's University *is* my business, at least until Sherry's murder is solved. And believe me,

Brent Redmond fraternizing with a young blonde is both out of the ordinary *and* disgusting."

"Even if Redmond is engaged in hanky-panky with one of the students, it's quite possible that she's of legal age. So technically, Brent wouldn't be breaking the law."

"If he's having a fling with a student, he's still breaking St. Priscilla's employee ethics code, not to mention that pesky little commandment about adultery. He's married, remember?"

"The whole thing could be perfectly innocent," said Terry, pausing to sip his coffee before continuing, "just plain old university business."

"I think I should ask Brent flat-out what he was doing that night."

"I wouldn't recommend it, Amanda. Take my advice, and just put Redmond out of your mind."

I sighed. "All right already. He's gone—kaput."

"Promise?"

"Promise," I said, with fingers crossed securely behind my back.

***

That Monday, as Aunt Sally and I were walking across the parking lot toward Raslin Hall, she asked, "What are all those thingamabobs on the light poles?"

"They're cameras. Sister Fred's amping up campus security."

She shook her head. "Move over, Big Brother. Big Sister's in charge now."

I didn't want to encourage her, but I had to laugh. "It's for our own safety, so you really shouldn't complain."

We walked past a blue Volkswagen beetle that was parked in one of the prime spots in front of the building. "I've seen that car before," I said. I briefly considered asking Aunt Sally if we could find a shady spot and wait for the Beetle's owner to show up but decided that the students' theses had to take priority over my curiosity.

At the front entrance, I rang the bell and waited, per the new protocol, to be buzzed in. Until the new digital key card system was put into place, a monitor had been installed at the reception desk so that the attendant could see visitors and, with the flip of a switch, keep an eye on several sections of the parking lot. Through the glass pane I could see Lynn Goodman, Raslin's full-time receptionist, come stomping angrily toward the door, her long, flame-red ponytail swinging back and forth like a pendulum on overdrive.

As she pushed the door open to let us in, she exclaimed, "This darned system Ralph installed doesn't work right. Useless, plain useless! And I'm not talking about the buzzer!"

"Look on the bright side," I smiled. "You'll only have to put up with it a little while longer. Meanwhile, think of all the great exercise you're getting."

Lynn dismissed the remark with an annoyed wave and resettled behind her desk, which was scattered with magazines. "Carole Ann said to tell you that they're all in a department meeting, but you should just go on up to the office."

Aunt Sally pointed at one of the magazines. "Can I borrow that *People*? I want to get the latest scoop on the Kardashians."

"Sure. Help yourself."

In the office, Aunt Sally dove into the magazine while I powered up the computer and pulled up my afternoon calendar of appointments. Half an hour later, I was sifting through student folders when the low rumblings of a heated argument came from outside the department. A young and angry masculine voice emitted a stream of expletives the likes of which I suspected had never before echoed throughout St. Priscilla's pristine halls.

"Aunt Sally, do you hear that?!"

But Aunt Sally was gone.

Then I heard another voice, this one all too familiar. "Listen, you tattooed excuse for a human being. Watch your damned language...this is a Christian university. I just asked you if you needed some help because you look like you're lost. And pull up your pants, while you're at it!"

The door to the hallway was open. The voices, which were escalating rapidly, were coming from the mezzanine. I hurried down the steps to see a young man in a tank top and baggy jeans set low on his hips. He wore a black fedora over a red bandanna, and his arms and neck were covered with tattoos, one of them a scorpion whose stinger emerged from the top of his shirt to target his jugular. An onyx scorpion ring was prominently displayed on the third finger of his right hand. He was shaking his fist at Aunt Sally and backing her dangerously close to the balustrade. "Listen, Granny, like I told you, I'm here to sign up!"

"I'm not your granny, you, you—"

"Can I help you?" I said, trying to keep my voice calm as I moved to position myself between my aunt and her young antagonist.

"I've been trying to tell this old bat that I'm here to sign up for my first class."

Aunt Sally gasped, indignant. "Old! I was just 72 on my last birthday!"

I placed a protective arm around her slight shoulders. "First of all, my aunt is correct in telling you that we don't tolerate profanity at St. Priscilla's." I directed a stern look at Aunt Sally. "From anyone."

"If he wants to sign up for classes," said Aunt Sally, "I guess that's a good thing, because he apparently doesn't know how to read." She pointed to a large poster near one of the stairways. "Look at those dates, or maybe you need to borrow my glasses. New student registration is Friday night." She folded her arms in smug satisfaction. "You're a little early, kid."

"Redmond told me I could come in and sign up with him any time. So just tell me where to find him."

"You're enrolling in an online program?"

"Yeah."

I glanced over the balustrade at the reception desk; Lynn Goodman was nowhere in sight. How was it that this threatening figure, obviously a Scorpions gangbanger, had been able to get into the building, apparently undetected by Security via the newly-installed cameras and monitors, and was wandering about freely through Raslin Hall?

Agitated, the Scorpion teetered on his feet. "I just need to know where Redmond's office is."

"Listen, kid, what you really need is to sign up for Manners 101," said Aunt Sally.

He was being awfully careful to avoid eye contact with me. Something was amiss, and I wasn't convinced he was here because of a pressing need to start his college education. I gave Aunt Sally a little push toward the English Department door. "You go on ahead. I'll be right in." Wondering where my sudden burst of confidence had come from, I turned back to the gangbanger. I really wanted to get to the bottom of his reason for being here. "Have you already decided on a major?"

"Major?" He screwed up his face. "I don't know. It really don't matter to me."

"It should matter, because you'll be taking your first major course right away. You don't want to waste time and money on a class you might not need or even want."

The youth clenched his fists and became visibly agitated once more. "Listen, lady, I'm getting tired of this back-and-forth business wit' you. I'm here to meet up with Redmond. Now lay off…and tell me where his office is."

I pointed toward the stairs. "Just go up the stairs and turn left. Mr. Redmond's office is at the end of the hallway, Room 225. Do you want me to—"

"I'll find it." And he was off and striding down the hallway, the waistband of his pants dropping precariously closer and closer to his knees.

"Wait!" I called after him. "What's your name?! I—I need to sign you in at the front desk." In truth, I had no intention of doing that—I just really wanted to know who this guy was.

He made a half-turn and said, "Jesse—Jesse Hycamp."

Inside the office, I found Aunt Sally calm and collected, and reading the magazine she'd borrowed from Lynn. "Are you all right?"

She waved off the question. "It'd take more than a twerp like that to throw me off my game. He's not one of the students you're gonna be helping, I hope."

"No, thank goodness, he isn't." I rested my hands on my hips and frowned. "Why did you disappear like that without telling me, anyway? To use your words, 'remember the buddy system.'"

"I had to use the little girls' room," she said. "Didn't think I needed anyone to hold my hand. I spotted the kid just hanging around on the balcony and thought I'd better see what he was up to."

I heard the door to the English suite swing open, and, afraid that Hycamp had returned, literally jumped out of my chair. Mike Kraemer, his face creased with concern, appeared at the office door. "I heard a ruckus out here earlier. Is everything okay? I was on a conference call and couldn't get away until now."

I assured him that all was fine. "Aunt Sally had a little run-in with one of our potential applicants. He said he had an appointment with Brent."

Mike frowned. "Give me a call if he shows up again, will you?"

"I don't think we have to worry about that. Besides, Carole Ann, Tony, and the rest of the department will be back from their meeting soon, so we won't be on our own very much longer."

Mike backed out of my doorway. "Speak of the devil—here they are now. I'll leave you ladies in their capable hands, then."

When I told Carole Ann what had happened, she said, "I'm sorry we weren't here. Not all our students come from stable backgrounds, so you don't always know what to expect."

"Aw, I wasn't scared," said Aunt Sally. "The kid looked pretty puny under all those tattoos."

Carole Ann went back to her desk just as my first student of the day arrived. I had two more appointments after that, both of which went well. When it was time to leave, Aunt Sally asked if we could stop for a coffee on the way home. "I need some caffeine. This babysitting gig is putting me to sleep."

We drove across the street to the Perk-Up Café, a refreshing change from the big-chain coffee shops that serve brews strong enough to curl your hair in grandé cups with prices to match. The shop was owned by a thirty-something couple, Abbey and Loren Spaith. Abbey, her generously freckled face intent on the task at hand, was filling the front display case with chocolate chip-oatmeal raisin cookies. Judging from the aroma that welcomed us as we walked through the door, they were fresh from the oven.

She wiped her hands on a blue gingham apron appliquéd with cups and saucers fashioned of bright yellow fabric. "I'm so happy to see you, Amanda. It's been a while."

"It's good to see you too, Abbey. This is my Aunt Sally."

Abbey nodded. "Nice to meet you, Sally. What can I get for you ladies today?"

"You don't have to ask me twice," I said. "I'll have a coffee and one of those cookies."

Aunt Sally said, "I'll have a tall skinny mocha latte, double chocolate shots, wet. And do you have any biscotti?"

"Boy, are you ever in the wrong place," laughed Abbey. "There's a Starbucks a few blocks from here on Tremont Street. If you're willing to rough it, though, I can add some chocolate syrup to your coffee and top it off with a dollop of whipped cream."

Aunt Sally pursed her lips in disappointment. "I suppose that'll be all right. I guess I'll take one of those cookies, too, unless you have some biscotti."

"You'll have to settle, I'm afraid," said Abbey, and placed a cookie on a small plate before pouring coffee into a ceramic mug.

"Where's Loren today?" I asked between sips and bites of homemade deliciousness.

Abbey frowned as she applied a cloth to clean the glass surface of the display case. "He's out in the alley, repainting the wall. We've been having a problem with graffiti the past few weeks. We called the police, but there really isn't anything they can do about it except increase their patrols."

"Graffiti? Did you see who did it?"

"We got a glimpse of them this last time—Loren pounded on the back window, and they ran off. There were three of them...they looked pretty wild—wore red bandannas under black fedoras."

"Scorpions," I said, my voice uneasy. "Someone from the Maricopa County Sheriff's Department just clued me in on them."

"A gang? Well, that's just great. We've been here for over five years, and, up to this point, we haven't seen any signs of gang activity in the neighborhood." Bending down to polish the bottom half of the case, Abbey peered through the glass at us. "Hopefully, they'll soon get bored with the neighborhood and move on."

"We just had some hooligan break into St. Priscilla's," said Aunt Sally, "but we gave him what-for, didn't we, Amanda?"

"That's a bit of an exaggeration. He didn't actually 'break in.' He was there to register for the university's online program. And all he did was use some rough language."

Aunt Sally set down her coffee cup too firmly. "The kid was trouble, Amanda. And I know trouble when I see it!"

"I wouldn't worry too much, Abbey," I said, refusing to react to Aunt Sally's histrionics. "I read somewhere that neighborhood universities and churches tend to keep gang activity in check."

"Well, I hope you're right." Abbey poured herself a cup of coffee. "I'd hate to see things go downhill around here."

Half an hour later, as we were on our way home, I noticed some fresh graffiti marring some of the other businesses lining Ridley Avenue, between the university and the on-ramp to the I-10, which would take us southeast from the university to Sun Lakes. I hadn't seen the graffiti when we'd driven past the other day. Among the flurry of unrecognizable symbols and numbers were several images of scorpions, which looked exactly like those etched into the two onyx rings I'd recently seen: the one I'd found in the Tomb…and the one worn by Jesse Hycamp.

Chapter Seven

While Terry cleaned up after dinner that evening, I went to my office, closed the door, and called Staatz. To my amazement, he actually answered. "Roy, can I ask you something?"

"Of course."

"I can't get the Scorpions out of my mind. Do you think they might have had something to do with Sherry's murder? How dangerous are they, really?"

"I have no reason to believe they had anything to do with the murder, but I can assure you that they're extremely dangerous."

"What's their story?"

"This gang is taking its cues from the King Cobras—their fathers, uncles, and older brothers. The Scorpions are young, relatively speaking, and technologically savvy—some are expert hackers—and they know how to play the system. We believe they're responsible for a number of Phoenix homicides, but so far no one's been able to pin anything on them. The murders they're suspected of having committed have all appeared to be random, so there are never any obvious motives or connections."

I took a deep breath. "One of them, Jesse Hycamp, just signed up for a program at St. Priscilla's."

"There's no law against that, Amanda. Now, if he's spotted committing a crime, that's another story. The fact that he's taking a class might actually be a good sign—maybe he wants to break loose from the gang and make something of himself."

"I hope you're right, but judging from his behavior, I don't think his motives are all that pure."

"We haven't seen any significant gang infiltration of the St. Priscilla's neighborhood. There've been some campus thefts—the dorm across from Cory Matuck's room was cleaned out—but we have no idea who's behind them—probably one or two of the students, is my guess."

"What about the scorpion ring I found in the Tomb?"

"Yeah, that's troubling. But like I said, these guys are smart. I find it difficult to believe that one of them would commit a murder and then be reckless enough to leave behind evidence at the scene of the crime."

"Roy, the Perk-Up Café across the street from St. Priscilla's has been having some trouble with graffiti. The owners have been in business for years, and they haven't had a problem until recently. I saw some of that graffiti, and scorpion images seem to be the main theme."

"If the café owners have a problem, they need to file a complaint."

"They have." I was at my computer so I Googled "Phoenix gangs" and clicked onto a site featuring a number of grisly murder scenes. The site informed me that an estimated two hundred street gangs are currently active in the East Valley. "Roy, have you completely ruled out the possibility that the Scorpions are involved in the Thatcher House thefts?"

"No, but—"

"Just humor me for a second. Say they *are* responsible for the thefts. Why would they be interested in a private Catholic college? I mean, the students here are from middle-class families. Most of them don't even have credit cards." I scrolled to the next page on Google, which featured a number of young men, all of them muscular, heavily tattooed, and standing or sitting in aggressive poses. But what was most terrifying was the look of pure hatred in their eyes.

"These types of gangs see college campuses as treasure troves," said Roy. "Dorm rooms are overflowing with computers, laptops, cell phones, iPads—you name it. High-tech electronics are a valuable commodity, and the stuff is fast and easy to move."

"But this is St. Priscilla's we're talking about, not the University of Arizona. I'd think the Scorpions would find a large public university much more lucrative. Could something else be drawing them here?"

"I can't think of anything. But you make a good point, which is why I think students—and not gangbangers—are responsible for the thefts."

"So there's nothing you can do about the gang?"

"Not until they do something to warrant my taking action. The Phoenix PD has been keeping an eye on them. They'll let us know if we have anything to worry about."

"That's reassuring, I guess." I Googled "Scorpions," but all I came up with was a whole lot of websites about the insects, one of which featured multiple close-up photos; I learned that out of almost two thousand species of scorpions, only thirty or forty species are capable of killing a person. *Well, that's a relief.* I backed out of the site and took a relaxing breath to see my "island paradise" screen saver appear. "While I've got you on the phone—have you come across anything new? What about the blood that was on the floor outside the Tomb? Were you able to get anything from that?"

"We confirmed that it was the same type as Sherry's, but that's it. We couldn't even get any decent prints. I'll keep you posted about any new developments, though."

"I hope you find something soon. Terry's starting to freak out. He's afraid the killer might still be running loose on campus."

"You can tell Terry not to worry. It's pretty clear to me that Sherry's murder was premeditated and that the killer was someone she knew. It's only a matter of time before we get him."

"Or her," I said, and paused before adding, "Sherry's killer could have been a faculty or staff member at St. Priscilla's, right? Or a student?"

"At this point, anything's possible. We've conducted extensive interviews, and so far there's nothing pointing me in any particular direction. All we have is the ring you found, and since it's circumstantial evidence—and all the Scorpions wear them—I wouldn't even know who to bring in first."

"What about those 16 missing files?"

"I haven't had time to look for them yet. I'm thinking that Sherry most likely didn't get to pull them. I promise to hunt them down soon."

"Yeah, it's a minor detail, so there's no rush."

"In the meantime, if you can come up with anything to reassure Terry, let me know. I need to hold him off for six weeks. That's how long my temporary assignment is, and I mean to finish it."

***

The next day, Aunt Sally and I stopped for lunch at the Palm Grove Club before going on to St. Priscilla's. To say that the meal met with her approval is an understatement—I was beginning to suspect that the real reason for her dislike of St. Priscilla's commons was the fact that it didn't have gin gimlets on the menu.

My first meeting of the afternoon was with a set of twins, English Lit majors who had, throughout their undergraduate and graduate programs, taken the same classes at the same times and with the same instructors.

I had a feeling they'd enjoyed playing a game or two with their professors à la *The Parent Trap*. The sisters, Becky and Blair Bennett, were identically cute, with big blue eyes and boyish haircuts. After going over their theses with them, a task that threatened to put me to sleep since both girls were writing on the works of Chaucer, I walked them out to the front office. "Bye, girls!"

"Later, Mrs. Winters!" they shouted in unison over their shoulders.

My next appointment hadn't yet arrived. Aunt Sally was deeply engrossed in a game of solitaire on my laptop, so I roamed out to the reception area and settled on the edge of Carole Ann's desk, hoping to partake of some light conversation that would rouse me from my literature lethargy. We'd just gotten into an interesting discussion of our favorite Netflix program when I heard the beep of my desk phone, an outside call signal, and hurried back to my office.

"You're actually going to answer that?" asked Aunt Sally.

"It's got to be a student," I said. "Anyone else would call me on my cell." I picked up the receiver. "Hello, this is Amanda Winters."

"Mrs. Winters, this is Cory—Cory Matuck."

"Cory, hi—this is a surprise…."

"Yeah, I know. I just need to talk to you about why I was in the sheriff's office the other day. I don't want you to get the wrong idea. Mrs. Winters, I had nothing to do with Miss Davenport's murder."

"Of course you didn't. Cory, I'm sure no one thinks that."

"There's something else I need to talk to you about. You're a detective, aren't you? You work with the sheriff, right?"

"I do sometimes, as a consultant."

"So whatever I tell you—do you have to tell your boss?"

"That depends on what it is. Cory, what kind of trouble are you in?"

"I can't talk right now. Can you meet me somewhere?"

I hesitated before answering. If Cory knew something about Sherry's murder, I should refer him directly to Roy, who wouldn't take kindly to my butting into his murder investigation by intercepting a potential witness. "If you know something, you need to tell Detective Staatz—he's stationed at the outpost where you were the other day. I'll go with you, if you want."

"Yeah, I met him the day you saw me. But I'm not ready to talk to him, and you can't say anything to anyone about this, either. Please, Mrs. Winters, you have to promise...."

Fear being an old friend of mine, I recognized it in Cory's voice. "I can promise you this. I won't say anything until you and I have had a chance to talk and sort through everything together. But then it's my decision whether or not to take it to Detective Staatz. Is it a deal?"

"Okay, but we can't meet here on campus."

"There's a restaurant in Sun Lakes called the Palm Grove. It's a private club, but I'll get there early and sign you in as my guest. How about seven p.m. tonight?"

"I can do that. See you then. And thanks, Mrs. Winters."

I spent the rest of the afternoon weighing possible reasons for Cory's need to talk to me. He said he had nothing to do with Sherry's murder, but could he have seen or heard something that might be connected to it? A video montage of every possibility, one more horrible than the last, began to flash through my mind like scenes through a child's View-Master: Each picture contained an obscure, dark figure holding a knife as it slowly crept up on Sherry, closer and closer with each click.

At the end of the day, as Aunt Sally and I made our way out of the department, Carole Ann said, "Before you go, I have to give both of you your new security key cards. Starting tomorrow, you won't be able to get into any of the buildings without them." She rummaged in a desk drawer and handed one to me and one to Aunt Sally. "Don't lose them. If you do, you'll have to come up with the $15 replacement fee."

We were headed toward the car when I spotted a mass of bright red among some oleander bushes at the edge of the parking lot. The flowers on those oleanders were pale pink, not red, so whatever was back there most definitely did not belong. I made a beeline for the shrubs to get a closer look.

"You're going the wrong way!" yelled Aunt Sally. "Arnold's over here in section B."

"Aunt Sally, look…just behind that oleander. Can you see it? What is it?"

"Whatever it is," she said, "it's something big."

We discovered that the "something big" was Cory Matuck. He was unconscious, his arms and legs sprawled out like a starfish. If he hadn't been wearing a bright red St. Priscilla's T-shirt, I never would have spotted him.

"Oh, no," said Aunt Sally. "Not another one."

I knelt down and placed my ear next to Cory's face. "He's breathing!" I pulled my cell phone from my purse, punched in 9-1-1, and gave the operator a quick description of Cory's injuries. From the looks of things, someone had taken a baseball bat to his head. I couldn't tell the extent of his wounds because there was too much blood, but I knew not to move him. "Cory," I said, smoothing his hair from his forehead, "help is on the way. Hang in there, guy." He didn't respond, but I repeated the words over and over because, even if he couldn't hear me, uttering those words gave me the illusion that I was doing something helpful.

Twenty minutes later, the paramedics had Cory in an ambulance. Sister Fred, huffing and puffing, her face red, came running toward us. "What happened? Is it one of our students?"

"Cory Matuck," I said. "It looks like someone gave him a good beating and tried to hide him in the bushes. They're taking him to St. Joseph's."

Sister Fred's body deflated like a balloon that someone had just poked with a pin. Her face looked drawn, as if she hadn't had a good night's sleep in a while. I wasn't surprised. She was responsible for the safety and well-being of over eight hundred students, and some lunatic killer might have just tried to claim a second victim on her campus.

"Amanda, could you do me a favor? Angie's gone for the day, and I could use some help. Would you please locate Cory's parents' contact information and bring it to my office? I need to let them know what happened and what hospital their son has been taken to."

"Of course." Sister Fred's request for my help was not to be taken lightly. I accepted it as an honor.

"I'll be phoning Detective Staatz," she said. "It doesn't seem likely that this is connected to Sherry's murder, but one never knows." She turned stiffly and headed back to her office in Raslin. For the first time that I could remember, she appeared completely bewildered. Even worse, she looked defeated. For her sake—for all our sakes—I prayed that Sherry's killer would be found soon. And now there was this new casualty: Cory beaten and tossed aside like a bag of roadside trash. I remembered my conversation with Roy about the Scorpions. Had Cory gotten himself involved with some of them? Was it a coincidence that he'd been attacked within a few hours of setting up a meeting with me? Had someone overheard him on the phone? I was starting to feel that same overwhelming sense of helplessness I'd felt after my godson Nathan's murder. I glanced at the screen on my cell phone—it was nearly six o'clock. I'd better hurry back to my office computer and look up the Matucks' contact information so I could get it to Sister Fred and get home. The day had been a long one.

"Aunt Sally, you go on home. Sister Fred's asked me to take care of something for her. I'll call Terry and have him pick me up."

She narrowed her eyes at me. "I don't know, Amanda. Are you gonna be all right alone?" She turned to gaze in the direction of Raslin Hall. "You know, without someone to keep you from going off the deep end?"

I sighed, not so much in response to her mistrust but because her question was all too valid. I was sick and tired of being afraid to do the things most people did as a matter of course. I had to figure this cluster C thing out. I *would* figure it out. "I'll be fine, Aunt Sally. I'll see you tomorrow."

As Aunt Sally headed toward Arnold, she stopped every few steps to turn around and make sure that I hadn't yet succumbed to a state of panic. I practiced some deep breathing exercises as I watched her get into her Caddy and exit the parking lot. I made it to my office without a hitch, where I booted up my computer, logged into the CRM, and waited impatiently as it flashed line after line of programming gibberish before the main menu appeared. Cory was the only Matuck in the system, so his parents' contact information came up quickly. I dashed off a printout for Sister Fred and took the elevator to the first-floor. I'd just passed the solarium next to Sister Fred's office when I literally ran into Laverne. "Sorry—I guess I wasn't watching where I was going."

Laverne smiled. "No problem. I should have been paying more attention. I just dropped off the weekly tuition report at Sister Fred's office, and I'm in kind of a hurry to get home." She glanced toward the main entryway. "Do you know what all the commotion was out there? I heard sirens."

"Someone attacked one of the students in the parking lot."

"Oh, no! Who was it?"

"Cory Matuck—the football player who works in the Registrar's Office."

She pressed her eyes closed and shook her head slowly. "Another attack—I can't believe it."

"And here we both are, completely ignoring Sister Fred's buddy system."

"It's not very practical at this time of the day—just about everyone's gone. I guess we could always call Security for an escort, but by the time they'd get to us, we could already be safely in our car and on the way home." She started for the double doors. "I'll see you tomorrow."

"Wait a sec, Laverne. Did you ever figure out that tuition statement for Samantha Baranski?"

She searched her memory for a moment. "Oh, you know what? It was just a fluke. She never should have been charged any tuition. Someone pulled up the wrong Baranski. Anyway, I drew up a letter of rescindment and mailed it out to her mother the day you brought the error to my attention."

"That's a relief. Thanks for taking care of it so quickly. I kind of felt responsible, since I'm the one who took the call."

Sister Fred was on the phone with Roy when I walked into her office. "Detective Staatz," she said, "this may very well be an unrelated event, but I felt it necessary to apprise you of the situation." She gestured for me to sit in one of the club chairs facing her desk. I sank into it with a sigh. The chair was soft leather, a rich chocolate brown, and very comfortable. I took the opportunity to close my eyes and enjoy the moment.

Sister Fred's voice cracked slightly as she spoke to Roy. "Thank you, anyway, but I feel it's my responsibility. I appreciate your offer, however. Yes, I'll be sure to do that. Good-bye." She replaced the receiver and rubbed her eyes wearily.

I handed her the printout of the Matucks' information. "This was easy to find. Cory's the only Matuck in the system."

"Thank you, Amanda." She placed her hand on the phone and said, "I'm not looking forward to making this call." She glanced at the paper, and her eyes widened in surprise. "Supai Village? This may be a problem."

"Why?"

"It's located at the bottom of Havasu Canyon. The Havasupai who live there have a reputation for not being very communicative with the outside world. The tribe is quite isolated."

I leaned forward in my chair. "Well, the Matucks have a telephone, so how isolated can they be?"

"They likely use the phone only for emergencies." She sighed. "I suppose I have to at least try, don't I?"

I rose from the chair. "Unless there's anything else I can help you with, I'll go ahead and call Terry and have him come get me."

"Thank you again, Amanda. I'm still all thumbs when it comes to our new computer system." She studied my face with concern. "Are you alone today?"

"I sent Aunt Sally home just a little while ago."

"And you're not…anxious?"

I smiled. "Well, I'm always anxious. But I'm trying to wean myself from having an anchor with me all the time."

"An anchor?"

"A companion—someone I trust—it usually helps to ward off panic attacks."

"I see. Well, I'll pray for you, Amanda."

"Thank you, Sister." Reluctantly, I rose from the comfy chair: I wouldn't have minded spending just a bit more time there, and, if allowed to do so, would probably have drifted off to sleep within minutes. "By the way, will Detective Staatz be looking into the attack on Cory?"

"Yes, he will. He was kind enough to offer to call Cory's parents, but I thought it best that the news come from me."

I nodded in understanding, thinking that I'd be devastated to hear that someone had attacked my son with some kind of blunt instrument, regardless of who that news came from. I didn't want to betray Cory's trust, but I felt that I should at least tell Sister Fred about his request to meet with me. "Sister, just hours before Aunt Sally and I found him in the parking lot, Cory called me to ask if I'd meet with him tonight. He sounded frightened—terrified almost."

"Terrified? Of what?"

"I don't know. He never got the chance to tell me."

"Perhaps you should let Detective Staatz know about this. He was told that Cory would be well enough to talk tomorrow. His injuries weren't as bad as they first looked—he has a concussion and some bruising, but he's expected to make a quick recovery."

"I'm glad to hear that. I'll give Detective Staatz a call tomorrow."

***

Before I had a chance to call Roy the next morning, he called me. "The kid has a hard head, and you can take that two ways: He refused to talk to me, and his injuries were bad but not life-threatening. That's because his wounds weren't left to bleed out—it's a good thing you found him when you did. His discharge is planned for Saturday—they just want to keep him a few more days for observation."

"He didn't tell you anything?"

"Not a thing. He said he wants to talk to you first." He cleared his throat. "Amanda, I suggest you hold off a while—give him a chance to think. I told Cory how lucky he was. If you hadn't called 9-1-1, he would have lost a lot more blood, and who knows where he'd be now. The morgue, maybe."

As soon as I disconnected from Roy's call, my phone rang again, and this time it was Jeff. "Mom, what's for dinner tonight?"

"You tell me."

"I could go for some of your roast beef sandwiches—you know, the ones you make with provolone and juice."

"Au jus."

"Yeah, that. And your homemade oven fries."

"You've got it."

"What time do you want me there?"

"I get home from work at around quarter after five. You could come early and let yourself in. I'm missing you big-time."

"How about I follow Dad home from work?"

"Perfect."

My first few hours in the English Department crept by slowly, only because I was so anxious to get home and start making those sandwiches and fries. At two p.m., I told Carole Ann that I'd asked Aunt Sally to take me home early. "I'm finished for the day, and my next appointment isn't until Friday morning."

"You go ahead, Amanda. Enjoy your dinner with Jeff. And you know what? Take tomorrow off while you're at it. You may want to rest up, because you're booked solid next week."

***

I was throwing some coleslaw together when Terry opened the garage door and came into the kitchen. "Before you ask...Jeff's parking in the driveway at this very moment." He peered through the patio doors and said, "Uh-oh—be right back."

I heard the front door opening, and seconds later Jeff entered the kitchen and gave me a big hug.

"Hmmm," I said, laughing. "Was that hug for me or for these roast beef sandwiches?"

"Both. Can I help with anything?"

"You can grab something cold to drink," I said, and brushed a lock of dark brown hair from his eyes. "Dad stocked the fridge with beer, so help yourself."

"Don't mind if I do." He popped the cap off a frosty bottle. "Where *is* Dad?"

"He's out on the patio, hosing everything off from last night's dust storm."

"Man, that was a bad one. I was out with Megan, and we had to pull over on the side of the road and wait for things to clear up."

"Megan? So we finally have a name."

"Oh yeah," said Terry. "He stepped inside and turned to admire the dust-free patio furniture as he continued, "I forgot to tell you. Jeff's dating Megan Carlisle. She works at the station."

I narrowed my eyes at Jeff. "How long have you been going with this girl?"

Jeff shrugged. "I don't know. A month, maybe."

"And I'm just finding out about it now? What's wrong with her?"

"Nothing's wrong with her." Jeff took a long sip of his beer. "It's no big deal, Mom. We're just going out and stuff."

"And stuff?" I said, raising my eyebrows.

Terry came over to the counter where I was assembling the sandwiches and stole a slice of roast beef. "These look so good. Can I set the table?"

"Sure. Change the subject. But yes, you can set the table. I guess we'll eat inside, since the patio furniture is soaking wet."

Over dinner, I learned that Megan worked in the station's IT department, where Jeff was completing his internship, and that she was the same age as Jeff (22) and an avid Cardinals fan.

"What does she look like?" I asked. "Is she pretty?"

Jeff looked at Terry. "I don't know. Dad, what do you think?"

Terry raised his hands in protest. "Oh no, you're not getting me involved, here."

Jeff laughed. "She's pretty, Mom. Her hair's kind of reddish brown—"

"—auburn," I said.

"Yeah, I guess. And her eyes are this really deep green. And she's smart."

I heaped more fries onto Jeff's plate. "So when are you going to bring her over for dinner?"

"Well, considering you're in the middle of a murder investigation, I thought I'd wait a while."

"Good idea," said Terry.

At Jeff's insistence, I brought him up to speed on Roy's findings.

"It must be hard to have to go through this again, a year after Nathan," he said.

"Yeah, it's awful. But I'm trying to keep focused on what's important—finding Sherry's killer."

"Any leads so far?"

Terry cleared his throat. "Your mom has a few. Have you ever heard of a gang called the Scorpions?"

A fry that Jeff had been about to pop into his mouth fell to his plate. "The Scorpions?!" He turned to me and directed his wide blue eyes squarely at mine. "Mom, you don't want to be messing with the Scorpions. They're bad news. Really bad news."

"I'm not 'messing' with them. They're barely on my radar. It's just that they've been a bit active in the St. Priscilla's neighborhood lately."

"I mean it, Mom." He placed his hand gently on mine. "Stay clear of them." He looked at Terry. "You've got to make sure, Dad. Seriously."

"I'll do my best. And your mom has already gotten the same warning from Detective Staatz—I'm sure she'll take your advice to heart."

***

Friday morning I called Roy from my office but had to leave a message. Since I had an email from the registrar, Patty LeBlanc, asking me to come see her at my first opportunity, I gave Aunt Sally her daily warning to stay away from my desk and my computer, declined her offer to "buddy up" with me, then headed down the hallway to the Registrar's Office. Patty was standing behind the counter and shuffling through a stack of forms. She looked up and smiled as I approached. "Hey, Amanda! How are you managing with those English students? Are any of them going to graduate on time?"

I laughed. "As far as I'm concerned, yes. They're all doing a super job with their theses."

"I have a big favor to ask you."

"Uh-oh. Here it comes."

She waved her hand at me. "Aw, it's nothing major." She set down her paperwork and patted it firmly with both hands. "Sherry represents the English Department at all our new student information sessions." Her eyes clouded with tears, and she rubbed them away before continuing. "At least she did…now that she's gone, there really is no one who knows the curriculum well enough to take over. No one except you, that is. Each of the faculty members knows their own courses, but as far as general degree requirements, they just don't have the experience you do."

"What about Tony? I mean, he's the assistant chair. I'm sure he knows the curriculum inside and out—he's overseeing the data conversion process for the English Department."

Patty nodded. "Tony knows his stuff all right. The problem is, he doesn't know how to communicate it. With potential new students, in particular, we want to be especially sure that they're getting all the information they need and that the answers to all their questions are clear."

"How many sessions are we talking about here?"

"For now, just the one scheduled for tonight. Sister Fred is already interviewing for Sherry's position, and from what I've heard, there are several excellent in-house candidates. Any one of them will probably be able to take over future information sessions."

"Tonight?! Wow, I wish you'd give me a little more notice."

"I'm sorry about that, Amanda. Things have been crazy around here."

"I guess I could manage. Uh, Patty, you know about my, uh—"

"Your panic attacks? Sure, I know. But don't worry, you won't have to stand in front of the room and give a presentation or anything like that. You just need to be on hand to answer questions. Okay?"

"Okay." I wondered if I should explain that my panic attacks often occurred out of the blue, and for no reason. I've had attacks while sitting on the sofa and watching my favorite cooking show on TV. But I decided to leave well enough alone. Why tempt fate?

"Perfect. I'll email you the details later today." She picked up the stack of forms and secured them with a rubber band. "I really appreciate you helping me out with this, Amanda."

I returned to the English Department to find a very flustered Carole Ann. My first thought was, *Now what has Aunt Sally done?*

But Aunt Sally had nothing to do with this particular trouble.

"Sister Fred just called," said Carole Ann. "Cory Matuck disappeared from his hospital room about an hour ago, and no one's been able to find him."

Chapter Eight

I didn't have much time to think about Cory
Matuck's disappearance, because I had only a few
hours to prep for that evening's session. Thankfully,
Aunt Sally had offered to stay late and drive me home
afterward. With no small amount of cajoling, I
convinced her to try the commons food once more,
since there wasn't enough time to grab a bite off-
campus. We could have a quick dinner downstairs and
have just enough time to stop back at the office and
gather the materials I'd be handing out to prospective
English majors that evening.

Just before the session was set to begin at seven
p.m., I made sure that Aunt Sally was safely tucked
away with her sudoku at one of the back tables and took
my place with the other department reps at a long table
at the front of the room. The group of potential new
students who showed up at the first-floor Cactus
Conference Room was small—no more than thirty or
so. I was relieved to note that Jesse Hycamp had
apparently gotten all the information he needed from
Brent Redmond the other day and was nowhere to be
seen. After the Admissions staff introduced themselves,
Patty did a quick run-through of the evening's agenda,
which was to include a number of short presentations
from various departments and colleges, culminating
with registration for first-semester courses.

Many of the female applicants, and some of their
moms, went goo-goo-eyed when Ian Malcolm,
Financial Aid director, took the podium. Ian always

looked as if he'd just stepped from the cover of GQ. Tonight he was dressed in a three-piece suit with matching red and gray paisley pocket silk and tie. He had dark, deep-set eyes and full lips set above a square chin. He took a sip from his water bottle and straightened his tie before setting about convincing the twenty or so attendees, and most importantly their parents, that the cost of their education would be well worth the rewards that were sure to follow.

After clearing his throat, Ian began his spiel. "I hope everyone's doing well this evening, and getting excited about taking that first step toward a promising future. Remember, education is something that you have to work at, and I mean work hard at, but it's the single most important thing you can do to ensure a happy, successful life for yourself." He passed a multi-ringed hand over the smooth surface of his shaved head, pausing to let his words sink in before continuing. "Earning a college education isn't easy, and, unfortunately, it isn't free, either. Still, there are many resources available to help you reduce the financial burden of your education."

I watched from the front of the room as our potential students began to squirm in their chairs while their parents exchanged nervous glances. I was sure that this was a typical reaction during the financial aid presentation. It was no secret that tuition costs in general were continuing to skyrocket, and neither was it a secret that the cost of living was also continuing to increase. People had other things to spend their money on, like food, gas, and clothing. Think Psychology 101 and Maslow's hierarchy of needs: People are unable to focus on abstract, intangible desires if their basic physical requirements aren't met. It would be ridiculous to assume that middle-class parents could shell out thirty to forty thousand dollars a year for tuition when many of them didn't know where the money for next month's mortgage payment would come from. Yet most parents still believed that education was a big step toward the proverbial American dream for their kids, and that if they didn't have the means to pay for it, the U.S. government would come to the rescue in the form of federal financial aid.

Ian stepped out from behind the podium and asked for a show of hands from students who'd already applied for financial aid. Nearly every hand went up.

"That's great. We offer three options for the disbursement of your federal funds: You can have them directly applied to your tuition bill, mailed to you in the form of a check, or direct-deposited into your savings or checking account. If you choose one of the last two options, you're responsible for applying the money to your tuition bill the same way you'd make payments on a credit card or car loan."

Ian paused again, surveying the faces in the room to evaluate their responses. He continued by telling them that their signature on the financial aid application was, in effect, a promise to the U.S. government that the money they received would be used for educational purposes only. "And here's something I want to stress: The application is free, as its title indicates. The funds you receive, however, are not. You're obligated to pay the money back with interest."

"What about Pell grants?" asked someone from the back row. "We don't have to repay those, right?"

"Correct. Grants are free money and are not repaid. Everyone who completes a financial aid application is automatically screened for eligibility for both loans and grants, most of which are based on financial need. And St. Priscilla's offers institutional scholarships to those students who qualify based on high school academic performance and, in some cases, demonstration of athletic ability."

After announcing that he'd be available to meet with students and parents after the session, Ian took a seat in the back of the room at Aunt Sally's table.

Patty took the podium, thanked Ian, and started the PowerPoint that introduced St. Priscilla's campus and degree programs. The presentation was colorful and slick, accompanied by a musical score that Marketing had determined would appeal to traditional-aged applicants who might be resistant to the idea of attending a private Catholic university.

After the PowerPoint, Patty asked if there were any questions before registration began. One of the parents stood and said, "I have one. What about the recent murder? And wasn't there also an attack on one of your students? Don't you people have any security here?"

Patty's face paled. "Mr....."

"Maris."

"I'll take it from here, Mrs. LeBlanc," announced Sister Fred as she strode through the doors to the room and made her way down the center aisle. Although she was as impeccably dressed as always, the dark circles under her eyes were new and made her look ten years older than her 64 years. "Mr. Maris, the Maricopa County Sheriff's Department has things well under control. It's true that one of our professional staff, tragically, was murdered; let me assure you, however, that the case is very close to being solved."

"And I got a mansion in Scottsdale I'll sell you for fifty thousand bucks." The comment echoed from the back of the room. *Aunt Sally!* I couldn't stifle my groan, which was loud enough for the chair of the History Department at the end of the table to hear, based on the look of annoyance he was aiming at me.

Sister Fred nudged Patty away from the podium and took her place there. "As for the student, that crime is currently under investigation; at this time, we believe the attack to be an isolated incident resulting from the student's involvement in some kind of illegal activity."

I whispered to Steve Holcumb, chair of the Psychology Department, who was sitting directly to my left, "What's she talking about? What illegal activity?!"

Holcumb simply shrugged and shook his head.

Sister Fred ignored the murmurings that filled the room. "In any case, additional security measures have been put into place. No one without an official key card can gain access to any of the buildings, and nearly fifty security cameras have been installed throughout the campus, both inside and out."

"Great," quipped Maris. "So we can view footage of our kids being attacked and murdered. Now tell me what you're doing to actually *prevent* them from getting stabbed or beaten to death!"

"We've taken actions—" began Sister Fred.

Maris ignored Sister Fred and instead engaged in heated conversation with his wife and daughter before getting up and hustling them out of the room. Several more attendees, obviously unaware of the recent events at St. Priscilla's until Maris raised the subject, also got up and, careful to avoid eye contact with any of the staff, hurried out the door. Only half the original crowd remained.

Sister Fred apologized for the interruption and said, "If any of you have concerns about safety or anything else regarding this university, please know that I have an open-door policy. If I'm in my office, I'll be happy to address your questions." She then nodded at Patty and motioned for her to return to the podium.

I was gathering some brochures to distribute when Aunt Sally, her flip hairdo bouncing wildly, trotted up to me. "Amanda! Some chubby guy in the parking lot is in trouble! We have to get out there right now!"

"What kind of trouble?"

"A bunch of gangbangers are closing in on him, and they're wearing those same hats as that kid from the other day—they must be Spiders."

"Scorpions?"

"Whatever. I was on my way to the little girls' room and saw the whole thing going down through the front doors. Hurry up—he could be dead by now!"

Ian Malcolm overheard the conversation. "Ladies, if there's some kind of disturbance in the parking lot, call Security and let them handle it. I don't think you should be getting involved."

"We won't," I assured him. "I'll just go to the front door and take a look. Will you call Security?"

He nodded. "I will, but what if students have questions about English programs?"

"Tell them I'll be right back."

I hurried out of the room after Aunt Sally, who'd already reached the front entrance. I pressed my face against the glass pane and surveyed the parking lot. It was nearly eight thirty, but with the addition of the recently installed security lighting, the entire parking lot in front of the building was clearly visible. I scanned the area, expecting to find another body, dead or wounded, stretched out on the macadam. Instead, I saw Brent Redmond, hands in pockets, strolling casually toward us. He was whistling.

In the background, a white van was slowly rolling toward the parking lot exit.

"Brent," I said, "what's going on? We thought you might be in trouble."

"Trouble?" he laughed and spread his arms wide. "There's no trouble here."

"But I saw—" began Aunt Sally.

"I don't know what you think you saw, Ms.—"

"—Mueller," I said. "This is my aunt, Sally Mueller."

He offered a handshake to Aunt Sally. "Brent Redmond. Glad to meet you." He shrugged and added, "Some kids thought the information session started at eight and that they could still get in. I told them they were too late and that there would be another session in a few weeks. That's it, plain and simple. There was no trouble whatsoever."

I watched the van as it turned right onto Ridley Avenue. "Aunt Sally said that those 'kids' looked like members of the Scorpions gang. You're sure they didn't threaten you?"

"Positive." He smiled at Aunt Sally and said, "Now that I think of it, I can see how you might have come to the assumption that I was in trouble. The kids *were* dressed kind of crazy." He put his hands in his pockets, and as he ambled toward the door, he gazed up at the moonlit sky and said, "It's a beautiful evening, isn't it?"

"Yes it is," I said, as three security officers burst through the front doors and ran out onto the parking lot. At the same time, one of Roy's patrol cars, lights flashing, appeared from around a corner and sped into the lot so fast that its front end left the ground. "We'd better get back inside," I groaned. "I'm going to have some explaining to do."

Aunt Sally, her face showing her frustration, said, "I know what I saw, Amanda. Those were Spiders—"

"Scorpions."

"Whatever. They tumbled out of that van and took a run at Redmond, who, by the way, I don't much like. He has beady eyes, and you'd need a magnifying glass to find his nose."

"How could you not like him when you only just met him?" I said as we headed back to the Cactus

Conference Room. "But I believe you. There's definitely something going on around here." I had a strong suspicion that Brent had lied about the "kids" in the parking lot, and I wanted to know why. And there was still the matter of Sherry's murder, Cory Matuck's attack, and now his disappearance from the hospital. Too many questions were constantly flooding my mind, and a single answer had yet to seep in.

Back inside, I apologized to Roy's deputies for the misunderstanding. Five students were waiting to ask me questions about various English programs. I was pleasantly surprised to discover that I remembered more than I thought I would, and I felt confident that I'd done a good job of representing the English Department. Sherry would have been proud.

After the last student left, as Aunt Sally and I were making our way to exit the building, Patty LeBlanc caught up with us. "Amanda, you were fantastic tonight!" She frowned. "But what happened out there in the parking lot?"

"Absolutely nothing. We thought Brent might be having trouble with some gangbangers, but he claims they were simply potential students who showed up too late for the information session."

"So, did you enjoy tonight?"

"I did, actually. I talked to some kids who really have a passion for English."

"Wonderful! That makes my next request easier."

My smile drooped. "Next request? What next request?"

"Could you help out at tomorrow's continuing student registration? Just for a few hours in the morning...."

"Oh, Patty, I don't think so. I don't have any experience with the new system."

"You don't need any experience. All you have to do is sit at the English Department's table in the gym and answer questions—pretty much the same thing you did tonight. And I'll make sure that you have all the information you'll need at the table."

"I don't know…."

"Please?" She glanced at Aunt Sally. "You can bring your aunt along."

"Gee, thanks." Aunt Sally glared at her. "Don't do me any favors."

Patty raised her hands and folded them in supplication. "I really need you, Amanda. This isn't meant to be a bribe, but I can offer you some coupons for free lunches at Ming's Dynasty."

Aunt Sally's eyes brightened considerably. "Free Chinese food? In that case, I'm in."

I closed my eyes and sighed. "It's only for a few hours?"

"Three, tops," Patty said. "Your table in the gym will be set up by 8:30 a.m. I'll see you then."

***

Even with Aunt Sally along to serve as my anchor, Saturday morning in the gym was more than uncomfortable. For starters, the room was huge, with high ceilings and multiple doors across its width. Footsteps bounced off the polished floor, and the raising of voices over the constant banging of books and folders being dropped onto tables gave me a serious case of raw nerves. Clusters of faculty and staff dotted the room, chatting in front of long folding tables that had been placed along the wall to hold urns of coffee and trays heaped with doughnuts and bagels. After Aunt Sally and I took our places at the English Department's table, I immediately focused on shutting out the noisy environment and reviewed the continuing student registration catalog that Patty LeBlanc had provided. It would be my task to advise English students on their major course sequence and answer questions from non-English majors interested in taking English courses as electives. I spotted Brent Redmond schmoozing with the deans and moving through the room as if he were hosting a cocktail party.

Aunt Sally had agreed to stand at one of the gym entrances to manage one of the long lines of students who'd been gathering in the hall outside the gym since six that morning. She waved at me now from her post at the double doors on the east end of the gym. I waved back and said a little prayer that she'd behave herself and not say anything that would instigate an all-out student riot.

I looked in vain for some sign of Cory Matuck. To remain eligible to play for the Desert Hawks, he had to make sure he was registered for his required number of full-time credits.

Brent Redmond, chocolate-frosted doughnut in hand, stopped at the table to greet me. "Hey, Amanda."

"Hi, Brent. I've been meaning to ask you how the new online business cohort is shaping up. Patty seems pretty excited about it."

He brushed crumbs from the front of his shirt. "Yeah, it's going gangbusters. I have more than fifty new students. In fact, I had to split the cohort into two groups."

"Wow…that *is* impressive."

Brent stood taller, assuming a stance of pride. "Students seem to love the idea of taking classes without leaving home. They never have to change out of their pajamas."

"I can see the appeal," I said. "Say, did you hear what Sister Fred said about Cory Matuck last night?"

His smile vanished. "Yeah, you never know with kids."

"I can't believe that Cory would be into anything shady. She couldn't have been implying that he was involved in a drug deal, could she?"

He shrugged and popped the last bit of doughnut into his mouth. "That I couldn't tell you." Turning his attention to the students gathered at one of the gym entrances, he mumbled, "Looks like the villagers are getting ready to storm the castle," and without another word, headed toward the College of Business table.

At precisely nine a.m., students began to pour into the gym to form separate lines in front of the tables. Tony Loduca came over with a small stack of manila folders. "I just pulled these files in the Tomb," he said. "They belong to English major re-entries who aren't familiar with the new courses, so I figured they'd have a lot of questions for you."

"Thanks, Tony."

"No problem. Looks like you have things under control here, so I'm going off-campus to run an errand." He checked his watch. "I should be back in an hour or so."

Four of the re-entry students stopped by my table, and as Patty had predicted, I had no trouble providing them information on the new curriculum. During a quiet moment, Patty came over to me. She glanced over her shoulder at the refreshments table, where Brent was hovering over huge trays of doughnuts. "I'm going to grab one of those chocolate doughnuts before Brent finishes them off. Want me to get you one?"

"No thanks. I'm a little nervous, and so is my stomach."

She waved her hand. "You're doing just fine. By the way, I gave your Aunt Sally my master key and asked her to grab some more course description sheets from the English Department. One of my student workers is going along as her buddy."

Just then a girl with multiple piercings and spiked hair rushed up to us. "Mrs. LeBlanc, I can't find Ms. Mueller. She was supposed to wait for me by the door."

"She was pretty anxious to get a break," said Patty, laughing and shaking her head. "But, Amber, I'm sure you'll be able to catch up with her if you leave now."

Nobody was laughing when Amber returned half an hour later to tell us that Aunt Sally was nowhere to be found.

Chapter Nine

Since the Math Department table was manned by two people, and, judging by the number of students in line, math was apparently not all that popular this semester, I asked one of the instructors to cover my table while I tried to hunt down Aunt Sally. I asked Patty if she'd come with me, and she readily agreed. "Don't worry, Amanda. I'm sure she's just in the ladies' room or something."

I glanced at my watch. "That thought doesn't make me feel any better. She's been gone now for nearly forty minutes."

We took the elevator to the second floor. It being a Saturday, the halls were empty, the door to the English Department was locked, and all the offices were dark. I pulled my key from my pocket, opened the door, and flipped on the light switch. "Aunt Sally, are you here?" There was no answer. We searched each of the offices, but there was no sign of her.

"Her purse is gone," I said, my voice numb.

"Do you think she might have gone out for a bite to eat?"

"Maybe," I said, not believing that for a minute. "If she has, I'm certainly going to give her a piece of my mind." With a last glance around the room, I clicked off the lights and relocked the door to the suite.

Back in the gym, the lines of students were shrinking. I asked several people if they'd seen my Aunt Sally, but no one had.

Patty sensed my growing sense of panic and put an arm around my shoulder. "Could she have just gone home?"

I shook my head. "No. She wouldn't leave me here alone." Tears were welling up in my eyes and blurring my vision so that I had to try three times to find my aunt's phone number on my cell. When I was finally able to make the call, there was no answer. I left a message even though I was beginning to doubt that she'd ever receive it. To add to my frustration, I was forced to place the question of her whereabouts on the back burner while I dealt with a sudden flurry of activity at my table. Half an hour later, the last of the students had left. I checked my phone for messages but came up empty. I called Terry and had to leave a message for him, too, and took my exasperation out on my cell by shaking it. *What good are these things if no one answers them?!*

Patty came over to offer some words of reason. "Amanda, if something happened to her here on campus, Security would have contacted us by now. And if she left and something happened to her, we'd likely know that, too. I mean, she had a driver's license and her university key card, right?"

I nodded. "She kept them in her wallet."

"So anyone would know to call the university if she were unable to call you herself. If you can wait a few minutes while I clean up, I'll give you a ride home." She started to gather up papers from the tables. "In the meantime, why don't you give Security a call?"

"I should have done that right away. Maybe she showed up on one of their monitors." I wiped my eyes with a tissue. "She can't just have vanished into thin air."

A security guard I'd never met answered the phone. "Security. Evie Woodard speaking."

I explained what had happened and asked her if she'd seen anyone who fit Aunt Sally's description.

"Other than the hall outside the gym, it's been quiet today." She went on to tell me that there hadn't been unusual activity on the monitors. "What's the make of her car, and where did she park? I can check to see if her car's still there."

I gave her a thorough description of Arnold and where we'd parked, and asked her to call me back as soon as possible, no matter what. As soon as I'd tucked my cell into my purse, the phone rang again. It was Dinah. "Are we still on for tonight?"

I'd forgotten that Terry and I had made plans to meet Roy and Dinah that night for dinner and dancing at the Palm Grove. "I'm afraid not—there's a problem." I explained that Aunt Sally was missing.

"Where could she be?!"

"I wish I knew, Dinah. Campus Security is checking right now to see if her car's still in the parking lot."

"Do you want me to call Roy?"

"Would you? He has patrols in the area already, and he could have them keep an eye out. I left a message for Terry, but he's in a meeting."

"So just in case...how are you going to get home?"

"Patty from the Registrar's Office said she'd give me a ride."

"Okay. Let me know when you hear something. If I don't hear from you by seven or you don't show up at the Palm Grove, I'll give you a call."

After the last student had left, Patty and I made our way up to the Registrar's office. She pushed a three-tier cart holding a huge, empty coffee urn and the scant remains of the doughnuts while I checked my phone for messages every two seconds. In the elevator, my cell phone rang, and I said a quick prayer that it was Aunt Sally calling with some reasonable explanation as to where she'd gone. But it wasn't Aunt Sally. It was Evie from Security calling to say that there was no sign of Arnold in the parking lot.

"I combed the entire campus, but I didn't find a car matching a description of your aunt's Cadillac. I'm sorry." She waited, giving me time to respond, but silence was the only response I could muster. "Actually, the fact that her car is gone is a good sign. It means she must have decided to go off-campus for some reason. Maybe she's running an errand?"

"Maybe," I said, and clicked off my phone without another word. I looked over at Patty and said, "Her car's gone." Tears that I'd been holding back now flowed freely. "Security thinks she just drove off somewhere and that she's all right. Patty, she wouldn't just leave without telling me."

"I hate to bring this up, but has your aunt been showing any signs of dementia? I mean, is it possible that she simply forgot about you?"

I shook my head. "Her mind is as sharp as a tack. She plays team trivia every week, and her team usually scores in the top five." I thought of her best friend, Esther Weinberg, who'd recently been diagnosed with early-stage Alzheimer's disease. "Although I suppose it's possible. Dementia has to have a starting point...."

"Well, I had to at least bring it up. It wouldn't be the worst thing in the world, Amanda. There's so much they can do with therapy and medications now."

A horrible thought suddenly occurred to me. "The other day, this kid named Jesse Hycamp—I'm sure he's a Scorpion gangbanger—got into a mix-up with Aunt Sally. He said he had an appointment with Brent. What if he came back, and he said something to her she didn't like, and she got into an argument with him...sometimes she says things without thinking."

Patty wrinkled her nose. "I doubt it. Why would he show up today? All the signs out front say 'Continuing Student Registration.' And what are the odds he'd run into your Aunt Sally again? Besides, how would a gangbanger get access to the building? He'd have to have a key card."

In my mind, I replayed the other day's altercation between Jesse Hycamp and Aunt Sally. "I don't know, Patty, but he got in at least once before. Maybe he snuck in with someone else."

"Our students know to be more careful than that, Amanda."

"You're right. I guess I'm just grasping at straws." When the elevator door opened, we pushed the cart over the metal threshold and into the hallway.

Then I remembered. "Hycamp said he was going to register with Brent for an online class. If he did, he'd have been given a key card, wouldn't he?"

She shook her head. "Online students aren't generally given key cards, since they don't attend classes on campus. Hycamp would have to submit a special request for one if he wanted to use the facilities here—both Ralph and I have to approve those requests, and I haven't received any this month." We arrived at the Registrar's Office. "Come in for a minute, Amanda. I want to check the computer to see if Hycamp actually registered."

A few minutes later, she found his name. "He's signed up for Brent's online business program. His cohort starts next week."

"So he was telling the truth. It's nerve-wracking to think that gangbangers are enrolling in our programs."

I told her about the graffiti that the owners of the Perk-Up Café had been dealing with.

"Yeah, I heard about that. And then there was the attack on Cory. I sure hope the Scorpions aren't staking a claim in this neighborhood—or on this campus."

"Speaking of Cory...at the information session the other night, Sister Fred mentioned that he'd gotten involved in some sort of illegal activity. I don't know Cory all that well, but I still don't believe it. What about you? You know him better than I do—what do you think?"

"Amanda, nothing surprises me these days. Kids— even good kids—get mixed up with the wrong crowd, get in over their heads."

"You think it's possible that Cory is into drugs?"

"Maybe. Maybe he was, and he changed his mind— wanted to get out."

"From what I've been learning about the Scorpions," I said, "it's easy to get in...and nearly impossible to get out. And I think the gang already has some sort of foothold on this campus."

Patty grabbed her purse and shut off the lights. "I hope to God you're wrong, Amanda." She glanced up and down the deserted hallway and took my arm. "Let's get out of here."

***

I called Roy as soon as I got home.

"I've already got a squad circling through the neighborhood," he said. "Dinah and I checked out Sally's house, and there was no answer...and no sign of Arnold." He sighed, and I knew he also suspected that something was very wrong. "Try not to worry. I'll call if anything comes up on my end, and you call me if you hear anything, okay?"

"Okay." Forgetting to say good-bye, I dropped the cell phone into my lap. I was sitting on the sofa in the living room and staring at the TV without knowing what I was watching when my heart began to pound and the room started to spin around me. A nausea that rose in my stomach quickly worsened, causing bile to escape up into my throat.

The attack lasted a good 15 minutes, and I was still shaking and covered with perspiration when I heard Terry and Jeff come in through the garage door. They entered the room while having an excited discussion about the previous day's Diamondbacks' win. "Hey, Mom, I need to pick up a few of my games. Megan's a game nut, and—"

As soon as they saw my face, the happy talk stopped.

Terry sat down next to me on the sofa and took both my hands in his. "You just had an attack, didn't you...I'm sorry. I'm here now."

"You didn't get my message." The tears came in a rush then, and my account of Aunt Sally's disappearance along with them.

Our landline phone rang. *She's dead. I know it. That's the morgue calling. Oh God, she's dead.*

Terry read my thoughts. "I'll get that." After an unbearably long sequence of "uh-huhs" and "hmms," he offered the phone to me. "It's Roy." In response to the look on my face, he said, "They haven't found her yet." He picked up my cell from the sofa. "You forgot to disconnect."

Trying to still the shaking of my hand, I gripped the phone. "Roy?"

"Now, Amanda, I don't want you to jump to conclusions. One of my squads found Sally's car. It was parked in an alley several blocks from the St. Priscilla's campus."

"But what about Aunt Sally? Where is she?"

"We still don't know that. Her handbag was locked in the trunk, along with her car keys and cell phone. Her wallet was inside the purse. I've had a car stationed outside her house for an hour, but there's been no movement in or out."

"Oh my God."

"Now listen to me. The fact that we haven't found her yet is probably a good thing. If someone hurt her, we'd have likely found her inside or near the car. She may be trying to find help. She wouldn't have been able to drive without keys."

"But why would she leave her car in an alley, with her purse and car keys in the trunk? That doesn't make sense!"

"We questioned the residents of the houses backing onto the alley, but no one recognized a photo of your aunt or saw who parked her car. Can you tell me exactly what happened this afternoon, beginning with the last time you saw her?"

"I was helping out with registration. Aunt Sally left the gym to get some papers from the English Department. I didn't see her leave, so I don't know exactly what time it was—it must have been around ten or so. I started to worry when she hadn't returned almost an hour later."

"I'm going to go ahead and issue an APB. She has to be somewhere. It's only a matter of time before we find her." He cleared his throat and asked, "Have you noticed her exhibiting any peculiar behavior lately? I mean, more peculiar than usual?"

I managed a weak laugh. "You, too? That's what Patty LeBlanc asked me earlier today. My answer was no then, and it's still no."

I pictured Aunt Sally roaming strange neighborhoods, alone and defenseless, without even a driver's license to help someone identify her if she was in trouble or hurt.

"Did she normally carry any cash or credit cards?"

"She always carries her MasterCard and a little bit of cash, not much. And she kept her driver's license and her St. Priscilla's key card in her wallet."

"We didn't find a key card or a credit card in her purse. And there was only a little bit of change in the coin compartment of her wallet."

"That can't be good." I thought of Jesse Hycamp, and what he might be capable of. "Would someone hurt a defenseless woman just to take what little she has?"

"I hate to say it, Amanda, but some people are capable of anything. Still, in this case, I think the possibility is remote. If she's hurt, I'm almost sure that we'd have found her by now."

"Well, if she *isn't* hurt, wouldn't you also have found her by now? Roy, you know as well as I do that if she were all right, she would have knocked on a door or stopped someone on the street for help. She would have used someone's phone to call me."

"Maybe she found a ride—maybe she's on her way home right now."

"Again, if that were the case, she would have found a way to contact me. Roy, I've been wanting to talk to you about something that happened last night in the St. Priscilla's parking lot. The assistant registrar, Brent Redmond—"

"I'm sorry, but I really just need to focus on finding your aunt right now."

"But this may have something to do with her disappearance. Aunt Sally saw Brent in the parking lot being threatened by Scorpion gangbangers. Jesse Hycamp and Aunt Sally got into an argument a few days ago, and he may have seen her again last night. What if he came back today to look for her and decided to scare her—or worse?"

"Amanda, I really don't have time to get into all that with you right now. All I want to do is find your Aunt Sally."

"I want to find her, too, Roy." He still wasn't taking my concern about Jesse Hycamp and the Scorpions seriously, but at least I'd been able to vent some of the thoughts that had been nagging at me. Maybe now I'd be able to think more clearly and come up with some of my own answers. "What about calling some of the other university staff? It's possible that someone saw something."

"My team's already on it. If you think of anything else that might help, give me a call."

Roy put Dinah on the phone. "Do you need anything? Want me to come over?"

"No...thanks. Roy's doing everything that can be done at this point. How was dinner?"

"We skipped the club tonight and ordered pizza. Were you and Terry able to get some dinner?"

"Terry's making grilled cheese and tomato soup, but I don't have much of an appetite."

"Well, try to eat something. I'll check in with you tomorrow morning, okay?"

I was still pacing the floor at 11 p.m. I tried three times to settle into sleep mode but couldn't get comfortable and gave up. With Terry snoring softly next to me, I turned the bedroom TV on low and flipped through channel after channel offering miraculous wrinkle creams, weight-loss aids, and hair-removal devices. I decided to do some reading and turned off the set. The novel I'd picked up at the library was bland, the characters cartoon-like. In the spirit of generosity I finished two chapters, but I'd reached the age where reading a book from cover to cover simply for the satisfaction gained by closure was no longer acceptable. Life was short. I tossed the book aside and blinked away tears as I tried to imagine, for the hundredth time since Roy's call, what had happened to Aunt Sally. Was Patty LeBlanc right about the possibility of dementia? Sure, Aunt Sally had memory problems: Sometimes she looked for her glasses when they were propped up on her head, and sometimes she couldn't remember where she'd put her keys, but those were the kinds of problems even Terry and I had from time to time, and I wouldn't say that we were in the early stages of Alzheimer's. I couldn't imagine that Aunt Sally would just leave me at St. Priscilla's, drive several blocks from campus, toss her purse into the trunk, and leave Arnold in a strange alley. I shook Terry's shoulder.

He sat up with a start. "What?! Did they find her?!"

"No. But I was just thinking—what if someone moved Aunt Sally's car to make it look like she'd left the campus. What if she's still there, in one of the buildings?"

"Why would anyone want to do that?"

I didn't want to think about the obvious. "Maybe she saw something that she wasn't supposed to see. She witnessed Brent Redmond being threatened. People who commit crimes don't like nosy people."

"You're not saying we should go look for her now...."

"That's exactly what I'm saying. Terry, just a week ago, Sherry was murdered at St. Priscilla's. I'm not going to lose Aunt Sally, too." As soon as I'd uttered the words, I felt gravity pulling me in two directions. My head was a cotton ball floating up into the stratosphere, and the rest of me was a two-ton block of concrete that someone had just heaved into a river. I pressed my eyes shut and willed the panic attack away. I knew that it was possible, even probable, that Aunt Sally was dead and that her body had been hidden somewhere at St. Priscilla's. If that were true, I'd never forgive myself. It was because of me and my ridiculous, baseless fears that she'd been placed in danger in the first place. When I'd had Evie Woodard from Security on the phone that afternoon, I should have insisted that she do a complete search of the campus right then and there—classrooms, meeting rooms, closets....

"Will we even be able to get inside any of the buildings at this hour?" said Terry, slipping into his shoes.

"We'll get in with my key card."

"Maybe we should call Roy and have him meet us."

"Yeah, we should do that." I punched his number into my cell. "I just hope and pray that we're not too late."

Chapter Ten

As I'd expected he would, Roy urged me to wait until morning to search the campus for Aunt Sally. "I'll bring in my team first thing, and we can scour the entire place from top to bottom."

"Roy, I'm not going to wait another minute, let alone until morning. Terry and I are leaving now— we'll check in with Security, start with Raslin, and take it from there. If you don't show, I'll understand."

There was an exaggerated sigh. "I'll let my patrols know you're coming. I'll be there as soon as I can." He paused. "I suppose you won't wait for me."

"You suppose right."

"Try to keep it low-key, will you? Sister Fred will have both our heads if we stir up the students now that things are just starting to get back to normal."

"Back to normal? I'm not sure if St. Priscilla's will ever get back to normal."

"Amanda—"

But I had to get it all out. "Nathan's murder nearly destroyed Dinah, Roy, and it still haunts us. We were left with a big, gaping hole that can't ever be filled. Jeff was Nathan's best friend, and he still has nightmares. And now it's happened again with Sherry's murder. This time, I'm leaving nothing to chance."

"I know, Amanda. I just meant that that all St. Priscilla's students want is to get on with their education, and they should be able to do that without fear. They should feel safe."

"But what if they're *not* safe?"

Roy had no answer for that one.

It was coming up on midnight, and the Raslin Hall parking lot was empty. Terry pulled up to the building's main entrance, and I was running up the front stairs before he even turned off the ignition. I swiped my key card and waited for the now-familiar half-hum, half-click before pulling the door open. The desk was deserted: No one was stationed there after six p.m. except during scheduled evening events, and no special event ever lasted until midnight. In the first-floor hallway ahead of us, a small group of female students in baggy pajamas and flip-flops emerged from the commons and disappeared through the side entrance facing Thatcher House.

I pressed the elevator button, and when it didn't work fast enough, opted for the stairs. I led Terry down to the basement's main hallway, which, especially at this hour, was no more than a dark tunnel. Inside the Security Department, a row of unattended monitors flickered dully. "Hello!" I called out, motioning for Terry to follow me into the room. I heard the distant flush of a toilet, and moments later Eddie Gruber stepped out of the washroom. His eyes widened with surprise when he saw me and Terry.

"Hi, Eddie," I said. "You remember my husband, Terry."

Eddie extended his arm and welcomed Terry with a hearty handshake. "Sure do...we met at the Christmas party last year. Nice to see you again, Mr. Winters. But what are you folks doing here at this hour?"

"I think my Aunt Sally may be in trouble—she might be somewhere in one of the campus buildings. Did Evie Woodard fill you in on her disappearance this afternoon?"

Eddie scratched his head. "Yes, she did, Mrs. Winters. Strange things have been happening around here lately. First Miss Davenport is murdered right here in the basement, then one of the students gets himself beaten to a pulp and vanishes into thin air from his hospital room, and now your aunt has gone and disappeared." He waved his arm at the line of monitors. "I'm beginning to think these things aren't worth their weight in salt."

The security monitors. "Eddie, have you looked at the security tapes from this afternoon?"

"As a matter of fact, Evie and I viewed them together. But they're not tapes. The system's digital, and it records everything directly onto DVDs."

"Did you see anything unusual anywhere on that footage? My aunt was supposed to be going to the English Department to pick up some papers."

Eddie pulled a handkerchief from his pants pocket. "The second-floor cameras are aimed at the entrances to all the offices and restrooms." He blew his nose loudly. "We didn't catch sight of her, though. Now, say she took a turn into the ladies room or got as far as the English Department door: The cameras would have seen that."

"Then she never made it to the office," said Terry.

"Is it possible for us to take a look at that DVD, Eddie?" I asked.

"No, ma'am. Someone from the sheriff's office came and picked it up hours ago. They got experts who might be able to find something that we missed from the day Miss Davenport was murdered. But I figure they won't find anything from today, because nothing was on it. I saw it with my own eyes."

Terry and I exchanged confused glances. "You saw what with your own eyes, Eddie?"

"Nothing, Mrs. Winters. I saw nothing with my own eyes."

"Okay, then," I said, shaking the fog of confusion out of my head. "We're just going to have a quick look around, if that's all right."

"Want me to come with you? If you need to get into the offices and such, you'll need a set of master keys, and you haven't been cleared by Ralph to have 'em. If I let you borrow my keys, I'd lose my job."

"I wouldn't want that," I said with a tired smile. "But I'd appreciate your coming along."

"Just give me 15 minutes to lock things up here and to turn on some extra lights."

"We're going to start with the English Department, and I've got a key for that—I checked it earlier today, but I want to have a second look. Oh, I almost forgot—Detective Staatz is on his way. He should be here shortly, so maybe it would be best if you're at the front entrance when he arrives so you can let him in. We'll wait for you on the mezzanine." At the door, I paused. "Eddie, have you noticed any rough-looking characters hanging around campus lately?"

"Gangbangers, you mean? I sure have, and I told Ralph, too. I must have had to escort at least eight of those delinquents out of Raslin just this week alone."

"How are they getting past the new security system?" I asked.

"Oh, all these kids are up on the new technology. They probably have some fancy high-tech card that they can use to override the locks, like the skeleton keys we had back in the old days. Or maybe someone's just letting 'em in."

"Did you see anyone on campus this afternoon who didn't belong?"

"I didn't see 'em, per se, but their van showed up on the security DVD Staatz took with him."

I took a deep breath. "Eddie, you just told us that you saw nothing on the security recording."

"Nothing but that white van in the north parking lot."

"But the cameras didn't catch anyone from that van entering any of the buildings?"

"Nope. And we would have seen those gangbangers for sure, since they stick out like sore thumbs. The guys wear those little black hats with the brims—you remember the kind, like Frank Sinatra used to wear back in the sixties?"

"Fedoras. Over red bandannas?"

"Yeah...strange combination, if you ask me. Frank would never have worn a danged scarf under his hat."

Terry's eyes had been fixed on the security monitors, and I now nudged him toward the door. "Thanks, Eddie."

"Glad to be of assistance, Mrs. Winters. I'll see you in just a bit."

The second floor offices were dark and deserted, as was to be expected after midnight. I unlocked the door to the English Department and flipped on the overhead light switch. Behind me, Terry said, "Sweetheart, she's obviously not here."

I stepped through the door and crossed the room to the faculty offices. Nothing had changed since I'd searched the suite with Patty earlier that afternoon. I turned back to Terry, who'd settled himself into Carole Ann's desk chair and was gazing intently at the screen of his smartphone.

"I don't even know where to begin," I said. "When Roy gets here, should we split up to search the buildings?"

"That wouldn't work, since Eddie is the only person with a master key. And you're the only other one with a key card to the building entrances." He slipped his phone into his shirt pocket. "Sorry, hon." His eyes added, *What were you expecting to find?* He stood and, always the gentleman, opened the door to the hallway and waited for me to pass through. I hesitated. Something was wrong. I turned around to examine the reception area one last time. There was nothing obviously out of place. I studied the surface of Carole Ann's desk—everything was as it should be. Then my gaze ran down the side of the desk and rested on the hook that normally held the key to the Tomb. It was empty.

"I think I know where Aunt Sally is," I said. "Come on, we've got to move fast!" As Terry pulled the door closed behind him, I pulled out my cell phone and punched the number for Security. "Eddie, bring your master keys and meet us outside the Tomb. And hurry!"

I pushed the elevator button. The doors swished open almost immediately, but it wasn't fast enough for me. Tears of panic flooded my eyes. If I was right, we would find Aunt Sally in the very same place where Sherry had been murdered.

As soon as we reached the Tomb, I used both fists to pound on the heavy door, all the while knowing that no one inside, alive or dead, could possibly hear the sound through the thick fireproof slab. "Aunt Sally! Aunt Sally, are you in there?!"

When I heard the clinking of Eddie's master keys as he came barreling around the far corner and down the hallway toward us, I forced myself to expel a breath. It was either that or pass out, which would do no one absolutely any good. I teetered on my feet, and Terry placed a gentle hand on my shoulder. "Amanda, let's move out of the way and give Eddie some room."

Eddie inserted the key into the lock and turned it. "Sorry it took me so long. Detective Staatz just got here. He's right behind me." He pushed the door open to reveal a small figure huddled on the floor next to a filing cabinet at the end of the row. Aunt Sally's head lolled against the wall. Her mouth was open, and her eyes were closed. Her eyeglasses had dropped, or had been knocked, to the concrete floor a good three feet from where she sat.

I rushed into the room and when I reached her, fell to my knees at her side.

Eddie said, "I'll call 9-1-1" and stepped out into the hallway. I touched Aunt Sally's face. It was cool and clammy. Her lips were cracked and flaky. I felt her pulse. "She's alive. We need to get her hydrated."

"Where can I get water?" asked Terry.

Roy appeared in the doorway. "I just passed a vending machine down the hall. I'll go."

When Roy returned with the water, I pressed the mouth of the bottle to Aunt Sally's lips. The water streamed down her face and dribbled off her chin. Within seconds, she started to come around, and her eyes fluttered open.

"Amanda?"

"Aunt Sally," I said. "You're going to be all right now. You're going to be fine."

She closed her eyes again, and managed a weak nod.

I held her hands between both of mine as we waited for the paramedics to arrive. I studied the floor around us. If someone had taken the Tomb key from the English Department, did they keep it, or did they toss it somewhere inside the room before slamming the door shut? "Terry, do me a favor and bring me Aunt Sally's glasses—they're over there on the floor. And could you also check the tops of all the filing cabinets and look around the floor for the Tomb key from Carole Ann's desk? It should be here somewhere."

Terry made a careful search, circling the room slowly several times. "I got it!" he said, and held out his palm to show me the key.

"No, that's not it. That must be Patty LeBlanc's master key. She gave it to Aunt Sally when she sent her to the English Department. It opens all the offices, but it doesn't work on the lock to this room."

Eddie, followed by the EMTs, appeared at the door.

As we watched the paramedics check Aunt Sally's vital signs and lift her onto a stretcher, Roy asked, "How in the world did she end up in here?"

"This was no accident, Roy. The key to this room is missing from Carole Ann's desk—which means that someone planned this. They took the key, they meant to lock Aunt Sally in this room—and they knew that there was a good chance she'd never make it out alive." I paused for a moment, then continued, "Roy, if I hadn't decided to come here tonight, I wouldn't have noticed that the key to the Tomb was missing. And it's more than likely that Aunt Sally wouldn't have been found until Monday—when it was too late."

He nodded soberly. "You're right. Thank God you didn't listen to me. This time."

Roy, with Terry and me close behind him, followed the ambulance to St. Joseph's Hospital. An ICU medical team consisting of a doctor and two nurses took pains to be gentle as they moved Aunt Sally from the gurney to a bed in one of the intake alcoves surrounding the circular desk in the nurses' station. Terry and I hovered outside the alcove, and one of the doctors smiled reassuringly as he drew a curtain around the bed. "We need to get some IV fluids started right now. There's a waiting room down the hall to your left." He noticed the look on my face and added, "She's going to be okay."

Roy checked the time on his phone and said, "Why don't we all go home and try to get some sleep? I'll come back in the morning and see if she's up to some questioning."

I remembered Cory, who'd disappeared from this same hospital just a few days earlier. "I'm afraid to leave her, Roy. Cory Matuck disappeared from this hospital."

"Your aunt Sally will be safe here, Amanda. She's in the ICU. She won't be left alone for a minute. I can talk to the staff and make sure that someone stays with her at all times, if it'll make you feel better."

"Yes, that would make me feel a little better. Thanks."

My cell rang, and Dinah's name appeared on the screen. "Dinah...hi."

"Roy texted me about Aunt Sally. How is she?"

"They're treating her for acute dehydration. But they say she's going to be all right."

"Thank God! Do you have any idea how long she was in that room, or how she got locked in?"

"It may have been as long as ten hours. I don't know, exactly. What I do know is that she didn't lock herself in. We'll know more when she's able to talk."

"Let me know if there's anything I can do."

"How about telling Roy to find whoever did this? That would be a good start."

As Terry and I drove silently home, I considered several possibilities as to who had locked Aunt Sally inside the Tomb, and how and why they'd done it. No matter how hard I tried, I couldn't come up with a reasonable explanation for her car being found in an alley blocks away from the campus.

Eddie Gruber said that Aunt Sally hadn't shown up on the security footage. I supposed that wasn't really unusual, given the fact that the internal cameras were positioned only outside restrooms and pointed toward office doors. She'd obviously never made it as far as the English Department. And no security cameras were focused on the Tomb door or anywhere else in the basement.

My mind wandered from Aunt Sally being locked in the Tomb to Sherry being murdered there. Sherry's estimated time of death was about half an hour before most of the university's employees were pulling into the parking lot. Raslin Hall would have been fairly empty, but still, no one would think twice about a staff or faculty member showing up early. Only a St. Priscilla's employee or student would be aware of the placement of the security cameras. Only a St. Priscilla's employee or student would know that Sherry made it a general rule to arrive at the office each morning before any of the staff. And only a St. Priscilla's employee or student familiar with the English Department would know about the key that hung in an inconspicuous spot on the side of Carole Ann's desk.

***

Since Terry had some errands to run after church, Roy offered to pick me up Sunday afternoon on his way to the hospital. I was happy to see that Aunt Sally's color, as well as her feistiness, had returned. She'd been moved to a regular medical floor and, her arms folded rigidly, was sitting up in bed and scowling at a bowl of green gelatin on her lunch tray. A young nursing assistant exhaled with relief as we entered the room. "I don't put the meal trays together," she apologized. "I didn't give her that gelatin—I promise."

"Don't give it a second thought," I said. "I'm sure it's not the worst thing my aunt's ever had for lunch."

"Oh yeah?" Aunt Sally gave the cup of gelatin a shake. "Look! It doesn't move!" She pushed the tray toward the nursing assistant. "You can take this away. How about bringing me a hot cup of coffee and a cheese Danish?"

The girl took the tray and hurriedly left the room.

There was one straight-backed chair in the corner, and I pulled it close to the bed, while Roy stood near the window. "Aunt Sally, I brought your glasses, your purse, and some clothes. I placed the purse on the nightstand. "How are you feeling?"

"Aw, I'm all right. For a while, there, I thought I was a goner." Her face softened when she asked, "How did you know where to find me?"

"I noticed that the English Department's key to the Tomb was gone and put two and two together." I glanced over at Roy, who was listening intently. "Can you tell us what happened? Do you remember anything?"

"I was about to unlock the door to the office so I could get those darned forms Patty wanted when everything went dark."

"Did you pass out?" I asked.

"No. Someone put something over my face...covered my eyes, my nose, my mouth—I could hardly breathe."

"Wait a minute—" I turned to Roy. "Eddie Gruber in Security said that she never showed up on the security footage. But there's a camera aimed at the door to the English Department."

"I had our tech guy take a look at the DVD. Several minutes of footage are missing."

"It was erased?"

Roy shook his head. "No. Someone disconnected the camera for about half an hour."

I nodded thoughtfully. "That confirms it, then."

"Confirms what?" Roy asked.

"Aunt Sally getting locked inside the Tomb was no accident."

Aunt Sally's voice rose an octave. "Geez, I could have told you that!"

I took Aunt Sally's hand. "Did you see who it was? Who attacked you?"

"No. They came from behind, the lousy cowards. Then they took me down the stairs. I heard the door swish open, and they made me grab hold of the railing so I wouldn't trip and fall. I guess they didn't want me to croak right there out in the open."

"You said 'they.' Was there more than one person?"

"Two, I think. The one who grabbed me was a guy." She studied the ceiling in thought. "Or it could've been a gal with really hairy arms."

"Did they say anything? Did you hear a voice?"

"I didn't hear so much as a sneeze. The next thing I knew, they pulled off whatever they covered my face with—some kind of scarf, I guess—and pushed me into the Tomb. The door slammed shut before I could get my balance and turn back around. I never got a look at them."

"What color was it—the thing they put over your face? Was it red?"

"It could have been black, white, or polka dot, for all I know. My eyes were covered until they pulled the scarf off and shoved me inside the Tomb. It took me a long time to find the light switch in there." She shivered. "By the way, I know they just cleaned the floor, but the rest of the place could use a good once-over."

"The main thing is that you're okay now. The doctor's keeping you overnight just to make sure you stay that way. Can I bring you anything?"

"No thanks. My Medicare's paying for everything, including this flimsy paper nightgown and slippers, so I might as well use what they give me. I just hope dinner's better than breakfast and lunch."

Roy stepped closer to the bed. "Sally, do you have any idea how your car turned up in an alley blocks away from the university—with your handbag in the trunk?"

"They messed with Arnold, too?! Is he okay?"

He gave her a smile of reassurance. "Arnold's fine. I had one of my team drive him back to your house."

"I left my purse on Amanda's desk in her office before we went to the gym, and that's the last place I saw it. And the last place I saw Arnold was in the parking lot, right where I left him."

"There were no credit cards or cash in your wallet."

She sighed. "I just had the one MasterCard. I'll have to call and report it stolen. And I guess I can kiss the twenty I had in my wallet good-bye."

Roy made a note on his iPad. "I'll take care of reporting the credit card."

"And I'll replace the twenty," I said. "After all, you never would have come to St. Priscilla's if it weren't for me."

Aunt Sally pursed her lips. "First I nearly get killed in a mine, then I almost suffocate inside a room-size coffin. I have to say, Amanda, you're going to an awful lot of trouble to get the measly inheritance I'm leaving you."

I patted her hand. "You just concentrate on getting better, okay?"

Roy pulled out his iPad. "I have one last question, if you're up to it…did you see anyone between the time you left the gym and the time you were attacked?"

"I saw Mike from the Business Office, but he was headed down the hallway in the other direction. I don't think he even noticed me." Her eyes suddenly glistened with tears. "Why would anyone want to do this? I could have died in there."

I wrapped my arms around her and hugged her tightly. "I don't know. But we're going to find out. And we'll make them answer for what they did. We'll make them pay."

Chapter Eleven

That evening I was sitting on a bar stool at the kitchen counter, my usual perch for kibitzing with Terry while he cooked, and drinking in the warmth of sharing a simple moment with the man I loved, along with the savory aroma of the dish he was preparing for dinner—risotto with asparagus and parmesan. By the way, I'm a pretty darn good cook, too, but since Terry finds a beer in one hand and a cooking utensil in the other relaxing, who am I to deprive him?

"I can't understand why someone would see Aunt Sally as a threat," I said. What other reason would someone have to kill her?"

"Probably not for a credit card and twenty bucks," said Terry. "But you have to admit, she sometimes has a way with words. She can be a bit, uh, grating."

"Certainly not grating enough for someone to want her dead!" The doorbell chimed. "Our dinner guests are here," I said, and hopped down from the bar stool. Roy had originally declined my invitation, but Dinah had persuaded him that a pleasant evening with friends would ease some of the stress that had been building up inside him during this case. And I figured that plying him with some good food and drink might loosen him up a little, maybe enough so that he'd share more of whatever he'd found up to this point in the investigation.

Plus, this was an opportunity to benefit from Dinah's logical thought process as well as Roy's inside knowledge and experience. I needed to share all the crazy ideas that had been caroming in my head since Aunt Sally's "near-death experience" in the Tomb—ideas that had been turning my brain into an organic pinball machine. Dinah would process them in her well-ordered, methodical way before re-gifting them to me in a tidy package that would likely make perfect sense. Roy would catch any false assumptions on my part and counter them with his own conclusions. Of course, experience told me that my "false" assumptions would, in the end, probably turn out to be right.

Dinah greeted me at the front door with a hug. "Mmm. Something smells wonderful!"

With satisfaction, I noticed that she looked as happy and healthy as ever. The lines that had been etched into her face during the months after Nathan's death had faded so that they were now nearly invisible. She was dressed in jeans and an apricot shirt that highlighted her olive skin. Her jewelry, as usual, was understated and elegant: a simple rose gold bracelet and matching earrings.

Terry handed Roy a Blue Moon and said, "Hope you're hungry. We're having roast chicken and risotto."

"How lucky are we," said Dinah to me, her tone conspiratorial, "that both our men cook like gourmet chefs?" She passed a bottle of wine to Terry. "Fess Parker Chardonnay—I know how much you love those Davy Crockett reruns."

Terry accepted the wine and kissed Dinah on the cheek. He was wearing a burgundy apron covered in a grapevine pattern. "Had I known you were bringing this, I would have pulled out my old coonskin hat. Now all of you head out to the patio. The weather's perfect for al fresco dining."

"Uh, no, it isn't," said Roy. "It's 102 degrees out there."

"Terry wants to show off our new swamp cooler," I said. "Please, just humor him."

Terry handed Roy a cold bottle of Stella. "It's an IceMaster 3000—makes a cool breeze that'll make you think you're on a sailboat in the middle of a Michigan lake in June." He slid his hands in a smooth, horizontal motion for emphasis. "You're going to love it."

"All right," said Roy. "But if I start to break out in a hot sweat, I'm coming back inside to watch you through the patio doors as you all melt into human puddles."

I took Dinah's left arm and Roy's right, and led them outside. We sat quietly for a while, sipping our wine and nibbling an assortment of cheeses that Terry had arranged on a small platter with some water crackers. The air was redolent with the fragrance of our Cat's Claw, a species of acacia that lacks the beauty of a rose bush but smells as intensely sweet. As Terry had promised, the swamp cooler made for a pleasantly cool evening, and we thoroughly enjoyed the twilight birdsong and the cheerful glow from the white Italian lights Terry had strung along the patio fascia.

Without explanation, I retrieved my laptop from its hiding place on the chair beside me and placed it on the table in front of me.

"What's this?" asked Dinah as she slathered some brie on a cracker. "You're not thinking of working now, are you?"

"No, not exactly," I said as I booted up. "I was just kind of hoping the two of you would help me figure out a few things."

Dinah pinned me with a wary look. "A few things about what?"

"About Sherry's murder—why Cory Matuck was beaten within an ounce of his life right after he asked to meet with me, and why Aunt Sally was attacked and thrown into the Tomb—the very same place where Sherry was murdered." I cleared my throat as I pulled up the Word document with my notes. "Also, why Brent Redmond lied when he said the Scorpions who showed up on campus the other night were merely an innocent group of potential students. By the way, they were in a white van—the same van, I suspect, that Eddie Gruber saw on the security footage the day Aunt Sally was locked in the Tomb."

"Uh, Roy?" Dinah gave him a tentative look. "Are you okay with all of us discussing your case?"

He took a sip of his beer. "Knowing Amanda, I don't think I have a choice."

"Point taken," said Dinah. "Where do we start?"

"We start at the beginning, with Sherry's murder," I said, my voice determined.

I opened to the first page of my Word document, on which I'd noted each incident or event that had taken place during the past few weeks. "Maybe we should try brainstorming. Let's see…Sherry called Mike from the Business Office the night before she was murdered to ask to meet with him; there was that list of student names and ID numbers that I found on the floor of the Tomb—and the scorpion ring—"

"Which you eventually handed over to me," said Roy dryly.

I waved him off before continuing. "Then there was that tangle between Aunt Sally and Jesse Hycamp the other day, and Aunt Sally getting locked inside the Tomb." I looked up, my gaze skipping to Dinah, then to Roy, then to Dinah again. "I just can't make sense of any of this."

"Do you see any possible connections?" asked Dinah, as Terry emerged from the house with the first tray of food.

"Not really," I said, studying the Word document, which was starting to look like Sanskrit to me. "I see only a whole lot of words and phrases that don't seem to be related."

Terry glanced down at my laptop screen. "C'mon, sweetheart. Put it away. Risotto is not a dish best served cold."

Reluctantly, I stowed my laptop under the table.

Roy half-rose from his chair. "Can I help?"

"No thanks," said Terry. "I've got it. But how about after we eat, I create an Excel spreadsheet? That way we can plot everything out on one page and maybe see some connections."

"You sure you want to take the time to do all that?" I asked.

"For you? Do you really have to ask?"

Dinner conversation focused on Aunt Sally's health status. "Will she be able to be discharged soon?" asked Dinah.

"She told us that they're going to 'let her out' tomorrow morning. Terry and I are going to pick her up at around ten."

"We're pretty sure the nursing staff will be happy to see us," added Terry. "According to the unit secretary, she hasn't been a stellar patient."

"No surprise there," said Roy.

"Come on, now, guys," I said. "Don't be so hard on her. She's been through an awful lot."

"That's right," added Dinah. "If I'd been locked in a basement room for several hours, I don't think I'd be a model patient, either."

After dinner, we went inside for coffee. Dinah and I settled on the sofa on either side of Terry, who had my laptop open on the coffee table in front of him, while Roy perched on the edge of the loveseat that was a part of our L-shaped sectional.

Dinah admired our freshly painted walls. "The room looks beautiful." We'd just finished covering the last of the blue paint that my mother had said kept the house cool "even during the heat of an Arizona summer." The new wall color was a pale taupe that, in my opinion, was just as cool and offered us the bonus of not having to buy all new furniture. I'm pretty sure Mom would have approved.

I put an arm around Terry's shoulder as I focused on the laptop screen. "Have I thanked you for being such a great husband?" I asked, as I watched him copy and paste the information from my Word document onto his spreadsheet.

"Not suitably, and not lately," he said. "Okay. Take a look at what we've got."

I looked at the spreadsheet. "Wow, I'm not sure if this is going to be all that helpful, but it does look pretty."

"I color-coded all the pieces of information so that, at a glance, you can see what's common to each event. For example, the Scorpions wear red bandannas. Whatever Sally's attackers used to cover her face—she called it a scarf—could have been a bandanna. He pointed out the columns headed Sherry, Scorpions, Cory Matuck, and Aunt Sally, then to the row entitled, Bandanna. I highlighted all those pieces of information with a red font because they all might be connected." He flashed me an apologetic look. "I also added a column for Dorm Thefts, but, as you can see, there are no obvious connections."

"Not yet, anyway," I said.

"Terry, maybe I should think about adding you to the consulting team," said Roy with a smile.

Terry laughed and shook his head. "You couldn't afford me."

***

Late Monday morning, Terry and I picked up Aunt Sally from the hospital. She insisted that she was well enough to come to St. Priscilla's with me that afternoon. "After that hospital food, even the stuff they serve in the commons looks good." After several minutes of arguing and trying to convince us that she was well enough to drive, she finally gave in. "I'll bet Arnold misses me," she said. "I'm driving tomorrow for sure. And no one better try and stop me."

Terry dropped us off at the university and promised to pick us up at five. The first thing I did was to check the screw on Carole Anne's desk for the key to the Tomb. Just as I'd expected, it was there, right where it was supposed to be. Whoever had taken it had replaced it—someone who could walk in and out of the English Department without being noticed. I immediately asked Aunt Sally to come with me to Security: The footage from that morning must have captured images of everyone who'd entered the department.

As long as we were going down to the basement, I thought I might as well take the opportunity to stop in at the Tomb and look for those 16 files that were on the list but unaccounted for.

"Aunt Sally, bring your sudoku book. This might take me a while."

When we reached the Tomb, Aunt Sally refused to go in. "No way are you going to get me in there again. I'll wait here in the doorway to make sure you don't get locked in."

After a few minutes, I muttered under my breath, "Okay—this is strange."

"What?"

"The 16 files that weren't recovered from the Tomb floor are all missing—every last one of them."

"So someone else has your same list and already took them," Aunt Sally said matter-of-factly. "Can't you just look them up in the computer?"

"These numbers go back too far. They haven't been entered into the system yet." I slid the last file drawer closed. "You know what I think, Aunt Sally?" My voice was numb, and my stomach did a flip-flop as the realization dawned on me. "I think Sherry *did* have the chance to pull all the files on this list before she was murdered. Whoever murdered her must have taken them. So if we can find the person who has them—"

Aunt Sally's voice was barely audible as she finished my sentence. "—we'll know who the killer is."

After we closed the Tomb door and made sure it was locked, we found Ralph at his usual place in front of the security monitors.

I asked to see that morning's digital footage. "Sorry, Mrs. Winters. There's no footage to look at. When Staatz took the DVD, I forgot to replace it. As a matter of fact, I just happened to think of it about five minutes before you walked in right now."

Another dead end.

Back in the English Department, I called Roy. "The 16 files you had me look for aren't here."

"What? Then where are they?"

"I wish I knew, Roy," I said, and explained my theory to him.

"I can't figure why someone would commit murder because of some old student files," he said. "If you think of something else, call me."

I spent a few hours reviewing all the work the students had completed on their theses the previous week while Aunt Sally busied herself with something new: a crossword puzzle. At around four, I decided to have a talk with Mike Kraemer. Aunt Sally said that she'd spotted him shortly before her attack. I was sure that Roy would get to him eventually, but I was anxious to hear if he'd heard or seen anything suspicious, and as long as his office was right down the hall from mine, it would be foolish of me not to just go ahead and satisfy my curiosity. Strike while the iron's hot, as they say.

As I approached the Business Office service counter, Laverne Hutchins greeted me with a concerned look. "Amanda, I heard about your aunt. How is she?"

"She's fine, thanks. In fact, she's back in the office with me today. I thought I'd take a few minutes to talk to Mike—is he free?"

"Your timing is perfect—he just got back from a meeting." She left her chair and opened a gate that gave me access to the office interior. "Come on in." She gathered up some papers and said, "I have to run these over to Ian. If Mike asks, tell him I'll be right back."

The door to Mike's office was slightly ajar. I knocked softly before entering and joined him on the other side of his desk, where he stood at an impressive bank of windows overlooking one of the manicured green spaces on campus, a small courtyard adjacent to Mesquite Avenue. A copse of tall Arizona pines prevented us from seeing the Perk-Up Café, which was directly across the street from this end of Raslin Hall. A large obelisk fountain bubbled in the near distance, and a flock of cactus wrens fluttered in its spray to drink and to cool their wings.

"You sure have a prime spot here," I said. "This view is a far cry from the one of the parking lot I get to admire from my window."

Mike chuckled. "If the English profs had this view, they wouldn't get much work done. They'd be gazing at the treetops all day and reciting Lord Byron to their students." He turned and sat on the wide window ledge. "So what brings you to my neck of the woods?"

"A question or two…maybe three."

With a broad grin, he said, "Should I be worried? I mean, you're with the sheriff's department now, aren't you?"

"On a consulting basis," I added with a smile, "but no worries—you're innocent until proven guilty. Remember the day after Sherry's murder, when my Aunt Sally and I crossed paths with you in the basement?"

"Sure." He flashed a perfect smile. "I'm not that old yet, Amanda. My memory's still pretty good."

"You were on your way to the Tomb. I was just wondering why. I mean, financial records are kept in the file room next door."

His jaw tightened perceptibly. "I have to go to the Tomb occasionally to match up old academic records with financial statements. Why do you ask?"

"I was just curious. I didn't realize the Business Office even had a key."

"We don't. Again, I have only an occasional need to get into that room. When I do, I usually borrow a key from the Registrar's Office. Sometimes I call Security to let me in."

"Do you mind telling me the names of the students you were looking up that day?"

"As a matter of fact, I do, Amanda. It's really none of your concern."

He was probably correct, there, but that didn't stop me from asking my next question. "Aunt Sally told me that she saw you in the hallway Saturday just before she was attacked."

"I do remember spotting her getting off the elevator and heading down the hallway toward the English Department. But I didn't see anyone else. Whoever ambushed her must have waited until I let myself into my office."

"So why did you leave the gym during registration, anyway? Aren't you supposed to be available in case students need to make payment arrangements?"

"I was gone for less than 15 minutes. There was something I had to take care of. With all due respect, Amanda, I don't feel that I have to explain myself to you."

Uh-oh. I hadn't intended to raise any hackles. I knew that if I didn't back off immediately, I wasn't going to get anywhere. "Mike, I'm not suggesting that you're involved in anything questionable. I'm just trying to make some sense of everything that's happened. If I see a piece that doesn't fit, I need to find out why."

"Aside from my leaving the gym and going to my own office, what other pieces, exactly, don't fit?"

"The suspect piece, for one thing. Detective Staatz hasn't been able to come up with anyone with a motive for killing Sherry. Here's another piece: Cory Matuck was attacked within hours of asking me to meet with him. He was frightened about something—I don't know what—but I think it has to do with Sherry's murder. Now he's disappeared from his hospital room without a trace. I still don't know what he wanted to talk to me about, who attacked him, or where he is now. And Aunt Sally...."

"They could all just be coincidences, Amanda. I mean, do you have any concrete evidence that would link Sherry's murder with the attacks on Cory and your aunt?"

"Not yet." I cleared my throat. "What do you know about the Scorpions?"

"Wow—that's an abrupt segue." He leaned back against the window ledge and folded his arms. "I know that they're a violent gang and that they've recently been seen in the neighborhood—and here on campus."

"Why do you think that is? What appeal do you think a private Catholic university holds for a bunch of gangbangers?"

"Amanda, not all students who attend Catholic colleges are saints. Unfortunately, some of St. Priscilla's students are likely buying drugs. And like any other street gang, the Scorpions are selling them." He shrugged. "It's unfortunate, but common." He moved to his desk and placed a hand on his mouse. As his computer screen jumped to life, he said, "I've really got to get back to work."

"Well, thanks for taking the time to talk to me." I paused at the doorway. "Do you think the Scorpions are capable of murder?"

He turned away from me and studied the scene outside his window. "Of course they are—you just have to pick up a newspaper to figure that out. But if I were you, I'd forget about the Scorpions and let Detective Staatz take care of them if he thinks they're in some way connected to Sherry's murder."

"One more question: Sherry asked to see you the day she was murdered. Do you know why?" I didn't think I'd get an answer, but I had to toss out one last seed to see if anything would sprout.

Again, he avoided eye contact with me and went back to staring out his window. "I have some advice for you, and I hope you'll take it: Stay out of this. Detective Staatz is in charge for a reason—let him do his job. Asking all these questions will only draw attention to yourself—the wrong kind of attention."

"If I was inclined to stay out of things, Mike, my Aunt Sally would be dead right now. So I'm thinking that I won't stop asking questions anytime soon, at least not until I start getting some answers."

"You're a stubborn woman, Amanda." He took a handkerchief from his pocket and wiped perspiration from his upper lip. "I have to warn you, though. You don't know what you're up against here."

"No, I don't—not yet, anyway. But you know something, Mike? I get the distinct impression that you do."

I left in frustration and barely glanced at Laverne as I passed her desk and let myself through the gate to the other side of the counter. I was certain that Mike knew more about the Scorpions, and about their possible connection to Sherry's murder, than he was letting on.

Outside in the hallway, I nearly collided with Jesse Hycamp. Today he was dressed like any other student, in jeans and a Desert Hawks T-shirt. The red bandanna and black fedora were missing.

"Well, hello again," he said, his face clearly showing his disdain for me.

"What brings you to campus this afternoon, Jesse?"

"Nothing that concerns you."

He moved toward the stairs, but I stopped him with a tug on his shirt sleeve. "Wait a minute. Can I talk to you for just a second?"

He spun around to face me angrily. "I have a right to be here."

"I know. Listen, all I'm asking for is just a few minutes of your time."

He surveyed the area around us. "What do you want?!"

"I want to know what you and your friends in the white van were doing here Friday evening and Saturday afternoon."

"Lady, I don't know what you're talking about."

"Do you think St. Priscilla students are easy targets?"

He made another move toward the stairway. "I don't got time for this."

"Do you know Cory Matuck?"

"Never heard of him."

"Here's a message for you and the rest of the Scorpions: There's no place for any of you on this campus. This university—and its students—are off-limits. And one more thing: If any of you had anything to do with Sherry Davenport's murder, Cory Matuck's beating, or the attack on my aunt, it's only a matter of time before whoever is responsible is arrested. Oh, and maybe you all should also remember that this state still has a death penalty."

"Lady, you are one crazy chick."

"You have no idea."

I watched him disappear down the stairs before continuing down the hallway to the English Department. I was shaking so badly that I had to stop and brace myself against a wall.

"Amanda, what on earth—are you all right?"

There was that ubiquitous question again, this time from Sister Fred.

I nodded. "Yes, thanks, Sister. I'm fine."

"What are you doing out in this hallway alone?" she asked, folding her arms. "Nobody can seem to remember that we're on a strict buddy system until further notice."

"I—I just had to make a quick trip to the Business Office," I said, my eyes scanning the hallway around us. "I don't see your buddy, Sister."

"Never mind about me, Amanda. You'd better get back to the English Department." Her voice softened. "I heard about your aunt locking herself inside the basement archive. I'm terribly sorry. How is she?"

I decided not to correct her assumption that Aunt Sally getting locked inside the Tomb had been an accident. "Oh, she's already back to her old, normal self."

"Well, tell her I asked about her." She moved down the hallway to the elevator, then turned back to add, "And please tell her to be more careful in the future."

I peeked over the railing to see if Jesse Hycamp was loitering in the reception area, but there was no sign of him. I may have gone too far with my threats. What had possessed me to bring up the death penalty?! I suspected that I'd just painted a huge target on my back—a target that had likely placed me squarely in the Scorpions' sights.

Chapter Twelve

Terry pulled up to Raslin Hall's main entrance shortly after 5:30 p.m. As Aunt Sally and I were about to exit the front door, Mike Kraemer suddenly appeared behind us, reached in front of us to grab the pull bar, and held the door shut.

I tried to push his arm away, but he wouldn't budge. "Mike—I'm not in the mood for games. Is there a problem?"

"Yeah, I think there might be. I told you that you've been asking too many questions, and now some people are having a problem with that."

"What people? Who are you talking about?"

Mike glanced nervously over his shoulder, but there was no one there. "You were seen coming into my office this afternoon. I don't know how, but someone overheard our conversation."

"Are you talking about Jesse Hycamp? I ran into him after I left your office, but how could he possibly have overheard us?" I remembered that Laverne had left the office to take some papers to Financial Aid. Had Hycamp simply walked into the Business Office after she'd left, and listened at Mike's door?

Aunt Sally said, "The Spiders probably have his office bugged."

"Scorpions," I said to her through clenched teeth. "Mike, did Sherry ask too many questions? Is that why she was murdered?"

"There are things you don't understand."

"So explain them to me."

He lowered his gaze to avoid mine. "I can't." He looked up again, his eyes despondent. "I'll be calling Detective Staatz when I get back to my office. Then he can decide how much to tell you, and when."

Terry appeared at the door and pulled on it. His voice, muffled, reached us through the glass panes. "Amanda, is everything all right?"

Mike let go of the bar, and the door opened.

I glanced uneasily at Mike and said, "Yeah, everything's good. You remember Mike Kraemer from the Christmas party, don't you?"

Terry extended his hand. "Of course. How've you been, Mike?"

Mike put on a happy face. "I'm good, Terry, and you?"

"Can't complain."

Mike disappeared up the stairs without another word.

"What was that all about?" asked Terry as we walked to the car.

"He said I was asking too many questions—the same thing he told me earlier in his office. He said someone has a problem with me."

"Who would that be?"

"I don't know. Maybe the Scorpion who's enrolled here...Jesse Hycamp. I ran into him today."

"If you ask me, everyone's starting to lose it around here," said Aunt Sally as we walked to the car. "I think he's a nut job."

"Mike *was* acting weird—paranoid."

Terry started the car. "Maybe he has good reason to be paranoid. Maybe it's time to back off, Amanda."

I suddenly remembered that, once again, I'd forgotten something back at the office, this time my key card.

Terry sighed. "Can't you just wait and get it tomorrow?"

"No, I can't. I wouldn't want anyone to think I'm irresponsible."

"If you go back now, someone will have to let you into the building. And they'll know you forgot your key card, which will still make you look irresponsible, only sooner rather than later."

"Lynn Goodman is at the desk right now," I said, opening the passenger door. "Lynn understands irresponsibility. She accepts it."

"That girl is starting to forget more things than my friend Esther," said Aunt Sally.

As I made my way back to the front entrance, there was a flurry of activity ahead of me. Lynn, supported on either arm by two students, stumbled through the door. Her face had changed from its usual mask of indifference to one of hysteria.

I ran up to Lynn and her student escorts. "What's wrong?!"

But she was unable to speak, and only shook her head in anguish. Tears were streaming down her cheeks.

I ran up the stairs, and another student opened the door for me. I immediately caught a flash of color from the corner of my eye, and turned to see a ghastly scene that was very much out of place on the glossy black slate floor of the reception area. Mike Kraemer, his neck twisted at an improbable angle, stared at me with vacant eyes. As I watched in horror, blood pooled from beneath his body in a macabre tide that slowly spread across the floor until it finally swept me into its current.

***

When I came to, Terry was kneeling over me. Sister Fred, a troubled look on her face, was right behind him and peering over his shoulder. "Amanda! Amanda, are you all right?!"

Again, with that question.

She held a Styrofoam cup out to me. "Here, drink. How are you feeling?"

I sat up and accepted the water gratefully. "Not my best." I glanced over to where I'd seen Mike Kraemer's body, hoping I'd imagined it—hallucinations, a new twist on this cluster C thing? But it was still there. I watched silently as a student bearing a stadium blanket sporting the university's Desert Hawks logo tiptoed around the pool of blood and placed it gently over Mike's body.

"Staatz and his team are on the way," said Terry. "Just sit still until you're sure you're okay to stand."

"I have to stop passing out like this," I said, rubbing the back of my head gingerly. Tears brimmed my eyes. "What happened?" I turned to Sister Fred. "Terry and I were talking to him just five minutes ago."

"He must have fallen over the balustrade. No one saw how it happened." She pulled a handkerchief from her sleeve and wiped her face. "Poor Mike." She looked at me, her eyes pleading. "Amanda, why is this happening? I—I don't understand." She shook her head sadly and stared up at the mezzanine. "If I didn't know better, I'd say that someone has put a curse on this university."

"It's no curse, Sister Fred." My gaze followed hers. "That balustrade is a good four feet tall. You can't possibly believe this was an accident."

"The alternative is too horrible to imagine, Amanda. But if it turns out that Mike's fall wasn't an accident, I'm afraid I'll have no choice but to close St. Priscilla's before anyone else is harmed."

Ralph Michaels came huffing toward us. Two members of his Security staff were heavy on his heels.

His eyes immediately took in the scene, and he wasted no time in taking action. "Lock down the building—no one gets in or out until Staatz gives us the all-clear. Jake, you hold down the front entrance. Lonnie, you take the back. Get Evie up here to secure the commons doors to the courtyard."

"Ralph," I said, as Terry helped me to my feet. "Did you see any gangbangers on the security footage this morning? Did you see that white van you mentioned the other day?"

"As a matter of fact, yes, about an hour ago. I went out to ask them what their business was. They said they were here to pick up one of their friends who's supposed to be a student here."

"You think the Scorpions had something to do with this?" asked Terry.

"I'm beginning to think so…yes." But the wailing of sirens drowned out my voice.

"There's the fire department," said Ralph. "I have to clear this area." After settling everyone in the commons, he returned to oversee the scene of the accident (or more accurately, in my opinion, the scene of the crime) and to wait for Roy's team to arrive.

The kitchen staff was just beginning to set up for dinner, so we helped ourselves to fresh coffee from a huge stainless steel urn. Sister Fred hadn't appeared surprised when I'd brought up the Scorpions with Ralph, and I was curious to know why. I asked her.

"I've tried to keep an open mind about those Scorpion boys—you never really know why someone turns to crime—what they've been through. But Detective Staatz did fill me in a bit on the gang, and I have to admit that it's possible they may be responsible for some of the recent…events. I've been president of this university for twenty years, and until lately there's

never been so much as a fistfight in the parking lot—
and now two people are dead. ”

"I was almost number two." Aunt Sally hovered
over our table, her eyes narrowed accusingly at me.
"You leave me sitting in the car, and all this time you're
in here having a coffee klatch?"

I held my cup out to her. "Here, Aunt Sally, take
mine. I haven't touched it. And please forgive us for not
coming out to get you. Mike Kraemer just fell to his
death, and we were a little preoccupied."

"So who's gonna be next, Amanda?" She shook her
head and headed off to another table, muttering, "Now I
know why I never went to college."

"The Scorpions have been seen hanging around this
campus, and two people are now dead. They're not
innocent boys, Sister Fred. They're thieves and
murderers. You have to consider the possibility that
they're responsible for everything that's been
happening here."

She took a sip from her mug, and I could see that she
was shaking badly. "Well, Amanda, I have to accept
your word for it. You were quite successful in helping
Detective Staatz solve your godson's murder." She
offered a weak smile. "And I trust you, even with all
your…issues."

"Thank you—I think."

"I was so naïve that when some of the students
began to report their concerns to me months ago, I
didn't recognize the problem for what it was. Now I'm
afraid it may be too late."

I glanced uneasily at Terry. "Is there something else
we should know"?

"Amanda, someone's been breaking into Thatcher
House—there have been thefts."

"Yes, Detective Staatz told me."

"In the past few months, nearly $200,000 worth of computers, smartphones, cash—even bicycles—have gone missing."

"I knew there was a problem," I said, "but I had no idea it was such a big problem." I was about to ask for more details when I spied Roy.

"Hello, Sister Fred." He stood over our table and fixed me with a curious look. "Amanda, how is it that you always seem to get to crime scenes before I do?"

Crime scenes. So Roy didn't think Mike's death was an accident, either. "I happen to be working here, remember?"

"That's right. I almost forgot."

"What do you make of it, Roy?" asked Terry.

"Nothing...yet."

"Detective, can I get you some coffee?" asked Sister Fred, beginning to rise from her seat.

He motioned for her to remain seated. "Thanks, but I'll get it, Sister. You stay here. I just have a few questions for everyone."

Roy returned with his coffee and sat down next to me and across from Sister Fred. "Okay. Can someone tell me exactly what happened?"

Sister Fred folded her hands in front of her and announced in a measured voice, "Our bursar, Mike Kraemer, fell from the mezzanine. Unfortunately, there appears to have been no witnesses."

"And there are no security cameras on that level," I added.

"Think for a minute," said Roy. "Did you see anything unusual inside the building today—or outside—anyone who didn't belong?"

"I ran into Jesse Hycamp in the hallway, but apparently he's now a St. Priscilla's student." I glanced at Terry. "Did you see anyone out of the ordinary?"

He shook his head. "No, but I wasn't really paying attention."

I told Roy about Ralph seeing some gangbangers he'd tagged as Scorpions in the parking lot earlier.

"I'll ask him about that." He lowered his head and studied me over the tops of his glasses. "Anything else?"

"I'm getting another cup of coffee." I cocked my head slightly to signal that he should follow me.

Taking the hint, Roy got up from the table. "I could use a refill, too."

As soon as we were out of earshot, I told Roy how, in his office earlier that day, Mike had warned me to stop asking questions. "He said that I might attract the wrong kind of attention, and that I could be placing myself in danger. And then, just minutes before his death, he stopped me and Aunt Sally at the front door as we were leaving. He warned me again, and this time he was nearly frantic. He told me that someone had a problem with me."

"Someone, who?"

"He wouldn't say. He told me that he was going to call you and tell you everything when he got back to his office."

"He never called me," said Roy.

"That's because he never made it back to his office." As I refilled my cup, I said, "Someone pushed him over that railing, Roy. I know it, and you know it."

"Maybe. Do you have a motive? Any suspects?"

"I don't have a motive yet, exactly. As for suspects, I had an interesting conversation with Jesse Hycamp."

"You said he's a student now, so—"

I focused my eyes on the floor when I interrupted him. "He may have taken a few of the things I said to him as threats against the Scorpions."

Roy performed a half-swivel on his feet and exclaimed, "Oh my God, Amanda. Please tell me you're joking."

"I wish I could tell you that, Roy. I—I don't know why I did it. The words just came out."

Roy gritted his teeth. "What, exactly, did you say?"

"Well, I may have mentioned the state's death penalty." I screwed up my face. "But now that I think of it, that wasn't really a threat, was it? It was more of a warning—"

Roy sighed. "I told you to avoid contact with the Scorpions."

"I didn't *try* to run into him, Roy. It just happened. Shortly before he died, Mike implied that someone overheard us talking in his office. The head cashier left for a short time, and I ran into Hycamp in the hallway just as I was leaving to head back to the English Department. Hycamp could have snuck into the Business Office, then overheard us talking about the Scorpions and Sherry's murder, and got spooked...maybe spooked enough to kill Mike."

Roy rubbed his eyes wearily. "We always seem to be coming up with new theories, but no new findings. Unless I can place Hycamp or anyone else on the mezzanine at the time Kraemer fell, I've got nothing. As far as I'm concerned, he's just another student."

I folded my arms in front of me. "Why didn't you tell me the truth about the Thatcher House thefts? About how bad the problem is?"

"Wait just a minute, Amanda. Where did you get the idea that I have to report every detail of every case I'm working on to you? You work for the department on a consulting basis—meaning that you know only what I want you to know."

"Roy, you told me I'm officially on this case. If I am, then I have a right to know everything—otherwise, what's the point?"

"Sorry. I guess I'm just tired…and frustrated. And I still don't think the thefts are related to Sherry's murder."

"What about Mike? You really don't think it was an accident, do you?"

"Kraemer's death is assumed to be an accident until it's proven otherwise."

"But you referred to 'the crime scene' earlier," I said.

"That was my mistake—a slip of the tongue. Do me a favor and forget it."

"Will you be checking out Jesse Hycamp?"

"Like I said, unless I have reason to suspect him of committing an actual crime, I have to leave him alone. Meanwhile, I want you to steer clear of him, and anyone else you suspect of belonging to the Scorpions. Understood?"

"Understood."

Before returning to the table, we poked our heads out into the hallway to assess the situation. One of Roy's men was assisting Ralph with students who were trying to enter the building's main entrance. Ralph must have been explaining what had happened, because the looks on the students' faces were in a collective state of flux, changing from curiosity to despair. Paramedics had already arrived and were in the process of transporting Mike's body to an ambulance via a side door.

"You know what?" said Roy. "I'd better get out there and do my job—talk to some people." He turned back to me and snapped his fingers. "I almost forgot. I talked to Travis Halloway, the agent who represented Sherry Davenport at the modeling agency. Shortly after she left the firm, she had to take out a restraining order against the guy, though he claims he wasn't stalking her. It was clear, though, that he still carries a big chip on his shoulder."

"Even after all these years? So he's a person of interest?"

"Absolutely. He doesn't have an alibi...says he was at home last Monday—alone, of course."

"I thought he lived in LA."

"He did until recently. He relocated to Phoenix a few months ago."

"Interesting," I said. "But Halloway couldn't have known precisely when and where to find Sherry alone. During the week, a student worker is stationed at the reception desk from seven a.m. until Lynn Goodman takes over at eight. Were you able to question whoever was at the desk then?"

"I talked to the student worker, and she insisted that only a few staff and faculty came through—no strangers."

"I still think the killer must be someone who knew Sherry—someone who knew her routine and the fact that she was always the first to arrive at the office. You might want to talk to Tony Loduca, by the way. He left the gym during Saturday's registration—he told me he was leaving campus to run some errands. I'm just thinking...he left at around the same time Aunt Sally went missing."

Roy made a note. "I'll check it out. But I'm not writing Halloway off just yet."

"Before you go, tell me...have you heard anything about Cory Matuck? I have a feeling he may hold the key to this whole thing."

"*Nada.* I've had his dorm watched since he disappeared from the hospital. He hasn't even come back to get his things."

"He's probably hunkered down with his family," I said. "If I were a kid in trouble, that's where I'd be."

Roy pulled out his iPad. "I'll drop in on them. Are they in Chandler?"

"No such luck. They live in Supai Village at the bottom of Havasu Canyon. It branches off the Grand Canyon, so it's not all that easy to get to. The only way into the village is by helicopter, pack mule, or horseback."

"The village must at least have phone service."

"Of course. But if your son told you someone's out to kill him because of something he saw, or because of something he knows, would you acknowledge his presence to some stranger on the phone?"

Roy sighed and shook his head. "It looks like we'll just have to wait for Cory to come to us." He took off down the hallway before I could voice my protest.

But my brain had already kicked into high gear. I figured that if Cory was hiding, he must have a pretty good reason, and it would take some convincing to get him back out in the open, especially after the attack in the campus parking lot. He'd reached out to me once. All things considered, I thought that I'd have a better shot than Roy of getting through to him. All I had to do was find him before he—or someone else—ended up dead. Terry waited at Raslin Hall's reception desk while Aunt Sally and I went up to my office, where I called up the Matucks' contact information for the second time.

That evening, I reached Maya, Cory's mother. Although she said that Cory hadn't been in contact with the family for over a week, the hesitation in her voice convinced me that she was lying.

The obvious course of action was to go to Supai Village and meet with Cory face-to-face. There was no way Terry would agree to pay the steep costs of helicopter transport, but he used to love convening with nature during Boy Scout camp-outs with Jeff. I just might be able to sell him on a relaxing horseback ride along a winding canyon trail.

Chapter Thirteen

During the week, I did some research to prep for our trip to Supai Village. I learned that horseback or mule transport into the canyon was out of the question because of my cluster C. Apparently more than one "nervous Nellie" had suffered panic attacks and plunged to their deaths on one of the narrow rock shelves bordering the trail. I guess I could have withheld information about my medical history, but then if my horse were suddenly to lose footing, causing me to take a fatal dive into the canyon, the insurance company would ultimately learn about my sin of omission and refuse to pay up on my accidental death insurance, leaving Terry high and dry. It took some cajoling and a bit of bribery, but Terry eventually agreed to cover the helicopter transport costs. In my mind, this was not completely the lesser of two evils, since I also have a flying phobia, but I had no choice: I couldn't very well magically twitch my nose or blink myself into the village.

During a phone conversation with Aunt Sally, I accidentally let the cat out of the bag about the trip, and Arnold pulled into our driveway ten minutes later. "Please take me along," she pleaded. "I've always wanted to see the Falls, and I've never had a chopper ride. It's on my bucket list."

"Is there anything that *isn't* on your bucket list?" asked Terry. "And do you by any chance remember what happened when we let you come along on our trip to Mexico last year?"

"I remember we had a little trouble because of some bad roads." She pressed her hands together in a gesture of begging. "I'll pay my own way, and I'll be good." She held up three fingers. "Scout's honor."

"I'd feel better about that if you'd actually been a Girl Scout," I said.

"Hey, I made it all the way through the Brownies."

"And *I'd* feel better if your memory was more accurate," said Terry. "Our trouble in Mexico was not because of bad roads."

"I'll behave." She crossed her heart and held up a hand. "Honest Injun."

"Aunt Sally," I said, and rolled my eyes. "We're going into a Native American village. These people deserve our respect, and if we let you come with us, you're going to have to watch your language. The expression you just used is extremely inappropriate."

She set her jaw and looked downcast "Sorry, Amanda," then added, "I don't get it—I mean, I didn't say "lying Inj—"

"—never mind," interrupted Terry. He sighed. "All right, you win. We leave Friday."

"What about the students, Amanda? Did Sister Fred hand you a pink slip already?"

"No, Aunt Sally, she didn't. I had only a few appointments for Friday, and I asked Carole Ann to reschedule the others for next week."

"I could be ready to leave bright and early tomorrow morning," said Aunt Sally hopefully.

"We're leaving Friday," said Terry. "Take it or leave it."

"I'll take it." She held a hand to her mouth and whispered an aside, "I hope he's not this grouchy during the whole trip."

Should we ask if Jeff wants to come along?" I asked, never passing up an opportunity to get up close and personal with our only child.

"Sure," said Terry, "but he'll have to square things with school and make sure he's not needed at the station Friday or Saturday."

"I'll give him a call right now," I said, clapping my hands together in anticipation.

***

Shortly after noon on Friday, our six-seat helicopter set down on a tiny landing strip nestled between Supai's Village Café and Tourism Office. In my opinion, riding a horse or mule down an eight mile-long treacherous path would have been a welcome option to the helicopter—cluster C or no cluster C. The young chopper pilot seemed to take great delight in fast dips and turns; my stomach remained in situ only because I was safely wedged between Terry and Jeff and had my eyes squeezed shut throughout the entire flight. Aunt Sally, however, enjoyed the bumpy ride, judging by all the "woo-hoos!" and "yippee ki yays!" she screamed into my ear from her seat behind me.

"Mom, you missed some great sights," said Jeff. "We passed right by Rock Falls—it wasn't even there until the flash flood hit the Canyon in 2008."

"Did you take pictures?" I asked.

"Nope." He laughed. "I tried, but every time I was about to get a great shot, the pilot took a crazy dip."

"Yeah, I noticed he liked to do that."

We ordered soft drinks at the Village Café and waited for our stomachs to settle before enjoying some Navajo fry bread tacos.

"Now what?" asked Aunt Sally as she inspected our stark surroundings. "You could have warned me that a person can't even get a danged gin gimlet around here."

Terry held up his hands. "I don't want to hear a single complaint from you, Aunt Sally. It took me three solid hours of redialing to get through to Reservations, and the woman I talked to said it takes most people days—sometimes weeks—to book a room. The Hikers' Lodge phone line is always swamped, and their new website has been down for a while. The only reason we even got a reservation is because the phone call just before mine was a cancellation for tonight."

Aunt Sally shrugged. "Well, if they refuse to tech up and join the rest of us in the twenty-first century, that's their problem."

"Aunt Sally, just enjoy your ginger ale and let me think for a minute," I said. "I have to figure out my next step."

Jeff had found a travel website featuring information on Supai Village and the nearby Falls. "It says here that alcohol isn't allowed in the village. If they find anyone with liquor, they get ejected."

"Oh brother, what the heck was I thinking, asking to come along on this trip?" muttered Aunt Sally under her breath.

Terry jabbed a finger at her. "Remember, you promised to behave. I can't stress enough that we all have to be extremely considerate of these people. There aren't many of the Havasupai Tribe left, and they depend on tourism to make a simple living here."

"According to this article," interjected Jeff, "they're called the *Havasuw 'Baaja,* or 'people of the blue-green water.' They consider the land to be sacred, and they do everything they can to preserve it. They don't allow pets or weapons here, either. And we can't leave any trash behind—we have to take it out of the Canyon with us when we leave."

"Humph," grumbled Aunt Sally. "At least we won't have to cart any empty liquor bottles out with us."

After lunch, we checked in at the lodge, a bare-bones motel with a sign warning that the rooms had no TVs and that Internet service was not guaranteed. Our single room, which was the only one available, featured two queen beds and a pull-out sleeper for Jeff.

"They need to fix this place up," said Aunt Sally. "I've stayed in more modern motel rooms than this one, and I'm talking the early sixties."

"There's likely not much money for updates," I said as I checked out the bathroom, which had a sink, a toilet, and a stand-up shower that was neatly tiled in white acrylic. "It must be expensive to live at the bottom of a canyon. Think of the costs of bringing in food, water, and other supplies. At least everything looks clean, and the beds seem comfortable."

"And the room's air-conditioned," added Jeff, checking his phone again. "It's supposed to get up to 105 degrees by four o'clock."

For some reason, Jeff was the only one of us able to get cell service. "Keep your phone charged," I told him, "it's our only means of communication right now."

"I will," Jeff assured me. "We'll need it in case of an emergency—according to the U.S. Department of Agriculture, the Supai Village is the most remote community in the contiguous United States." He frowned. "Uh-oh—this article also says that emergency services aren't always available."

Aunt Sally groaned. "Great. No alcohol, and no EMTs." She glanced at me. "My odds of survival were better when you got us trapped in that mine, Amanda."

Aunt Sally was not interested in venturing out into the heat, so despite our misgivings, we left her alone in the room with her sudokus while Terry and Jeff accompanied me to the Matucks' house. Since the village is less than two square miles and has a population of around two hundred, the house was relatively easy to find. The one-story, brown clapboard dwelling was one of several clustered at the base of a cliff outcropping. A petite woman in her mid-forties was tending raised garden beds under a rustic pergola consisting of a canvas canopy atop a plain wooden structure. In an effort not to startle her, I cleared my throat before using the traditional Havasupai greeting, "*Gam'yu.*"

She turned to us with a tentative smile and used a hand to shade her eyes from the sun. "Yes? Can I help you?"

I extended a hand. "Mrs. Matuck?"

Her smile morphed into a concerned frown. "And you are…?"

"Amanda Winters. I talked to you on the phone the other evening. And this is my husband Terry and my son Jeff."

She used her skirt to brush soil from her hand and accepted my handshake. "I told you—Cory's not here. I have no idea where he is."

"Mrs. Matuck…."

"Maya."

I smiled. "Maya, I'm—we're—not here to hurt Cory. We won't even try to persuade him to come back with us." I met her eyes with a sober gaze. "I just need to talk to him. St. Priscilla's is in trouble: Two people have already been murdered, and I think Cory may know something that would help us find whoever's responsible."

"I'm very sorry that you came all this way for nothing," she said. "Even if I knew where my son was, I wouldn't tell you."

The front door of the house creaked open, and Cory stepped out. "Mrs. Winters, what are you doing here?"

"Cory!" Maya exclaimed. "I told you to stay inside when strangers come around."

"Mrs. Winters isn't a stranger," he said with a smile. "She's a friend."

Cory's bruises had changed from their original blend of red, black, and blue to a sickly hue of greenish-gray.

"I'm glad to see that you're healing," I said. "But it wasn't the smartest thing to do, leaving the hospital without your doctor's permission."

"I had no choice." He studied Jeff with curiosity. "Are you a St. Priscilla's student?"

"Naw, I'm a grad student at ASU."

I looped my arm through Jeff's. "I'm sorry…Cory, this is my son Jeff and my husband Terry."

"Desert Hawks, huh?" said Terry as he admired Cory's T-shirt. "You're on the football team?"

"Yeah," he said, and shook his head in frustration. "And I've already missed four practices."

"I have a feeling Coach Martin will forgive you, considering the circumstances," I said.

"I don't know about that, Mrs. Winters." Cory shifted his weight from foot to foot while his gaze took in the surrounding area. "Are you sure no one followed you here?"

Jeff chuckled. "Thanks to the wild moves of our chopper pilot, not even a CIA drone would have been able to follow us here. And my dad got the last open reservation for tonight."

"The people I'm thinking of are pretty creative. If they want something, they tend to get it."

Maya motioned us toward the house. "Please, let's go inside. I have some fresh lemonade."

The Matucks' living room was small, and the furniture worn but comfortable. The blinds had been closed to keep the midday sun out, so the room was as dark and cool as a fall evening. Terry, Jeff, and I settled on a floral-upholstered sofa, while Cory, with a heavy sigh, fell into an easy chair. Maya disappeared into the kitchen and returned a few minutes later with a tray of glasses filled with iced lemonade.

"I'll leave you to talk to Cory," she said. "If you need anything, I'll be just outside." She directed a meaningful gaze at her son. "Your father will be home in about half an hour, so I hope you can finish up by then."

Cory nodded.

"Thanks, Maya," I said. "We promise not to keep him long."

As soon as Cory's mother was clear of the house, I said, "Cory, Mike Kraemer is dead. I think he was murdered. And someone tried to kill my aunt."

"No way!" He hung his head in his hands. "Man, I can't believe this is happening."

"Just exactly what *is* happening? Do you know something about Miss Davenport's murder? Is that why you wanted to meet with me?"

"I'm not sure of anything, Mrs. Winters."

"You must know something," I said, beginning to lose my patience. "Whatever you wanted to talk to me about last week sounded pretty urgent. And why did you leave the hospital without telling anyone? I find it hard to believe that you'd jeopardize your status on the team, or your academic standing, by taking off like that without good reason."

Cory glanced at Jeff as if apologizing for what he was going to say next. His face was twisted in a mask of despair when he said, "Someone called me at the hospital and told me that if I talked to you, we'd both be dead by the end of the week."

"How could they know that we'd planned to meet? Did you tell anyone?"

"No. Someone must have overheard me. I was calling you from the commons, and it was pretty crowded."

"Do you remember seeing anyone loitering around you while you were on the phone?"

"No. But Mrs. Winters, they seem to know everything that goes on at St. Priscilla's."

"The Scorpions, you mean?"

He nodded. "The guy who called me said I should tell you that you're asking too many questions. He said you need to back off."

"That's what Mike Kraemer told me just before he died." I closed my eyes at the memory of Mike's broken body on the floor of Raslin Hall's reception area. "Did you recognize the caller's voice?"

He shook his head. "No. I never heard it before."

"Cory, at least you must be able to describe your attackers. Were they members of the Scorpions? Were they wearing red bandannas under black fedoras? Did they have scorpion tattoos?"

"Please, Mrs. Winters, I can't—"

"Yes, you can."

Jeff took a long drink of his lemonade. "You might just as well tell her what you know. My mom doesn't give up easily."

"Detective Staatz can arrange for protection for you," said Terry. "He'll guarantee your safety."

Cory's eyes brimmed with tears. "No one can guarantee my safety, not now. I can tell you this much: The Scorpions have been stealing from the rooms at Thatcher House."

I emitted a dry laugh. "I'd pretty much figured that out already. But what does that have to do with the murders of Sherry Davenport and Mike Kraemer?"

Cory made a point of not meeting my gaze. "Nothing. I mean, I don't know. I don't have any evidence about Miss Davenport's murder, or anything like that."

"The day I saw you at the sheriff's outpost—did you tell Detective Steele any of this?"

He shook his head. "No."

"At least tell me who's helping the Scorpions. Is it a teacher? A staff member? Another student? Who?!"

"I can't tell you. Not now, not after—" He bowed his head. "Don't you get it, Mrs. Winters? There's something more than just the Thatcher House thefts— something big. I just don't know what it is—but they must think I know more than I do, or they wouldn't have beaten the daylights out of me."

"What about Mike Kraemer? Where do you think he fits into all of this?"

Cory shook his head slowly. "I don't know anything more than what I've told you. I guess he must have found out about whatever Miss Davenport knew—the thing that got her killed."

"If you tell Detective Staatz what you've just told us, he can use the information to at least put a stop to the thefts. There's also a good chance he'll even find if someone at St. Priscilla's is helping the Scorpions, and why. Don't you want that?"

"Of course I do. I want things to go back to the way they were." He looked up with tears in his eyes. "I want to feel safe again."

Chapter Fourteen

The copter ride out of the canyon Saturday morning was no less terrifying than the ride in, but I managed to keep my eyes open long enough to admire the turquoise waters of the Havasu Falls. Sun stars glinted off the massive spray, and for a few long moments, I forgot all about the fact that we were weaving through canyon walls in a small whirlybird. We had a different pilot this time, a man of about seventy who, to my chagrin, kept turning away from the control panel to flirt with Aunt Sally. We also had an extra passenger: Cory had decided at the last minute to come back with us. I offered him our guest room when he insisted he wasn't ready to go back to Thatcher House.

After dropping off Aunt Sally and Jeff, we pulled into the driveway to discover an attractive young blonde sitting on one of the chairs in our small front courtyard.

"Oh no—what's *she* doing here?" muttered Cory. "Mrs. Winters, no one can know I'm here."

"Okay, then hunker down out of sight back there, and Terry will pull right into the garage." I turned around and added, "Who is she, anyway?"

"Alana Christopoulos. She's on St. Priscilla's cheerleading squad. Her brother Zach is on the football team. She likes me, but I have no use for her. She's pretty stuck-up."

"She couldn't possibly have known that you were planning to stay with us. So what's she doing here?"

"I don't have a clue."

"There's only one way to find out," said Terry, as the garage door slid closed behind us. He unlocked the door to the kitchen. "Amanda, how about you go ask her what she wants while I rustle up some food?"

I dropped my purse on the kitchen counter and hurried straight through the living room to the front door. Alana, standing with arms crossed, looked relieved to see me.

"Alana"? I said.

Her pretty face distorted with anxiety, she glanced over her shoulder and said, "Hi, Mrs. Winters. I don't think we've ever met...how did you know my name?"

I craned my neck to check out the street in both directions but saw nothing and ushered her inside. "I've seen you around campus." Using Cory's information, I added, "cheerleading squad, right?"

She nodded.

"I'm assuming you're here for a reason. Is something wrong?"

"I need to talk to you, Mrs. Winters. I left two messages...."

"We've been out of town," I explained. "Can I get you something to drink? Iced tea, maybe, or a soda?"

"I could use some iced tea," she said thankfully. "I've been waiting outside for hours."

"Then I'm glad we didn't decide to stay away an extra day," I said with a smile. "You must be hungry, too. I'll ask my husband to bring something."

I popped into the kitchen to see that Terry was already making ham sandwiches. He handed me two frosty glasses of iced tea with lemon wedges. "Here. This'll be good for a start." With a wink, he added, "You might want to ask Sister Fred to compensate you for all the extra student advising you've been doing."

"Not a bad idea," I said with a laugh. "Where's Cory?"

"In the guest room, unpacking."

"Um...could you move my computer out to the kitchen counter when you get the chance?"

"Can't you just use the laptop?"

"I could, but I have a lot of stuff on my computer—you know, about Sherry's murder investigation. I'm sure Cory wouldn't snoop, but I'd feel better if I could keep my eyes on it."

Back in the living room, I settled on the sofa next to Alana and handed her a glass of iced tea. "Okay...tell me what's going on."

"Something very bad is happening at St. Priscilla's."

"That's obvious," I said. "Two people have been murdered within the past couple weeks."

"I don't know anything about the murders, but whatever's going on, I think that my brother Zach is involved."

"Involved, how?"

"He won't tell me. He's scared—really scared. And since he's been working on Mr. Redmond's project, he seems tired all the time. He's been walking around like a zombie or something."

"Mr. Redmond's project?"

"It's a beta test to try out some new assignments for an online business program. Zach claims that the work is easy—the assignments are just time-consuming. But he's been staying out late most nights—hasn't been sleeping much."

"Alana, I don't think you came here to talk about Mr. Redmond's project or your brother's sleeping habits. What's really on your mind?" It suddenly occurred to me that based on her hair color and style, Alana could be the young woman who'd dropped off Brent Redmond at his truck that night in the university parking lot. For her sake, and mine, I hoped she wasn't. I already had more than enough on my plate.

"I came here because everyone knows you've been asking questions about the Scorpions. Zach's been hanging around some of them, and I was hoping you could help me—help Zach."

I frowned, attempting to remember who I'd had conversations with about the gang. There was Roy, but he wouldn't be sharing our discussions with St. Priscilla's students—and, of course, Sister Fred, Patty LeBlanc, and Mike Kraemer. I couldn't imagine any of them talking to students about me, or about my interest in the Scorpions. "Do you think Zach would agree to talk to someone with the sheriff's department? Someone who'd be very interested in hearing what he has to say?"

"Not a chance. That's why I came to you."

I sighed and sipped my tea. "What makes you think he'll talk to me?"

"His girlfriend told him how cool you are."

"Who's his girlfriend?"

"Tanya Lauren. She's one of the grad students you've been helping."

Terry came out with a tray of sandwiches. "Here you go, ladies. Let me know if you need anything else."

"Thanks, Terry." I made quick introductions. As soon as he disappeared back into the kitchen, she asked about Cory.

"He and Zach are good friends," said Alana. "Cory's doing assignments for the beta test, too."

"I don't see how these guys are managing to squeeze extra assignments into their full course loads."

"They probably stay up all night working on them. That's why Zach's been looking like one of the walking dead."

"Did you know that Cory was attacked in the university parking lot last week?"

Alana nodded. "Zach thinks he's going to be next."

"Why would he think that?"

"I don't know. He won't talk to me about it, that's for sure."

"Is Zach taking drugs? Is he buying them from the Scorpions?"

Alana looked up in shock. "No way. He doesn't take so much as a cold tablet unless it's absolutely necessary."

"Sorry. I had to ask."

"I don't understand what the Scorpions have on him, but it's like he's hypnotized. The other day, one of them showed up in the commons while we were having lunch, and Zach took off with him without a word. He left half his lunch untouched, and if you knew anything about Zach, you'd know how weird that is."

"Who was this guy? Do you know his name?"

"Jesse something."

"Jesse Hycamp?"

Alana nodded. "Yeah."

I settled back against the sofa cushion and sighed. "Why did Zach send you instead of just contacting me himself?"

"He totally freaked after Cory was attacked. Like I said, he's scared. He wants me to arrange a meeting with you—someplace out of the way."

A dry laugh escaped my lips. "Sun Lakes is about as 'out of the way' as you can get. I don't expect you'll find any gangs around here, unless it's a gang of golfers on their way to the nineteenth hole."

Alana shrugged. "I'm just the messenger, Mrs. Winters. I'm sorry, but Zach won't come near your house." She pulled a small piece of paper from her purse and handed it to me. "This is his phone number. He wants you to call him as soon as possible."

"Okay, I'll do that. Now, is there anything else I should know?"

"No." She set down a half-eaten sandwich and rubbed her hands on her jeans. "But, Mrs. Winters...do you know where Cory is?"

I remembered the fear in Cory's voice when he spotted Alana outside our house. "I haven't seen him since the morning he was taken to the hospital." I felt bad lying to her, but Cory obviously didn't want her to know his whereabouts, and I had to respect that.

I stood and moved toward the front door. This conversation was going nowhere, and Alana's sudden interest in Cory, who, at that moment and unbeknownst to her, was in my guest room, was beginning to make me feel uncomfortable. "If I hear from Cory, I'll be sure to email you." I opened the door, wondering if I'd have to eventually just push the girl out onto the front stoop. "I have some unpacking to do, but I'll call Zach a little later."

"Could you call him now?"

"*Right* now, you mean?"

Alana nodded.

"All right, then." I closed the front door again and gestured toward the sofa. "Why don't you sit back down and finish your sandwich?"

I grabbed the landline and punched in the number Alana gave me while she popped a tuft of bread into her mouth and chewed thoughtfully. Zach answered immediately.

"Zach? This is Amanda Winters. Alana's with me— she says you want to talk to me."

"Thanks, Mrs. Winters. I didn't know who else I could trust."

"Can't you just tell me whatever it is you want to tell me right now? I mean, you don't think your phone is bugged or anything like that, do you?"

"Maybe. I don't know."

"You're kidding."

"No, I'm not. Just about anyone can hack into a person's cell—all they need is the right app and your number. They can even read your texts and track your location." Zach was silent for several moments, and I was afraid he'd hung up. "I don't want to get you into any trouble, especially after what happened to Miss Davenport."

"Based on what Alana shared with me, Zach, if you don't tell me what you know about the Scorpions and what they're up to at St. Priscilla's, someone else is liable to get hurt, or worse."

"I do want to talk to you, Mrs. Winters, but I can't leave my apartment right now. I need you to come here."

The fact that this could be a trap briefly entered my mind, but before I even knew what I was saying, I'd agreed to meet him. I jotted down the address he rattled off, and I said I'd be there at 7:30 that evening. I was counting on Terry not being too tired from our trip to drive me. If he was, I'd find someone else to take me.

***

"Absolutely not! Amanda, you are not going to meet with anyone, especially some kid who's cozying up to the Scorpions. Some kid you don't even know!" He looked at the address I'd handed him. "And I have no idea where this even is. Why couldn't he meet you somewhere out in public?"

"Because he's afraid." Cory stood in the doorway to the kitchen. "The Scorpions play for keeps, Mr. Winters, and Zach has reason to be afraid. I was lucky."

Terry hoisted his hands up into the air. "I rest my case."

"Well, I'm going to be at this address at 7:30 tonight, one way or another," I said. "I promised him."

"I'll take you," said Cory, "if someone drives me over to Thatcher to get my car."

Terry's response to that offer was a look of rage. "No way, Cory!" He redirected his anger toward me. "Have you completely lost your mind?! Amanda, people have been murdered! For once, I'm grateful for your cluster C, since, in this case, your inability to drive more than a few blocks might just save your life, because there's no way I'm taking you." He glared at Cory again. "And no one else is taking you, either."

I blinked back tears. I could take harsh words from pretty much anyone except Terry. I couldn't remember a time when he didn't support me in anything I'd set my mind to do. And my mind was set on talking to Zach Christopoulos. I always felt one hundred percent safe with Terry. I really didn't want to ask anyone else to drive me—if Zach was being watched by the Scorpions, I didn't want to draw further attention to Aunt Sally or Dinah. But since Terry was adamant about my not going, I had no choice.

I called Dinah's cell. She was in the middle of showing a house but immediately agreed to come pick me up at seven. "Of course, I'll drive you. Just give me the address quick, so I can load it into my GPS."

As I hung up, my stomach began to churn, and the room started to spin. Wonderful...the last thing I needed right now was a panic attack. I didn't have time for this; it was almost six-thirty. I closed my eyes and willed the vertigo to stop. It didn't. I tried to focus on what the meeting would be like—what information Zach would be able to give me. He'd asked me to come alone, but I couldn't ask Dinah to wait outside in the car for me. Zach would just have to trust me. Now all I'd have to do is trust him.

***

The setting sun was barely peeking over the mountains as Dinah and I made our way north along Arizona Avenue. We would take Arizona as far as we could, then go west on Broadway until we hit a series of narrow streets with unfamiliar names that would zigzag us into central Phoenix. When small, free-standing stores with barred doors and window signs hand-lettered in Spanish began to outnumber the strip malls, and brightly painted casitas replaced the gated communities, Dinah said, "We're not in Chandler anymore. Are you sure that kid gave you the right address?"

"I'm sure. Why?"

"Because the last time we were even close to this neighborhood, we were with the guys on our way to that club—you know, the *Rock 'n Bowl.*"

"I remember it well." There'd been a DJ spinning records from the plush leather interior of a pink Chevy convertible on the street level and a bowling alley/restaurant on the basement level. At the club's entrance, we'd been admitted by a gray-haired lady with twinkling eyes and a sweet smile who collected a small cover charge. After an hour of dancing to great fifties and sixties music, we'd gone downstairs to check out the bowling alley and have a bite to eat. At ten p.m., we mounted the narrow staircase back to the first floor only to find a tattooed goon wearing a leather jacket over a bare chest playing techno-rap. At the door, the little old lady had been replaced by a bouncer whose day job could have been sumo wrestling.

"That night, Roy made me promise never to come back to this neighborhood alone."

"But you're not alone. I'm with you."

"I'm surprised Terry agreed to this."

"He didn't, actually. I snuck out the patio door."

"Great. So now we're both in trouble...again." The light turned red. "Where are we going, exactly?" asked Dinah.

"I gave you the address."

"Yeah, I know. But is it a house? A restaurant? A bar? What am I looking for?"

"An apartment building, I think."

The light turned green, and before Dinah could move, the car immediately behind us collided with the Audi's rear fender.

"Oh no...." she groaned, and checked the rearview mirror before pulling over to the curb.

I turned around in my seat to see three young guys scrambling out of an old green Taurus. They were all wearing black fedoras over red bandannas.

"Dinah, we've just been rear-ended by a trio of Scorpions."

There was a sudden, loud click of the door locks as Dinah checked them. Two of the men approached her door, and she unrolled the window an inch. The third man was making a show of inspecting the Audi's fender. He saw me watching him and grinned as he ran a hand along the side of the car and came to stand outside the passenger window. One of the guys looked to be Hispanic, one Native American, and one Asian. I had to give the Scorpions extra credit for practicing diversity.

The man closest to Dinah's window tapped the glass lightly. "I'm so sorry—I really gotta get my brakes checked. Are you ladies all right?"

Just then my cell rang. It was Terry. How I wished I'd listened to him. "He—hello, darling," I said.

"Don't you darling me, Amanda. Where the heck are you?"

"I'm with Dinah."

"With Dinah, where?"

"I'm not sure at the moment. Can I call you right back?"

"You'd better not be on your way to meet with that Zach character."

"I'm a grown woman, Terry, fully capable of making my own decisions. I'll call you back when I can." I disconnected, but kept a firm hold on my phone in case I had to call 9-1-1.

"Lady," said the Scorpion closest to Dinah's window. "I suggest you come on out of there for just a minute so we can check out your bumper."

"Dinah, don't get out!" I whispered frantically.

All three were now standing outside Dinah's window, and I could clearly see the scorpion tattoos on their arms and the signature scorpion rings on their fingers. I craned my neck to see if anyone was around that we could summon for help, but cars whizzed by without pause, and no pedestrians were in sight.

Dinah gave them her sweetest smile and said, "Please, don't give my bumper a second thought." And with that, she started the Audi and pulled away from the curb with a screech of tires. She tossed me a side glance and said, "Amanda Winters, what did you get us into this time?"

I peeked over my shoulder. "They must have followed us from Sun Lakes, which means that they're watching my house."

She glanced in the rearview mirror. "Well, it looks like we've lost them. And if you believe the Scorpions are watching your house, Roy needs to assign some patrols to your street." The GPS told us that our destination was two blocks ahead. "I'm going to find a parking spot around the corner so we're not in plain view in case they come back."

Zach's address was attached to a nondescript stucco building with apartments on the second floor and a nail salon, closed for the night, on the first floor. A small window in the front door revealed five mailboxes just inside and a steep staircase bathed in murky yellow light. None of the mailboxes had nameplates. I tried the door, and it was locked, so I rang the single doorbell. A voice from a small, staticky speaker said, "Yeah?"

"I'm looking for Zach."

The door unlocked with a loud buzzing sound.

"Now what?" asked Dinah.

I shrugged and slowly started up the stairs. At the top was a long, narrow hallway, as dimly lighted as the stairway, with five doors. Suddenly, one of them opened with a painful creak, and a face half-covered with an unruly mop of black hair stuck out into the hallway.

"Mrs. Winters?"

"I'm here with a friend. Are you Zach?"

"Yeah."

There came a sudden pounding on the front door below us, and Zach's face immediately morphed into a white fright mask that appeared to be suspended, unattached to a body, in the darkness. "Holy crap, Mrs. Winters! Get up here, and fast!"

I turned around to see the three Scorpions that had rear-ended Dinah's Audi. They were peering through the glass pane and obviously intent on breaking down the door.

Dinah pushed me up the stairs ahead of her. "That door sounds like it's going to give any minute! Get up these stairs—and make it fast!"

Chapter Fifteen

Zach grabbed us by the sleeves, physically pulled us into the apartment, and slammed the dead bolt shut with a loud *crack*.

"What do they want?!" I asked, my breath coming in short gasps.

"Nothing good, that's for sure," replied Zach. He noticed that Dinah had pulled out her cell. "Who are you calling?"

"9-1-1."

He grabbed the phone from her hand. "You can't do that."

"Oh, yes I can. Now give me my phone!"

"If you involve the police, we're dead. Maybe not today, but soon." He peeked out into the hallway. "They're gone—for now. Here's your phone back."

I exchanged glances with Dinah. I knew that we were both wondering whether or not to run right then and there, and forget all about the meeting with Zach—forget about the ridiculous notion that he could tell me anything that would help me find Sherry's killer. Terry was right. I had no business getting involved in murder. Here I was, a grown woman playing detective. I was pretty sure private investigators needed to be licensed, and they certainly had to be trained in the art of self-defense. Not only did I not have a P. I. license—I didn't have any means to defend myself, and even if I did, my efforts could be rendered useless by a sudden panic attack. Negative thoughts streamed through my consciousness like a high-speed train through an ever-darkening tunnel, inviting anxiety to settle in and do its worst. *Focus, Amanda.* I took a seat on a sofa covered with an old sheet and concentrated my efforts on not bursting into tears.

"I'm here now, Zach," I said, "so you might as well tell me whatever it is you wanted to tell me. And you'd better talk fast, because I have a feeling those guys will be back with some sort of battering ram."

"While you're doing that, I'm going to call my boyfriend and have him meet us here," said Dinah, and, phone in hand, wandered into a tiny kitchenette. She didn't mention that her boyfriend happened to be a deputy commander with the Maricopa County Sheriff's Department.

My eyes pierced Zach with a laser-sharp gaze. "Your sister told me that you've been hanging around with the Scorpions. She doesn't get it, and neither do I. You're a college student on a football scholarship. Why risk it all to cozy up to a bunch of juvenile-delinquent losers? And why are you suddenly so afraid of them now?"

"I kind of got tricked into something," said Zach, and plopped down wearily on the sofa next to me. "And now I can't get out of it."

"Tricked into what? Get out of what?"

"Something big—bigger than the rooms at Thatcher House getting ripped off."

I rose to my feet. "Well, Zach, there's no point in my staying here another minute if you won't give me details." I pointed at Dinah. "By the way, the boyfriend this lady just phoned is with the Maricopa County Sheriff's Department." I made a show of checking my watch. "And he should be here in about five minutes. You can tell him what's going on, or you can tell me. It doesn't really matter to me at this point."

"The Scorpions are the ones ripping off the rooms in Thatcher House."

"That's obvious. I believe you mentioned 'something bigger'...."

Zach's gaze abruptly dropped to the floor. "I'm not sure about that, but if I tell you what I know about the thefts, can I get—what do you call it—immunity?"

Dinah and I exchanged glances. "I don't have the authority to do that, Zach," I said. "That'll be up to the detective in charge of the investigation. You really don't have anything to lose at this point, do you?"

"I never stole a thing. I'm kind of what you'd call a look-out. I feed them information about the comings and goings at Thatcher—you know, which rooms are going to be easy targets, and when." He looked up defensively. "I told them I was done with them, and now they want to take me out—like they tried to take out Cory."

My stomach did a flip-flop. "Was—is—Cory involved with the thefts?"

He shook his head slowly. "No. But they think he knows something about whatever else they're into, and they also think he told you about it."

"Zach, Alana's staying in a room at Thatcher, isn't she? By helping the Scorpions target the campus, you've actually placed your sister in danger along with the other students. Why did you do it?"

"It seemed like an easy way to make some extra cash. They gave me fifty bucks for every room they hit. It was a stupid mistake, but like I told you, I'm done with it."

The shrill ring of the doorbell made me jump.

"That must be Roy," said Dinah. "I doubt that the Scorpions would be polite enough to use the doorbell." She stuck her head out into the hallway to get a clear view of the door. "Yep, it's Roy."

Zach used the intercom to buzz Roy in. "Is he the detective in charge?" he asked me. "The one you were talking about?"

"Yes—Detective Roy Staatz. You have to tell him everything you know about the Scorpions and what they're doing at St. Priscilla's. You're going to have to tell him about your role in all of this, too. Agreed?"

He nodded his head and shoved his hands into the pockets of his jeans. "Yeah. Will he arrest me?"

"I don't know, but considering that there have been two murders at St. Priscilla's, you might be able to use whatever you know as leverage."

I motioned for Dinah to follow me into the kitchenette for two reasons: First, I wanted to give Roy and Zach some space and privacy to talk. Second, I wanted to avoid a confrontation with Roy as long as possible. I'd taken the brunt of his anger a few times, and I wasn't ready to face it now. I knew he wouldn't be happy about my getting Dinah involved in this mess.

"Hey," I said to Dinah. "Zach has a coffee press. I could use a cup—how about you?"

"That sounds good, actually."

I measured coffee into the beaker and poured boiling water over the grounds. Dinah was searching the cupboards for coffee mugs when the doorbell blared again. The bell was in the kitchen, so it was loud enough to make us both jump.

"I hope those aren't the Scorpions back with reinforcements," muttered Dinah.

"Not to worry," I said, which was a phrase I didn't use very often. "Roy's here, and he's armed."

I heard the buzzer sound, and a few minutes later Terry's voice, which was tinged with no small degree of panic. "Uh-oh, I think I might be in trouble," I said. I strolled into the living room and smiled sweetly. "Hello, darling. Care for a cup of coffee?"

Terry stared straight ahead at the wall. His jaw was clenched, and he was not smiling. "We'll talk about this tomorrow," he said, and glanced at Roy and Zach, who were standing off in a far corner of the living room. "Are you finished here?"

"I guess so." I gave Dinah a quick side-glance. "Uh, sweetheart, you didn't park too far away, did you?"

"Why?"

I shrugged. "No particular reason."

"I'm parked behind Roy's squad."

"Good...good." I retrieved my purse from where I'd left it on the end table next to the sofa. "Dinah, will you be all right if I leave now? Will Roy follow you home?"

"Oh, don't worry, Amanda." Roy had overheard me and, from across the room, interjected, "I'll be following her home."

Dinah mouthed the words *I'll call you tomorrow* as I trailed Terry out into the hallway. It was late, and there were few people on the street. To my relief, there was no sign of the Scorpions. As we drove south toward the freeway that would take us home, we passed buildings marred by graffiti marked by scorpions and other symbols I now recognized as the gang's emblems. Terry didn't utter a word until we pulled into our garage.

He opened the passenger-side door and said, "Well, I suppose we'd better deal with this now—get it behind us."

I pushed ahead of him into the kitchen and dropped my purse on the counter. "Deal with what and get what behind us?"

He threw his keys down onto the kitchen table—a little too emphatically—and said, "Do you have any idea of what the crime statistics are like in the neighborhood you dragged Dinah to tonight—the neighborhood you dragged *yourself* to?"

"No, I don't. Let me remind you that I'm an adult. I know that sometimes you think of me as a child because of my cluster C, but I can't let it get the best of me. I have to do what other adults do. I have to make decisions and be able to carry them out. At the very least, I have to try and get to the bottom of what's been happening at St. Priscilla's. I have to do it for Sherry, but, maybe even more important, I have to do it for me."

He came around the table and stood in front of me. His arms enveloped me, and I basked in the sensation of curling up in a safe and cozy cave. For me, reactions to most events, even the simple ones that people experienced every day, could be summed up in two words: *fear* and *avoidance*. I avoided any situation that was new—anything over which I didn't have complete control. I was afraid to drive, afraid of going to new places or walking into a room full of people. For pity sake, I was even afraid to answer the phone.

"You're not the easiest woman to live with, Amanda," Terry said, "but I wouldn't ever want to live without you, not for a minute. What you did tonight wasn't all that smart, but I understand why you did it." His eyes clouded with tears. "I don't know what I'd do if anything ever happened to you."

Then, as if to place an exclamation mark at the end of his sentence, he kissed me: a sweet, lingering kiss that drove out all the doubt I'd had about his willingness to forgive me for my careless lack of judgment.

***

Monday morning, Carole Ann called to tell me that she'd rescheduled last Friday's appointments. "Since you have no appointments today, I thought that maybe you could use an extra day to relax."

I called Aunt Sally to let her know that we both had the day off and got busy reorganizing the spreadsheet of events and clues I'd been building from the original version created by Terry. I inserted *Suspects* and *Motives* columns, and after adding elements from the conversation I'd had with Mike the day before his death, a few more possible relationships surfaced. Admittedly, any of these links could be coincidental, but I didn't want to assume anything at this point. My thoughts traveled back to the day of Sherry's murder. As the chair of the English Department, Sherry would have access to a great deal of information related to student records. Those 16 missing files must have some significance. But what was that significance? Mike Kraemer had mentioned that Sherry was upset. But what had upset her?

I remembered some things I'd heard and read about murder cases: Murder victims most often fall prey to people they know. Despite the ongoing trend of slasher movies about carloads of college students eliminated, one by one, by some deranged killer, very rarely are people murdered by maniacal strangers. Something else I remembered pertained to motive: One had to follow a trail that typically led to sex, money, or revenge. In this case, the only obvious sex scenario I could think of involved Brent Redmond. Although I still considered the possibility that Terry and I had caught him in a late-night rendezvous with a St. Priscilla's student, I doubted he was the type to actually be in a clandestine relationship with a young woman. I mean, he was married, fifty pounds overweight, and just plain annoying. I crossed Brent off my list, then uncrossed his name for two reasons: There's no accounting for taste, and I had to admit that I didn't have enough information to eliminate anyone as a suspect—a money- or revenge-related motive might yet surface.

I thought about what Zach had fessed up to. Although he was giving the Scorpions information about the Thatcher residents, he didn't have access to their schedules and other details. Someone else at the university must be helping the gang plan their heists—someone with access to information about the students' class schedules, extracurricular activities, planned trips home, and anything else that would leave dorm rooms unattended. Computers, cameras, smartphones—all of these, Staatz had said, were favorites of thieves and could garner huge sums of money from fences who made lucrative deals with eager markets. Someone other than Zach, with his "fifty dollars a hit" arrangement, was making a tidy profit from the Scorpions' thefts.

And what about the "something bigger"? There had to be a link between that and the campus thefts, given the fact that, according to Zach, the Scorpions thought Cory knew something about it and had passed it on to me.

I called Roy. "After Terry and I left Zach's apartment last night, did he tell you about anything else that's going on at St. Priscilla's—something other than the Thatcher House thefts?"

"No. After you left, the kid clammed up. And I'm glad you called, because I need to tell you never to involve Dinah in your dangerous wild goose chases ever again. I mean it."

"I-I'm sorry, Roy," I said, and disconnected.

I sat down on the living room sofa and rebooted my laptop. Who at the university would have a motive to cooperate with a dangerous street gang? Who would be capable of murder? I couldn't think of anyone on the staff or faculty at St. Priscilla's, at least anyone I knew—other than Zach Christopoulos—who would knowingly become involved in any kind of criminal activity. Everyone I knew played by the rules, at least on the surface. However, I mused, rules were broken every day, even by the most virtuous among us.

Since he was now a victim, I crossed off Mike Kraemer's name, then immediately re-added it. It was possible that Mike had become involved with the Scorpions and then changed his mind, making himself a target. Or maybe Mike hadn't been murdered after all. If Sherry discovered that he was involved in something illegal and confronted him with it, he could have panicked and killed her. Then, consumed by feelings of guilt and despair over what he'd done, he'd committed suicide. Mike had access to all kinds of student information, but what would be his motive for getting involved with the Scorpions in the first place?

Another person with full access to information, primarily through her secretary, Angie, was Sister Fred. The very idea of Sister Fred directing the Scorpions in their criminal activities between morning chapel and her administrative responsibilities was absurd, to say the least. Moreover, it was more than obvious that she loved her students. I added Sister Fred's name to my sheet, then quickly highlighted it in yellow as a caveat. I didn't know if she had been required to take a vow of poverty, but as the president of a large private university, she was well-compensated and would be an unlikely subject to be lured into a life of crime.

Who else? Ian Malcolm, director of Financial Aid? I hated to think of Ian as a criminal who was capable of murder, but he was a logical suspect: With his flashy looks and winning charm, Ian could easily get away with a crime, with no one the wiser. Was Ian aiding and abetting the Scorpions' theft ring in exchange for a percentage of the take? Ian had access to student schedules and dorm assignments. Maybe Sherry found out about his involvement with the Scorpions and had asked to meet with Mike to discuss it. Then Ian had found out, somehow, and killed both Sherry and Mike before they had a chance to go to the police with their suspicions. Still, Ian as the killer didn't quite make sense. As director of Financial Aid, why would he, with a salary that was more than adequate to cover his expensive tastes, risk his career for some extra spending cash?

I reconsidered the possibility that the killer was a student. Students are able to enter Raslin Hall at any time without arousing suspicion. Still, Sherry wouldn't have been able to move the heavy anvil to prop open the Tomb's iron door—the door had to have been closed after she'd entered the room, which meant that her murderer had a key. The only student I knew with access to that key, by virtue of his work-study in the Registrar's Office, was Cory Matuck. Had Cory been playing the innocent victim to divert suspicion from himself? Reluctantly, I added "Cory Matuck" to the Suspects column.

There were some obvious other additions, based solely on opportunity: the English Department faculty. They passed Carole Ann's desk—and the key dangling from its hook—every day. Had Sherry denied a raise to one of them? Had she turned someone down for a promotion? Then there was Ralph Michaels and his entire Security staff, including Eddie Gruber and Evie Woodard. Any one of them could have easily taken the department key and followed Sherry to the Tomb early that morning. I added "Faculty" and "Security staff" to the column.

I also added Lynn Goodman and Laverne Hutchins. As the Raslin Hall full-time receptionist, Lynn had her finger on the pulse of the university and always knew where everyone on campus was and what they were doing. Plus, her shift at the desk didn't start until eight a.m., so she also had opportunity. My only problem with Lynn as a suspect was that she didn't have obvious access to the Tomb key. Laverne Hutchins was a weak prospect; nevertheless, I added her because she was likely a confidant of Mike's. Maybe he'd shared Sherry's suspicions with her, and she'd reacted by killing them both. Then I then typed in "Tony Loduca," since his absence from the gym during Saturday's registration strangely coincided with Aunt Sally's disappearance. And maybe his promotion to assistant chair wasn't quite good enough for him. Maybe he aspired to a position that was one step higher—only Sherry had been in the way.

Finally, I typed in "Carole Ann Trebley." Although I doubted that getting overlooked for a promotion qualified as a motive for murder, Roy seemed to think it was a logical supposition. Aside from Sister Fred, Carole Ann was the last person I'd suspect of murder. I remember Sherry telling me about the day a bat had somehow gotten inside the English Department. While some of the faculty members had armed themselves with whatever they could find, including brooms and transom window poles, Carole Ann managed to throw her sweater over the creature and toss it through an open window to freedom, sweater and all. Carole Ann Trebley wouldn't hurt any creature, human or otherwise.

My Suspects column was now full to bursting; my Motives column, unfortunately, was woefully lacking." My brain was now buzzing like a hive of phobic bees. I turned off my computer and took a glass of Chardonnay out to the patio. I needed to figure out what to do next. Lulled by the combination of wine and fresh air, I nodded off and dreamed that Terry, I, and a 10-year-old Jeff were setting up a picnic at the edge of a lake. I laid out a red-checked cloth on a wooden picnic table while

Terry watched Jeff, who was laughing and frolicking in the water with a dog: a puppy with kind eyes and a grin that looked weirdly human. When I awoke half an hour later, my head was clear, and I knew exactly what my next step would be.

Chapter Sixteen

The next morning, shortly after arriving at the university, I sent Aunt Sally to fetch us some coffee from the commons. I was expecting twin grad students Becky and Blair Bennett, and I wanted to make sure that the three of us would have a good twenty minutes alone in the office. The twins shrieked with excitement when I asked if I could borrow their dorm room in exchange for a Friday night at the Clarendon, one of the trendiest hotels in midtown Phoenix.

"You won't be using our room as a secret love nest or anything like that, will you, Mrs. Winters?" asked Becky. "Because that would not be cool."

"That would be an emphatic no," I said. "Believe me, the room will be used for a legitimate purpose. I just can't tell you what that purpose is—not yet, anyhow."

"Is it official police business?" asked Blair.

"Mrs. Winters works for the sheriff's department," corrected Becky, "not the police department." She turned wide blue eyes on me in a direct gaze. "Are you going to use our room to hold a stake-out?!"

I gulped, wishing I'd thought to be prepared with a good reason for using the twins' dorm room. "Uh, something like that. If you want to change your mind, I won't blame you. I'm sure I can find someone else...."

"Oh no! You can definitely have the room!" said Blair. "Have you seen the swimming pool at the Clarendon, Mrs. Winters? It's gorgeous...it has this beautiful cascading waterfall, and it's surrounded with humongous pots of hibiscus and palms. It looks like Maui or something."

"The Republic named it the 'most awesome pool in the Valley' last year," Becky chimed in.

"But we don't want to come back to a trashed room," added Blair soberly. "You know, bullet-riddled walls, blood-stained carpeting, dead bodies all over the place—"

"I don't anticipate anything like that," I said, suddenly doubting the truth of my words. "Your room will be fine. But a condition comes with this deal."

"Condition?" asked Becky.

"What condition?" asked Blair.

"You can't tell a soul about this. I mean it. If you tell anyone, I'll come after you for the $250 I'm paying for the room."

"What about our parents? Can we let them know where we'll be? We told them we'd be on campus all weekend, but they're really spooked about the murder and check in with us practically every ten minutes."

"You can tell your parents, but that's it, and they have to keep it to themselves. Not a word to anyone else—that means no friends and no parties—got it?"

The twins looked at each other for a moment, just to make sure they were on the same page, and replied in unison, "Got it!"

We made arrangements for them to stop by the English Department before leaving for the night to hand their key card over to me. I'd just secured my bait. Now all that was left was to impale it on a sturdy hook and give it a good hard cast to see what I could catch. I decided that my first stop would be Ian Malcolm's office.

"Hey, remember the buddy system," said Carole Ann as I passed her desk on my way out of the office.

"I'm just going down the hallway to Financial Aid. When Aunt Sally gets back with our coffee, tell her I'll be back soon."

I found Ian in his office reclining in his leather swivel chair, argyle-covered feet on top of his desk. His shoes, a highly polished pair of Doc Martens, were positioned neatly on the floor next to his chair.

"Hey there, Ian. It looks like you're having a good day."

He lurched upright in the chair, his foot knocking a stack of papers from his desk. "Amanda, hi. What's new in the wonderful world of master's theses?"

"Oh, nothing much." I assumed a casual pose on the corner of his desk and observed his face as he slipped into his shoes while simultaneously gathering up the errant papers. "I just need some advice. I mean, you have much more experience dealing with students' problems than I do."

"What seems to be the trouble?"

I just talked to a couple of English grad students, the Bennett twins, and they're a bit worried."

Ian frowned. "Becky and Blair, the Chaucer girls?"

"Those would be the ones. They're involved in some kind of book fair in Flagstaff Saturday, and their dorm room will be left vacant Friday night. The twins are kind of worried about security. And I don't blame them. I could open my own store if I had just half the fancy high-tech stuff they described to me: laptops, iPads, cameras…you name it, they have it."

"Why don't they just pack up the things they're worried about and take them along to Flagstaff?"

Uh-oh. Good question. "I…uh—I think they're sharing a hotel room with some kids they don't know too well, so they don't feel comfortable about leaving the stuff in the room with strangers. And they certainly wouldn't want to leave that expensive equipment in the trunk of their car."

That seemed to satisfy Ian. "Well, they're going to be gone for only one night. What could happen?" He rose from his chair and shook his head. "I'd tell them not to worry."

Next I stopped at Brent Redmond's office. He was on a phone call, so I hovered in the doorway and listened, something I never would have considered two weeks earlier. Desperate times, however....

"Listen, Troy," he was saying, "I need those assignments for the beta test completed by the end of the week." He paused for Troy's response, which, judging by the tone of Brent's voice, was not to his liking. "Well, if you don't need the money, I can assign them to someone else." He slammed the receiver down and, spotting me in the doorway, said, "What?!"

I was speechless for a moment. I'd never heard of paying students in cash for participating in a beta test. And why did Brent always act as though he were up to something?

I repeated my spiel about the twins' unattended dorm room and tried to catch a glimmer of inordinate interest. There was none, but I figured it was because Brent was preoccupied and still thinking about his phone call with Troy. "I mean, I reassured the twins that their things would be safe, but now I'd feel responsible if something happened," I said. "You know?"

"If you're so worried about it, why not have a talk with Ralph? Maybe he can put your fears to rest. Besides, I don't see why you'd feel responsible if anything *did* happen. If campus Security and Staatz's team can't stop the thieves from ripping off the students, what could *you* possibly do to prevent it?"

"You're right. I guess there's no use worrying about it." I turned at the door. "Is everything going okay with the beta test?"

"Who told you about the beta test?"

"Uh, you did, actually. I just heard you mention it during your phone conversation." Another fib, but I couldn't very well throw Alana under the bus.

"It's going just fine. Why wouldn't it be?"

"I don't know. It sounded to me as though you were having trouble getting some of the test assignments done. Do you need more help? I could ask some of the English grad students; they can always use a little spending cash...."

"Not necessary." He sat down at his computer and started typing. "And students are getting elective credit for their work on the test—no cash is involved. Now, if you'll excuse me...I'm getting slammed with applications for online courses."

"Wow, that's a good thing, I suppose. Are you sure there isn't anything I can do to help?"

"No thanks. I just need to schedule some extra course sections and contact instructors to see who can cover them. I should have everything wrapped up by next week."

Just to remind him of the reason for my visit, I said, "So you don't think the Bennett twins need to worry about leaving their dorm room unattended Friday night?"

Brent's beady eyes aimed an annoyed look at me. "Amanda, I have more important things to think about right now—and I'm sure you do, too."

Right. Like why you just lied to me about how you're paying students for working on that beta test.

Before heading back to the English Department, I stopped in and shared my fears about the twins with Lynn Goodman at the reception desk. Given Lynn's penchant for gossip, I figured that would be the fastest way to spread the word about their unguarded dorm room. Back in the office, I went through my story about the Bennett twins with Tony Loduca. He was also dismissive. "Amanda, with all the extra patrols around here lately, I wouldn't worry."

"That's a good point. By the way, did Detective Staatz ever talk to you about the attack on my Aunt Sally last Saturday?"

"So I have you to thank for my being summoned to his office for questioning. Amanda, why in the world would you suspect that I had anything to do with what happened to your aunt?"

"I don't, Tony. I thought that since you left the gym just before she disappeared, maybe you saw her—saw something...."

"Well, I didn't see a thing. After leaving the gym that day, I drove over to Office Max for some supplies. Detective Staatz said he's going to talk to the manager to confirm the time I checked out at the counter. It's pretty humiliating...I'm a regular customer at that store."

"I'm sorry, Tony." But I doubt he heard my apology, because by the time I'd offered it, he was already halfway to his office.

Just as Aunt Sally and I were getting ready to leave for the day, the phone on my desk beeped the signal for an outside call.

I had a bad feeling about this one. "Aunt Sally, would you do me a favor and get that?"

"You're standing right there, Amanda."

"I know. Please?"

With a sigh, she picked up the phone. "Sally Mueller here." After listening for a moment, she handed me the phone. "You can relax...no one died."

I accepted the phone and said, "Hello? This is Amanda Winters.""It's Jennifer Baranski. Remember, my sister was billed by mistake?"

"Of course, I remember. How are you, Jennifer?"

"I'm fine. I just wanted to thank you for taking care of that mix-up. I feel bad because I came down on you so hard when I called that day. I'm sorry."

"There's no need to apologize. All I did was give your message to Ms. Hutchins in the Business Office. She's the one who drew up the letter of rescindment."

"Letter of rescindment?"

"You know, the letter confirming that the original statement was an error."

"Oh, we didn't get any letter. Someone named Laverne called and told my mom not to worry about the statement, that it was just a mistake and to ignore it."

"Are you sure?"

"Yep. My mom mentioned that she'd feel better if she had something in writing from the university. But Laverne said she'd already taken care of everything and that my mom should just tear up the statement."

"Well, as long as everything's good...."

"Everything's fine. Thanks again."

"Aunt Sally, do me a favor and have a seat. I just need to look something up, quick, before we leave."

I rebooted my computer, pulled up "Course Schedules" for the current academic year, and searched under the name "Baranski." There was no schedule for a Samantha Baranski—if she'd registered for the current semester and then cancelled due to her illness, the classes would show as having been dropped, along with the drop date. I backed out of "Schedules" and pulled up a list of active students. There were no other students named Baranski. Laverne had lied when she told me that someone "had pulled the wrong Baranski" from the student list. She'd also lied to me about having sent out a letter of rescindment to Jennifer's mother. But why?

Next I pulled up course schedules for Zach and Cory, and I wasn't surprised to see that neither of them were assigned a one-credit elective for Brent's beta test. It was possible that Brent would enter the elective credit after they'd completed the test, but the usual way an independent study, which was the classification for a beta test, was handled was to create a course name and number, add it to the student's schedule, enter "0" in the credits column, and then change the 0 to the correct number of credits when the study was completed. The only thing I knew for sure, at this point, was that I was sick and tired of the lies. No matter what it took, I was going to get to the truth.

***

"What do you mean, we're going to have an overnight at St. Priscilla's?" asked Terry. I'd made the mistake of blurting out my plan while he was pouring wine, and before I'd finished, there was a small puddle of Chardonnay on the table.

"Think of it as a mini-vacation," I said.

Knowing I'd have to be well-armed for this particular battle, I'd made Terry's favorite dish for dinner that evening: homemade mac and cheese, panko-breaded chicken cutlets, and corn on the cob. "We'll be staying in one of the dorm rooms. Terry, this may be my only chance to get to the bottom of what's going on at St. Priscilla's. I believe that the Thatcher House thefts are related to Sherry's murder. I think she was killed her because she learned that someone on the staff or faculty is involved in something else. If we catch the thieves, they'll lead us to the person in charge." I explained my plan to catch the Scorpions in the act and braced for the response I knew would be coming.

Terry's voice was remarkably calm—scary calm. "Okay. So the thieves break into the twins' room. Then what?"

"Then we call Security and 9-1-1. Roy has a team on campus right now. If we need them, they can be there within minutes."

He rested his chin in his hands. "So you think the thieves will break into the Bennett twins' dorm room, and when they find us there, instead of the high-priced technical gadgets they came for, they're going to sit down and shoot the breeze with us until Staatz comes to arrest them?"

"Of course not...but I'm sure we'll think of something." I wrinkled my nose. "And would you please not use the word 'shoot'?"

"Why not tell Staatz your idea and let him handle it? He could assign some of his team to stay in the girls' room."

"Roy wouldn't even consider it—he'd think it was a big waste of time and resources. Besides, even if he thought it was a good idea, he'd never admit it. And then, just to make sure I wouldn't follow through with my plan, he'd bar me from campus until he completes his investigation."

"How do you know the Scorpions are even going to fall for this?"

"I don't. But I figure we don't have anything to lose."

"We have a lot to lose. Amanda, this isn't just a bunch of unruly kids we're dealing with. These are hardened criminals who steal, murder, and worse."

"What's worse than murder?"

"You don't want to know."

"Well, anyway, even if nothing comes of this, it still might be fun. We can pretend we're college students having a secret rendezvous. And I'll pack lots of food…it'll be like a picnic." I remembered my dream—the picnic at the lake—and suddenly envisioned a puppy with big brown eyes that gazed knowingly into mine. "Terry, have you ever thought about us getting a dog?"

He tossed me a curious look. "Not since Jeff was little, and you put the kibosh on the idea. Why?"

"No special reason. I've been thinking…a dog might be good company for me when you're at work."

"I don't know, Amanda. A dog comes with a lot of responsibilities: training, vet bills, food costs—"

"Okay, just forget it. Sorry I brought it up."

"Getting back to this plan of yours…I'm still not convinced. I'm sure there are better places for a mini-vacation than a dorm in a Catholic university. Does the room even have cable?"

"I don't know, but we won't be watching TV, anyway. We can't have any lights on, either. The room's supposed to be empty for the weekend, remember?"

"That's right. Well, we could bring the mini-lantern and some cards. I promise to shuffle very quietly." He narrowed his eyes at me. "You're going to owe me big-time for this, Amanda Winters."

Chapter Seventeen

That Friday after work, I told Aunt Sally to go home without me. "Terry's taking off early, so we thought we'd try that new Italian place on Roberto Street for lunch."

"You know I love Italian, Amanda," she said, her eyes droopy.

"We'll take you along the next time. This is kind of a date."

"Okay, but don't forget your promise—I know I won't." On her way out, as she walked past Carole Ann's desk, I heard her say, "I'm leaving now, so make sure you know who makes it outta here without tossing her cookies."

As soon as I thought the coast was clear, I turned off my computer and breezed out of the office with a quick good-bye wave to Carole Ann.

"Boy, someone's in a big hurry to start the weekend," she laughed.

"That's an understatement."

Just to make sure that Aunt Sally hadn't stopped for the latest gossip from Lynn Goodman, I paused at the mezzanine balustrade and peered down at the first-floor reception area. Lynn had one of the front double doors propped open with her foot and was engaged in conversation with someone just outside. I couldn't hear what she was saying, but I could tell by the tone of her voice that she was agitated.

"Lynn, is everything all right down there?!" I called out.

I must have startled her, because she jumped back from the door, just enough for me to see past her shoulder to catch a glimpse of a black fedora atop a red bandanna. Without another word, I hurried down the stairs. By the time I'd reached the first floor, Lynn was behind the desk and gathering up stacks of magazines.

"Who was that at the door just now?"

"Some kid asking questions, but I took care of it. I'm getting ready to close up here for the day." She looked up from her magazines. "Any big plans for the weekend?"

"Not really," I said with a self-conscious tremor in my voice. "You know, just the usual. Dinner out somewhere—maybe a movie with Terry."

Ian Malcolm and Brent Redmond, the scents of their respective colognes mingling to herald their arrival, came jogging down the stairs together. At least Ian was jogging. Brent's movement was more of a lopsided shuffle.

"Uh, Brent, someone's waiting to talk to you out in the parking lot," said Lynn.

"Who might that be?"

"One of your beta-test students," she said, her eyes darting uncomfortably from me to Ian, then back to Brent.

Was she referring to the "kid who was asking questions" at the front door? I knew for a fact that he wasn't just some "beta-test student." Yet another lie, this one from Lynn: She knew as well as I did that the "kid" at the door was a Scorpion.

He checked his watch. "Well, I can give him five minutes," he said, and continued on his way to the front entrance, with Ian right behind him. "You ladies have a good weekend."

"Amanda, I was thinking what you said about the Bennett girls being so worried," said Lynn as she tossed her stack of magazines into a drawer. "They're going to be gone for only one night, aren't they?"

"A lot of the recent dorm thefts have happened on Friday nights," I said. "They have good reason to be worried."

"I guess I'm just not as much of a worry wart as you and the Bennet twins." Lynn shut down her computer. "Well, I'm out of here. Time to let the inmates take over for the weekend."

"Then I guess I'll see you Monday." I waved good-bye as I walked out the door and pretended to make a call on my cell. After I was sure that Lynn, Brent, and Ian had all cleared the parking lot, I searched out a place where no one would be likely to notice me while I waited for Terry. A sudden wave of nausea gripped my stomach as I began my lone walk along the side of the building. I noticed a secluded spot in an exterior stairwell leading down to the basement and headed toward it. I'd feel sheltered there, and less susceptible to anxiety.

When Terry pulled into the lot, I waved him down, jumped into the passenger seat, and told him to park as far as possible from Thatcher House, behind the Edward Anderson Theater. There was a concert that evening, and, at least for a few hours, our car would blend right in with those belonging to the patrons. We stayed close to the perimeter of the parking lot and its tree-lined border as we walked toward Raslin Hall, circling the building before making our way toward Thatcher House.

"I don't want Security to see us, so we have to hurry," I said as we plodded our way toward the residence hall, both of us carrying bags containing the mini-lantern, food, and a deck of cards to keep us occupied in case no one showed up.

"What do you have in here, a ten-pound bag of potatoes?" asked Terry. "My arms are already numb."

"Quit complaining, sweetheart—we're here."

Terry set down his bag and shook out his arm before taking my bag so I could swipe the Bennetts' key card. There was a click, and a moment later we were inside the building. I decided to avoid the elevator and led Terry up the stairs to the second floor. I knew that many of the resident students, including the two RAs, would already be on their way to their parents' homes for the weekend or getting an early start on their weekend partying. The Bennetts' room was at the rear of the building, overlooking the south parking lot. It was less cluttered than most dorm rooms I'd seen, with just enough furniture to make it cozy: two neatly made twin beds, two desks placed side-by-side in front of the single bank of windows, two matching chests of drawers, and one purple loveseat in front of a small flat-screen TV. I walked over to the window, checked out the parking lot below, and closed the blinds most of the way, leaving just enough space between the slats to allow us to look outside without drawing attention.

I inspected the room for a suitable hiding place. If someone did break in, we wouldn't want to be caught out in the open. We needed the thieves to take a few minutes to search the room before finding us, giving us enough time to call for help. I figured that any one of Ralph's team would have a slim-to-none chance of catching the thieves before they got away, but maybe they'd at least be able to get a description of a vehicle and a license plate number.

"Okay, let's make a plan," I said, as Terry started to unpack the food on one of the desks. I walked over to a door and opened it. "This closet might work, though it would be awfully tight." I put my hands on my hips and surveyed the tiny space. "Thankfully, claustrophobia isn't one of my issues."

"Yeah," said Terry. "Wonder how you missed that one? But you can forget the closet. It would be the first place they'd look." He inspected a bag of chips he'd taken from a bag. "These aren't the ones we usually buy."

"The store was out of the ones you like. Sorry."

He tossed the chips onto a desk and walked to the bathroom door. "I know this might sound lame, but we could hide in the tub behind the shower curtain. It might give us a few extra minutes to call for help while the thieves are cleaning out the room."

I shrugged. "It's not like we have options. The bathtub it is."

Terry pulled some plastic food containers from the shopping bag and set them on the desk. "Hungry?"

"Not yet. As a matter of fact, I might be too nervous to eat until this is all over and done with."

We shared quiet conversation in the dark room, with only the small lantern for light. We spent a few hours playing canasta, and it was midnight when Terry said, "I'm starving." He rummaged through one of the bags and said, "We've got ham on rye with spicy brown mustard and a side of potato salad. Still too nervous to eat?"

"I think something would have happened by now if it was going to. Let's eat."

"I hate to admit it, but this has been kind of enjoyable. All we need is a campfire and s'mores."

"I don't think the Bennett twins would appreciate us building a campfire in their room. And I have a feeling the local fire department would also frown on it." I reached across the desk that was serving as our table and took his hand. "I just want to let you know that I appreciate you going along with my crazy scheme."

He laughed. "Why do I suddenly feel like Ethel Mertz?" He took out two sandwiches and said, "Seriously, it took me a while, but over the past year I have to admit that I've learned to trust your...sleuthing instincts."

Sandwich in hand, I paused before taking my first bite. "So...can we talk about my dog?"

"There you go again with the dog. Who's going to take it for walks? You break out in a cold sweat whenever you're alone and venture more than a foot past the end of our driveway."

"I wouldn't be alone, Terry. I'd have my dog with me."

"We'll talk about it, okay?"

"Promise?"

"Yes, I promise—we'll talk about it."

I threw my arms around his neck. "Thanks, darling! I promise to feed it, and walk it, and brush it, and vacuum up after it, and—"

"Amanda—"

"What?"

"Never mind." He took a bite of his sandwich and chewed thoughtfully before continuing. "Okay. You know what Aunt Sally said about you the day we brought her home from the hospital?"

"No, what?"

"She said that you were one hell of a gumshoe."

"Really?"

"Really. She—" He suddenly drew a finger to his lips, then pointed toward the door. Someone was in the hallway just outside the room. In one fell swoop, Terry turned out the lantern, pushed the remains of our meal into the shopping bag, and shoved everything under one of the beds. We heard the sound of a key being inserted in the lock.

"They have a key! How do they have a key?!" I whispered as Terry pushed me through the bathroom door and into the tub. We pulled the curtain closed in front of us just as the door to the room opened with a groan. When Terry reached behind his back and pulled a revolver that had been tucked into his waistband, my stomach roiled with the sudden realization that we could both be in real danger—the kind that involves blood.

"Don't worry," he whispered. "It isn't loaded."

"Why would you bring an empty gun?!" I whispered back. "It'll just make the thieves mad, and we won't have any way to defend ourselves!"

Someone might be about to get seriously hurt, and it was now too late to change my mind and get the two of us out of this situation. If anything happened to Terry, I would never forgive myself. I felt the familiar surge of terror as it caused my heart to race and tiny sparks of blue lightning to flash in my peripheral vision. Taking some strange comfort in the fact that, this time, there was good reason for my panic, I clutched Terry's arm and squeezed my eyes shut. I opened them again as I remembered my cell phone. I tried to pull it from the pocket of my skirt, but the thing wouldn't budge from its tight quarters. I heard a soft rip as the pocket tore, releasing the phone. I squinted at the tiny screen as I scrolled through numbers in search of the one for Security. I uttered a silent curse as I realized that I'd left my readers in my purse, which was now inside one of the bags under the bed. All I could see were rows of fuzzy symbols. I silently mouthed to Terry "I can't see" and held the phone up to his face. He quickly found the number for Security and pressed it. I could hear Eddie Gruber's distinctive voice say, "Yep. Gruber here."

Terry widened his eyes at me as if to say, *What now?* If I replied to Gruber, there was more than a good chance that whoever had entered the room would hear me. I shrugged and whispered into the phone. "Emergency! Room 205B, Thatcher House!"

"Say again?" Eddie's response was so loud that I worried it might have been heard in the other room.

The thieves, however, were still noisily opening and closing dresser drawers, which meant they had not heard my whispered warning or Eddie's response. It was impossible to know for sure how many there were out there: no more than two or three, I thought. Someone opened the closet door; I heard the creak of hinges as it swung open. I figured it would be only a matter of seconds before they came into the bathroom to search the medicine cabinet for drugs.

"Call 9-1-1!" Terry whispered. Just then, the phone slipped from my hand and made a loud *clank* as it hit the bottom of the tub. Our only hope, now, was that Eddie had gotten the message and that he was doing something about it.

In his right hand, Terry had his revolver raised and aimed straight ahead. His left arm was wrapped around my waist, so tightly that it was starting to interfere with my breathing.

The door to the bathroom opened and hit the wall with a bang seconds before the shower curtain was pulled aside with a *whoosh*.

Chapter Eighteen

A kid wearing a St. Priscilla's Desert Hawks T-shirt and jeans gawked at me from above a red bandanna that covered most of his face. The bandanna didn't stop me from recognizing the person behind it: Jesse Hycamp. I wasn't sure what Hycamp found more shocking—the fact that I was standing in the tub, or the fact that I was standing in the tub with a man holding a gun. I tried to mask the look of recognition in my eyes and moved closer to Terry, who still had a firm grip on his bulletless gun.

"No need to panic," I blurted out. "The gun's empty."

Terry immediately followed up by saying, "She's lying. It's fully loaded and ready for action." He cocked the trigger. "So I suggest you just relax until the cops get here." He glanced at his watch and added, "which should be in about three minutes."

There was movement behind Jesse, and two other masked students wearing Desert Hawks gear appeared in the doorway behind him.

"Who are these guys?" The question came from a tall, muscle-bound "kid" who was squeezed into a St. Priscilla's T-shirt that appeared three sizes too small for him. "They're way too old to be students."

"Gee, thanks," I said.

Jesse's response was to back out through the bathroom doorway. I guess Terry's gun, bullets or no bullets, had done the trick.

The door to the hallway slammed shut, and I jumped. Jesse had bolted, and I was pretty sure he wasn't going for help. "Damn," muttered the other "student," whose scorpion tattoo, along with the red bandanna, tagged him as a gang member despite the St. Priscilla's T-shirt and cap.

"So now what?" the giant Scorpion asked.

His friend's response was to pull a gun from his waistband and point it at my head. He fixed Terry with a cold stare. "Hand over the gun, or I blow off her face."

I nudged Terry, hoping he'd take it as a warning to keep quiet. We didn't want to press our luck and get the armed Scorpion more riled up than he already was. I had a strong suspicion that his gun was actually loaded.

Instead, Terry, his voice dripping with bravado, said, "I just changed my mind about you relaxing until the cops get here. In fact, if I were you, I'd take a cue from your friend and get the hell out of here before campus Security shows up."

"But they're even older than we are," I added for good measure. "So you'll have plenty of time to get away if you leave right now." Regardless of whether or not Security arrived before or after the Scorpions got away, the fact remained that I'd recognized Jesse Hycamp as one of the would-be thieves: It was therefore only a matter of time before Roy arrested him and his partners in crime.

The muscle-bound Scorpion took off, and we were left alone to face his armed companion. When I saw his hand waver, I realized that, regardless of his intent, it might be only a matter of seconds before the gun would go off. Had Terry not been holding onto me, I would have taken a free fall to the tub floor. The Scorpion's voice was muffled by his bandanna, but there was no mistaking his growing impatience. "I said—hand over the gun!"

Terry nodded in submission and reached out his right arm as if surrendering his weapon. In the flash of an instant, he pitched the gun squarely at the Scorpion's face while pushing me down into the tub with his left hand. The Scorpion's face burst into a bloody spray. He went down hard, his hand grabbing the shower curtain and pulling it loose in a profusion of pink vinyl. Plastic daisy hooks scattered across the floor, and the metal curtain rod broke free of the wall with a sharp *crack*. The fallen Scorpion tried to get up but slipped on the tile, which was slick with his own blood, and fell awkwardly back to the floor, twisting his leg. All I could think of was how I was going to explain this mess to the Bennett twins.

Terry wrestled the gun from the Scorpion's hand and placed it in the sink where it would be out of reach, then helped me to my feet. "Are you all right? I didn't know what else to do. I had to get you out of the way."

I rubbed my left elbow, which was already turning purple where it had hit the rim of the tub. "I'll live," I said, my eyes focused squarely on the figure slumped on the floor, his right shoulder propped against the wall.

Terry knelt beside the Scorpion and inspected the damage. "You'll need some stitches, and it looks like they'll have to reset your nose, but you'll make it." He pulled a towel from a bar next to the sink and soaked it with some cold water before handing it to the boy, who looked to be no older than 18. "Here. Hold this up to your face."

"I'm calling Roy." I didn't know if I'd be able to sufficiently gather my wits about me, or stop shaking long enough, to accomplish that task. I was completely responsible for this near-catastrophe. I could have gotten Terry killed—gotten both of us killed.

"You know this kid?" Terry asked. The Scorpion was now groaning in pain as he sat on the floor.

"Not this one."

Eddie Gruber, eyes wide, rushed into the room while I was on the phone giving Roy a quick and dirty explanation of what had happened. "What in the Sam Hill is going on here?!" he said, his eyes bulging even wider as they took in the bathroom scene and Terry kneeling over the bleeding Scorpion. "Where are the Bennett girls?!"

I retrieved my purse and dropped my phone into it. "They're not here—they're safe." I glanced at Terry. "Roy's on his way."

"Who's the bloody kid?" asked Gruber. "One of our students?"

"I highly doubt it. He needs some medical attention, but he'll be all right. There were two others, but they got away."

Ralph Michaels erupted into the room and ran squarely into Eddie, nearly knocking him off his feet. He regarded the strange tableau: Terry on the floor, kneeling beside what appeared to be a badly hurt student decked out in Desert Hawks clothing. Smears of blood and daisy shower rings dotted the white-tiled floor, creating a bizarre work of pop art, a study in pink, yellow, and red. "What happened here?"

"Terry—my husband—agreed to help me stake out the Bennetts' room in an attempt to catch the theft ring in action." I smiled at Terry. "And we did."

Ralph pulled a tiny leather-covered pad from his jacket pocket. "Who gave you the okay to conduct a stake-out on St. Priscilla's premises?"

"No one, but…."

Ralph pointed to the two guns, the empty one in Terry's hand and the loaded one in the sink. "Who do the guns belong to?"

"This one's mine, but it isn't loaded," said Terry. "That one's loaded—it belongs to the kid, here."

Ralph moved away from me and over to the window to observe the parking lot below. Sirens blasted as fire engines, paramedic vans, and squad cars careened across the macadam and screeched to a halt outside Thatcher House. Within minutes, the tiny room was buzzing with activity. EMTs and two of Roy's uniformed officers entered with guns drawn: One of them was Deputy Caroline Steele, and the other was a part-time deputy named Frank Schmidt. I was relieved to see that Roy wasn't with them. I wasn't prepared for the dressing-down that I knew was to come. I began to feel a sense of dread as I watched Schmidt, his face expressionless, motion for Terry to stand. While Steele placed the guns in two separate plastic bags, Schmidt wrenched Terry's hands behind his back and cuffed them with zip ties.

"Ow!" The pain in Terry's eyes as he looked at me was more than physical. I could see accusation in them, too. And I didn't blame him.

"Wait, no!" I cried out. "You're arresting the wrong person!"

I tried to get close to Terry, but Schmidt backed me off with two hands. "Ma'am, you're going to have to stay back, or we'll have to cuff you, too."

"But he's not the criminal. He used that gun to defend us! And it wasn't even loaded!" I pointed at the Scorpion sitting up against the tub, where two paramedics were working on bandaging his nose. "That's your criminal! He belongs to the Scorpions gang—he's one of the thieves who's been burglarizing this building."

"Guns, loaded or not, aren't permitted anywhere on this campus, Amanda," said Ralph. "You know that as well as I do."

I heard Roy's familiar voice and turned to see him winding his way through all the official personnel. "Clear out this room," he ordered Steele. "We don't have space for all these people in here right now. Everyone outside except you"—he pointed at me— "Terry, and necessary medical personnel." He turned to Schmidt. "I'll take it from here, Frank. You and Caroline can take off now."

Ralph started to speak, and Roy shut him down with a raised hand. "Take your crew back to the Security Department. I'll be down as soon as I'm done here."

Ralph nodded his head and led Eddie out the door. I could hear him muttering under his breath about being "kicked off his own crime scene." He was clearly not happy about being dismissed.

"Sit." Roy gestured for me to perch at the foot of one of the beds and walked over to the bathroom door to talk to the EMTs. A moment later, he released Terry from his cuffs. "You're lucky that kid wasn't hurt worse than he was, or I'd have no choice but to take you in." He pulled his iPad from his jacket pocket. "Okay, tell me what happened. I need details."

I told him about my plan to stake out one of the dorm rooms in hopes of catching the Scorpion's theft ring. "There were three," I said, "but I recognized one of them—Jesse Hycamp. He took off as soon as he spotted me in the tub with Terry."

"You were in the tub?"

"When we heard them outside the door, we hid behind the shower curtain so we'd have a few extra minutes to call Security," Terry explained.

Roy brought out a paper pad from his pocket, scribbled something on it, and handed it to me.

"What's this?" I asked, bewildered.

"It's a citation for trespassing. You may be under contract with St. Priscilla's, but breaking and entering is still a crime."

"But I didn't break in. This is Becky and Blair Bennett's room. They gave me permission to use it." I held up the key card. "See? They gave me their key card to the building." I showed him the room key. "And their room key." I retrieved my phone from my purse and handed it to him. "Call them. They'll tell you."

To my surprise, Roy scrolled through my directory, found the Bennetts' number, and placed the call. He moved to the hallway so I couldn't hear what was being said. My stomach was beginning to act up, and I was feeling drained and woozy. I was happy to see the paramedics place the Scorpion, who was now wide awake and fixing me with a venomous stare, onto a stretcher. That meant the bathroom would soon be available for the retching that, at the moment, I was struggling to suppress.

Terry reached over and took my hand. He didn't have to ask me what was wrong. He was familiar with the signs and knew I was fighting off a major panic attack.

Roy returned and reached for the citation he'd just handed me. "You're off the hook on trespassing. But don't get your hopes up. I'm thinking obstruction of justice—interference with an official police case. Do you realize that you could have gotten both of you killed?" He shook his head and muttered, "Lord, Amanda, we've been through this before." He redirected his attention to Terry. "And you?! You bring a gun onto this campus—into this dorm room?! Really?!" He shook his head in disgust.

"That guy the EMTs just carted out," I said, my voice shaking with anger, "is a Scorpion who came here to commit burglary and threatened to, and I quote, 'blow her face off,' 'her' being me. Terry used his gun to save my life, and I wouldn't expect him to do anything less." I narrowed my eyes at Roy in defiance. "No shooting was involved. Terry's gun is empty—no bullets."

Again, Roy pulled the citation pad from his pocket, wrote something on it, and this time handed it to Terry. "Well, nevertheless, your hero is getting a citation for bringing a weapon onto this campus."

"I have a permit for that gun," Terry said.

"I guess you didn't see the signs plastered all over campus—you know, the ones with pictures of slashed-out guns on them with captions that say, 'No weapons beyond this point.'"

I felt that I had to remind Roy exactly who the real criminals were in this scenario. "I don't know how many times I've brought up Jesse Hycamp's name, and you kept saying that you can't do anything until he actually commits a crime. Well, now he has—at least he was about to, until Terry and I stopped him. So you can go ahead and bring him in for questioning." I glanced at Terry. "We're willing to serve as witnesses."

Roy got on his cell and called Steele. "Caroline, put an APB out on Jesse Hycamp."

"The Scorpion the paramedics just took out—have you ever seen him before?" I asked.

"His name's Sam Ramirez. He's got quite an impressive rap sheet for someone so young. He also happens to be a person of interest in the murder of a 15-year-old, a rival gang member."

"Will you be talking to him today?"

"As soon as the hospital clears it." His mouth broke into a brief smile. "As much as I hate to admit it, Terry, you did us all a favor by throwing that gun at him. He's slipped through our fingers more than a few times."

"Excuse me." I raced to the bathroom and, pink daisies crunching under my feet, made a hasty path to the commode. When I emerged ten minutes later, Terry and Roy were seated side-by-side on one of the beds, elbows resting on their knees. Both of them looked exhausted.

"Feel better?" Terry asked.

"Yes, thanks."

Roy rose from the bed. "I was just telling Terry that this stake-out idea of yours was way over the line, and—"

"Cory Matuck's staying at our house," I interjected. "I'm sure he knows more than he's saying, and I think he might be ready to talk to you now."

"What makes you think I can get him to talk? I tried when he was at the hospital, and he bolted out of there without telling me a thing. I had Caroline try to get through to him the day you were at the station, but even she couldn't get a word out of him."

"You have to at least try, Roy. Someone at St. Priscilla's is pulling the Scorpions' strings. Both Cory and Zach Christopoulos have said so. And I think they have a good idea of who that person is—they just haven't been able to come to terms with it, or they're just too plain scared to tell anyone. Another thing—the thieves didn't break into the Bennetts' room any more than Terry and I did. They had a key card to this building and what must have been a master key to all the rooms. And did you notice how Ramirez was dressed just like a regular St. Priscilla's student? That's how they've been getting into the building unnoticed— they're blending in. They can simply walk into Thatcher House whenever they want, into whichever room they want. It's the perfect cover."

Although he'd stopped taking notes, Roy appeared to absorb everything I'd been saying. When I was finished, he said, "Try to keep Cory at your place until noon tomorrow, will you? It'll take me the rest of the night to clear things up here. I have to stop in at Security to talk to Ralph, and then I need to go back to the station and see where we are with finding Hycamp. The sun'll be up long before I get to the hospital and question Ramirez."

After Roy left, Terry and I walked out to the parking lot in silence. Finally, I blurted out my apology in a rush of tears. "Terry, I'm sorry! I could have gotten us killed. I can't even think what—"

Terry stopped me in my tracks, put his arms around me, and kissed me as if his life depended on it. "Amanda, I love you. We both survived, and your stake-out idea worked. And despite his threats about having us arrested for obstruction of justice, I think Roy's beginning to realize that you've contributed a lot to this investigation."

"I love you more than anything, you know."

He smiled. "Yep, I know. It's part of your charm."

***

Terry and I both slept until the alarm clock woke us at noon Saturday. Over lunch, I related the events of the previous night to Cory. "Detective Staatz will be here sometime this morning. He wants to talk to you."

Cory shook his head slowly. "I have nothing to say to him." He frowned. "And you lied to me. You said that you were going to be house-sitting for your Aunt Sally last night."

I touched his arm. "Cory, we couldn't tell anyone about our plan. You know that, don't you?"

"All I know is that you don't trust me."

I was about to respond but was interrupted by the ringing of our landline. "It's Dinah," said Terry, handing me the receiver.

"Hi!" I said, evoking every bit of cheerful energy I could muster.

"Roy told me all about your adventure," she said, "or should I say 'misadventure.' I'm calling to see if you've recovered yet. My gosh, Amanda, you could have been killed! What were you thinking?"

"Hey, we caught the thieves—at least one of them. And Roy will get the other two soon, I'm sure."

"I think you need a break from all this excitement. Are you up for lunch tomorrow?"

"Just you and me?" I didn't think Roy would be too keen on a social get-together with Terry and me. At least not yet.

"Uh-huh, just you and me. I'll pick you up at 12:30."

As long as I was in phone mode, I decided to call the Bennetts to warn them about what they'd find back at their dorm. Since they were always together, the problem was which twin to call, Becky or Blair? I decided to approach it alphabetically. "Becky, it's Mrs. Winters."

"Mrs. Winters, the sheriff called us, like in the middle of the night! We told him we gave you permission to use our room—that was okay, wasn't it? Did something bad happen?"

"That's what I'm calling about. There was an, uh, accident, and I wanted to fill you in before you walked in and saw the blood—"

"Blood! Please don't tell me that you killed someone in our room!"

"Of course not. I used your room to stake out the Thatcher House thieves, and it worked. But one of the would-be thieves was hurt."

"Seriously?!"

"Just a broken nose, is all."

"I didn't figure you for a violent person, Mrs. Winters."

"My husband did the nose-breaking, and it was an act of self-defense. Your room is fine, for the most part. There was some damage to the bathroom—nothing major. Maintenance and Housekeeping are going to take care of everything today, and I'll cover the expense of a new shower curtain. Are you enjoying the hotel?"

"It's fantastic! We're in the pool right now. We pretty much have the whole place to ourselves."

"Great. Well, I wanted to warn you about the bathroom, just in case." I'd almost forgotten to ask a very important question. "Becky, wait! Did you or Blair ever give a copy of your room key, or your building key card, to anyone?"

"No way."

"I didn't think so." I let out a cleansing breath. "You girls enjoy the rest of your day. Checkout's at three p.m."

"Thanks for everything, Mrs. Winters. You're the best!"

After hanging up with Becky, I peeked through the window and said to Terry, "I thought I heard a car in the driveway—Roy's here. I opened the door and before he could step inside, asked, "Did you have a chance to talk to Sam Ramirez?"

"I just came from the hospital."

"Did he tell you anything?"

"Yeah, after I promised to put in a good word for him with the D.A."

"And...?"

"Before I tell you anything more, I want to hear what Matuck has to say."

"Where *is* Cory?" asked Terry.

"He's right over there on the...." I turned to an empty sofa. "Oh, no...Terry, go check out the guest room—and the bathroom."

A moment later, Terry, looking distraught, returned to the living room. "Cory's gone. And it looks like he took all his stuff with him."

Chapter Nineteen

"Now what?" I went back to the front door, stepped outside, and looked up and down the street, but there was no sign of Cory. I turned to Roy. "While we're trying to figure this out, how about a cup of coffee? I just made some."

"No thanks." He folded his arms and looked at me as though I were directly responsible for Cory taking it on the lam yet again. "You told him I was coming here, didn't you?"

"I felt I had to—he was already upset that I lied to him about where we were last night. How was I to know he'd take off again?"

Roy took a step toward the door. "Well, I can't wait around for him to come back—I have too much work to do. Just give me a call if he shows up again."

"Wait," I said, and stood in front of the door to block his exit. "I have to know what Ramirez said."

"He confessed to being involved in the Thatcher House thefts."

This was beginning to feel like pulling teeth. "Well, yes, I already assumed that he was involved, since Terry and I caught him red-handed in the Bennetts' room. What about the St. Priscilla's employee who's working with the Scorpions? Did he give you a name? And did he say anything about the murders?"

"Amanda, yes, he did give me a name, but I can't tell you anything more until I have the person behind bars. I'm not taking any more chances with this case. Just when I think I'm getting a handle on things, something new pops up to complicate matters." He pointed a finger at Terry. "Like an armed citizen holding an unapproved stake-out in a student residence hall."

"Come on, Roy," I said. "You admitted that you wouldn't have Ramirez if Terry and I hadn't pulled off that stake-out. You owe me."

"I can tell you this. Someone at the university has been orchestrating the campus thefts in exchange for a hefty cut of the profits. As far as this person being involved with the deaths, I don't have any evidence at this point. One could speculate that Sherry found out who was behind the theft ring and that she was murdered to keep that person from being exposed."

"Laverne Hutchins in the Business Office lied to me about sending a letter of rescindment to a student who was mailed a tuition statement by mistake. Brent Redmond lied to me about paying students with cash for their participation in a beta test. And Lynn Goodman lied about talking to a Scorpion the other day."

Roy gave me a quizzical look. "What does any of that have to do with my investigation?"

"I don't know that it has. But I've been witness to quite a few lies from St. Priscilla's staff, lately, and I can't figure out why. I just thought you should know."

"In my job, I've learned that most people lie every day, for all kinds of reasons—sometimes for no reason at all. I wouldn't give it too much thought."

"That's a bit cynical, isn't it?" I said as I moved aside to let him pass.

He didn't respond but walked silently to his car, got in, and pulled out of the driveway.

"Let's open that bottle of champagne left over from New Year's," said Terry.

"You really feel like celebrating right now? With champagne? Before noon?"

"Yes, and if you don't help me drink it, what's left in the bottle is going to go flat."

I shrugged. "Okay. I guess we've earned a little day drinking after last night."

In the kitchen, Terry reached into the back of the fridge and pulled out our lone bottle of Cook's. We sat at the table, sipping from crystal flutes and engaging in small talk about Dinah and Roy, about the possibility of getting a dog, about Jeff and Megan, whom—in Jeff's absence—Terry felt free to describe as "lovely and sweetly nerdish." For a little while, things felt good. Things felt normal. Then abruptly, stark reality returned in a dark cloud of anxiety.

"I've got to find Cory before the Scorpions do," I said. "They're going to be especially nervous now that Sam Ramirez has been arrested. Will you drive me over to Thatcher? Maybe Cory went back to his dorm."

Terry's eyes practically popped out of their sockets. "Are you kidding me, Amanda?! Go back to Thatcher House?! Today?! After all the trouble we just got into?!"

"Well, as long as you don't bring your gun along—"

"—no, Amanda. You can just put that idea right out of your head. I'm not driving anywhere. Both of us are staying right here for the rest of the day." When I got up from the kitchen table, he added, "And don't call Aunt Sally, or Dinah, or Jeff to ask them to drive you to the campus, because if you do, I'll call Roy and tell him what you're up to. We witnessed an attempted crime by a dangerous gang. The Scorpions could be watching our house right now."

"Terry, they were wearing masks. I probably wouldn't even be able to point any of them out in a lineup."

"You recognized Jesse Hycamp, and he knew it. That's why he ran."

Defeated, I returned to my chair at the kitchen table.

Terry poured a second glass of champagne for each of us. "Let's spend a few productive minutes trying to figure out Roy's next step. Which St. Priscilla's employee do you think he's going to arrest?"

"I'm thinking Ian Malcolm. He's the director of Financial Aid. He works with money all day long—chances are he's become quite fond of it."

"Mike Kraemer worked with money, too."

"Yes, but I don't think even Roy would arrest a dead person."

I set down my empty flute, rose from the table, and said, "Terry, I can't just sit here and wait for who knows how long. If we leave right now, we might be able to catch up to Roy and follow him; it's the only way we'll be able to find out who he's about to arrest."

"You want us to stalk Roy Staatz, a deputy commander of the District 1 Maricopa County Sheriff's Office?"

"I wish you wouldn't put it that way. You make it sound so...ridiculous."

"It *is* ridiculous. We'd never catch up to Roy. We don't even know where he's going. Have some patience, Amanda—you'll probably get an update tomorrow during your lunch with Dinah."

"You're right. At this point, it would make far more sense to go back to Thatcher House and look for Cory than to try and follow Roy."

Terry groaned. "I told you, no. I already have to pay a huge fine for bringing my gun onto St. Priscilla's campus. I don't even want to think about what Staatz would do if he found out I drove you back there. Not to mention we've both been drinking—the last think I need is a DUI."

"Bringing the gun to campus was your idea, if you recall. If I'd known that you were even considering it, I would have said no."

"Why don't you call that friend of Cory's...what's his name? The football player friend you and Dinah met the other night. Have *him* try to find Cory."

I perked up immediately. "Zach Christopoulos! That's actually a really good idea."

"Well, I do have them every now and then."

Zach answered on the first ring.

"Zach, it's Amanda Winters."

"Listen, Mrs. Winters, everyone knows what happened at Thatcher House last night. And someone in particular isn't at all happy about it.

"I stifled a scream of frustration and gritted my teeth. "Zach, will you please tell me who that 'someone' is? I'm tired of all the dancing around here."

"I only know for sure who the messenger is. I've been told to keep my mouth shut and to have nothing more to do with you, or else."

"Or else what?"

"Or else I can go ahead and cancel next semester's courses and use the refund as a down payment on my casket."

"Well, I actually just called to ask you to do me a small favor."

"Sorry, Mrs. Winters—no."

"I need to find Cory—fast. Surely you can just check around campus to find out if anyone's seen him...."

"I can't do it—sorry."

"Okay, Zach. I'll try to find Cory without you."

***

"We're not going off on some wild goose chase, Amanda! I mean it this time. I don't want you going back to that apartment. I don't even want *me* going back to that apartment. We're going to stay right here and let Roy handle this."

"Terry, I'm sure Zach knows who at St. Priscilla's is working with the Scorpions. We have to convince him to come clean about it, and the only way to do that is to talk to him face-to-face."

"Amanda, just please try to relax. You're going to work yourself up into another panic attack."

But I couldn't relax. At dinner, I tried to eat the left-overs Terry reheated for us, but I couldn't. I tried to concentrate on an episode of my favorite cooking reality show, but I couldn't. Every ten minutes or so, I jumped up to check the landline to see if it was working. I thought for sure Roy would have called by now with some news. He knew how badly I wanted to be kept in the loop, and, after all, I was officially on his payroll. I deserved to know what was happening.

"Why doesn't he call?" I said as we locked things up for the night.

"Where's your cell phone?" asked Terry. "Doesn't Staatz usually call you on your cell?"

"Oh my gosh! Where did I put it?!" I checked my purse and the pockets of the shirt and pants I'd worn that day. "It's not here!"

We searched the entire house, all the usual places. My cell phone wasn't anywhere.

Terry's eyes brightened with an epiphany. "The car! I'll bet it fell out of your purse. It wouldn't be the first time."

I hurried to the garage door, flipped on the light switch, and pressed my face against the passenger-side window. Just as Terry had suspected, my cell phone was on the floor, half-hidden under the seat. I checked for messages, and sure enough, there was one from Roy. As I listened, I shook my head in disbelief.

"What?!" pressed Terry from the kitchen doorway.

"Roy arrested Lynn Goodman."

"The redheaded receptionist with the ponytail?!"

"She had the security clearance, Terry. She had access to all the buildings and maintained detailed calendars for all the resident students. I even saw her talking to one of the Scorpions yesterday, but I never made the connection."

"What about Sherry's murder?"

"Roy didn't say anything about a murder charge. I'll call him right now."

"Maybe you should wait till morning," said Terry. "It's kind of late."

"If I'm going to get any sleep tonight, I have to call him now, and if you're going to get any sleep tonight, he'd better answer."

I made the call, but neither Terry nor I got much sleep that night.

***

I tried Roy again the next morning but had to leave another message. Despite the fact that I didn't allow my cell phone out of my sight for a minute, it refused to ring. I was starting to think he was avoiding me. Terry left to run some errands, and I started an editing project I'd been putting off: a science article about the effects of fast food on the morbidity of monkeys in the Amazon rain forest. At 12:30, I went outside to wait for Dinah to pick me up for lunch. Within minutes, she pulled into the driveway.

Aunt Sally was in the back seat. "Surprise!" she said, leaning forward eagerly. "This is going to be great! Woo-hoo! Girls night out!"

"It happens to be 12:30 in the afternoon," I reminded her.

"I ran into Aunt Sally this morning at Bashas," said Dinah. "And—"

"No need to explain," I said, having learned long ago the importance of choosing one's battles.

"So where are we going for lunch?" asked Aunt Sally. "Italian? Chinese? Thai?"

"I thought we'd try that new French café in Chandler," said Dinah. "French Vi's."

Aunt Sally's face morphed into a mass of frown wrinkles. "French fries?"

"No," chuckled Dinah. ""Vi is the owner, and she's French, or so I gather."

"I guess that'll be all right," said Aunt Sally. "But I'm not eating any snails."

We were settling at a table by the window when a call came through on my cell. I checked the screen and said, "I have to take this. It's Roy."

"So much for your break," sighed Dinah.

"Amanda, I know you're probably at lunch with Dinah right now, but I thought you'd want me to call you with an update."

"It's about time, Roy. I was beginning to think I'd never hear from you."

"I arrested Lynn Goodman for her involvement in the Scorpion theft ring. Thanks to Ramirez's signed confession, we have enough to make the arrest stick."

I scowled into the phone. "You already told me that in last night's message. I thought you said you were calling with an update. An update is something new—this isn't new."

"What's new is that I've cleared Goodman in Sherry's murder. We checked her alibi, and it's airtight. Her neighbor saw her leave her house at 7:30 the morning of the murder. She never could have made it to the university until an hour past the estimated time of Sherry's death."

"So you still don't have a suspect?!"

"I wish I could tell you otherwise, but no. It looks like there's no connection between the thefts and the murder. And the circumstances surrounding Mike Kraemer's death remain inconclusive. We still can't be sure whether it was murder, suicide, or an accident."

"What about Cory Matuck? Do you have any idea where he is?" *Or whether he's even still alive?*

"Well, he hasn't called me, if that's what you mean. And I really don't have the time or the resources to be scouring the streets looking for someone who doesn't want to be found."

"What about Jesse Hycamp?"

"Haven't found him yet, but it's only a matter of time before we get him—Ramirez has given us some good leads." He paused for a moment and said, "Can you hand the phone to Dinah for a second?"

"Sure." I passed the phone to Dinah. "Roy wants to talk to you."

A moment later, Dinah smiled and said, "I love you, too," and passed the phone back to me.

At least some things were moving along nicely.

After the server took our orders, I shared Roy's news about Lynn Goodman.

"Then I guess this lunch is a celebration," said Dinah. "No more thefts at St. Priscilla's."

I shook my head. "It's way too early to celebrate—if you want to believe Roy, that is."

Dinah frowned. "What are you talking about?"

"Roy still has no suspects in Sherry's murder, and he still believes that Mike's death might have been an accident. But I think I've come up with some answers for him."

"Why didn't you tell him that over the phone when you had the chance?" asked Dinah.

"I want to be sure. If my theory turns out to be wrong, he'll never ask for my help on a case again."

While we waited for our server to bring the check, another call came through on my cell, and this time it was Zach Christopoulos. "I have some good news, Mrs. Winters. I found Cory."

After a moment's silence, I asked, "Zach, just tell me. Where is he?"

"He's here in my apartment. He didn't know where else to go. He says the Scorpions are after him again, and this time they mean to kill him."

"Did you call 9-1-1?"

"No, Mrs. Winters. They don't send anyone if you only think that you're going to get killed."

"Please, just don't let him leave. I'll be right there."

Zach's response was a click as he disconnected.

"Dinah," I said. "I think I just found the person who can confirm that my theory is right. Remember the apartment we visited the other night? Zach Christopoulos' apartment?"

"How can I forget?" Then, with a look of distrust, she added, "Why?"

"Because Cory's there right now, and I need to get to him before the Scorpions do."

"Amanda, Roy would be extremely upset with me if I went back there, to put it mildly."

"It could be a matter of life and death," I said.

"Well, if you put it that way...."

I left a message for Roy asking him to meet us at Zach's apartment. Then I called Terry and left a message for him. In Dinah's car, I experienced a pang of guilt at knowing that I might be about to once more place her and Aunt Sally in harm's way. But I felt I had no choice: Not only did I believe that Cory could confirm my suspicions, I believed that he was correct in thinking his life was in danger. My hope was that Roy would show up before anything major happened.

Half an hour later, Dinah parked on the street in front of Zach's apartment building.

"You and Aunt Sally wait out here for me," I said. Although I really needed their support, there was no way I was going to let my cluster C take precedence over their safety. Dinah protested until I persuaded her that there was nothing to worry about.

This time, I was wrong.

Chapter Twenty

The door to the building was unlocked. I stepped
into the dimly lighted hallway and stared up into an
even darker hallway before making my way up the
stairs. A twinge of unease prompted me to reach into
my purse for my cell phone. I checked the time. When
would Roy get here? I had no idea, since I didn't even
know if he'd received my message yet. It would be up
to me to make Cory understand that he'd be safe in Sun
Lakes with Terry and me until the source of his fear
was eliminated. I'd persuade him that Roy could be
trusted. I wanted everything to be nicely packaged for
Roy, so he could tie the final string and arrest the
monster who'd murdered Sherry and, very possibly,
Mike. I reached the top landing, and Zach's door
opened before I had a chance to knock. But it wasn't
Zach who'd opened the door. It was Jesse Hycamp.

I turned for the stairs and grabbed the railing to
make a quick descent, but Hycamp caught me by the
collar and jerked me back into the apartment. The living
room was dark. The window blinds were drawn, and
the air was thick with smoke from the kind of cigarettes
you couldn't find on the service-counter shelves at
Safeway. Through the haze, I could plainly see Cory.
He was seated in an armchair in a corner of the room.
Although conscious, he had obviously sustained
another beating that had opened the wounds from his
earlier run-in with the Scorpions.

"Angel, our visitor's here," said Hycamp to the giant
Scorpion I recognized from the Thatcher House stake-

out. He pushed me roughly onto the sofa. "Watch her. I'm just going to check outside to see if her old man's car is out there." His eyes nailed me with a smoldering gaze. "Don't you move. I'll be back in a minute."

Angel, whose massive, tattooed arms bulged with muscles, held the butt of a revolver that was poised for another blow to Cory's head. I had a short window of opportunity, here, and I knew I'd have to act fast.

"Angel," I said, surprised to hear that my voice was cooperating with my brain. "That's funny. Your name doesn't fit you at all. Now, 'Knucklehead' or 'Dimwit'—either of those would work."

I'd hit a nerve. Angel whirled toward me in a bizarre pirouette that appeared strangely delicate for someone so huge. Taking advantage of the moment, Cory stumbled out of the chair and threw his own linebacker frame at Angel's legs. The Scorpion fell like a sack of wet concrete, landing squarely on top of Cory. The gun was knocked from Angel's hand and skittered across the floor. I immediately went after it and was bending down to pick it up when a familiar voice said, "Not so fast, Amanda. Step away from the gun."

It was Brent Redmond, and Jesse Hycamp was right behind him.

"Brent," I said, slowly rising to a full standing position while trying to figure out how to grab the gun, aim, and, if necessary, actually get it to shoot. "I wish I could say I'm surprised to see you here."

I pulled out my cell and punched random buttons, hoping to connect with someone…anyone. In one fluid motion, Brent came over to me and yanked the cell phone from my hand.

He turned to Angel. "Get up off the floor and get your gun."

Angel did as he was told.

"Give it to me."

Angel handed the gun to Brent.

The room began to spin, and my breathing grew ragged and shallow. This was a familiar sensation: I knew that I was about to die. And judging by the pure evil in Brent's eyes, this time it might be the real thing. I shut my eyes tightly. *Stop. Stop! No panic attack—not now!* I opened my eyes with the sudden realization that my symptoms could be due to the pungent fog of funny smoke I'd been inhaling. Maybe I wasn't having a panic attack at all. I willed myself to refocus.

Brent jerked the gun at me. "You couldn't just mind your own business, Amanda?"

Cory, who'd remained on the floor up to this point, got to his feet, his weight causing the floorboards to creak. Brent cocked the trigger. "Hold it, Cory. Take a seat over there on the couch—you too, Amanda."

I had to engage Brent somehow. I had to get the gun away from him. *Oh God, please let Roy be pulling up to the building right at this moment.*

Cory spoke up, his voice numb. "You wanted me to talk, Mrs. Winters. I'm ready to talk now—I guess I have nothing to lose."

Brent smiled. "You're right, Cory. You have nothing to lose—and neither do I. So go ahead. Talk away."

I knew what Brent meant by his having nothing to lose. He'd decided to kill us, so how much we knew no longer mattered. I hoped Cory's story would be a long one.

Cory touched a tentative hand to a fresh wound on his head, and when he drew it away, it was full of blood. He absently wiped his hand on his jeans as he began his account. "Miss Davenport found out that a lot of the online students Redmond's been signing up for classes are fakes—he's been registering Scorpion gangbangers for full credit loads, which makes them eligible for federal financial aid. But they never actually take any classes."

That's all I needed to confirm that my theory was right. The "something bigger" that Zach had alluded to was financial aid fraud, and Brent was behind it. "Your beta test is a fake, too," I said. "After I heard you talking on the phone with a student about paying him for completing some test assignments, I started to wonder. I came to the conclusion that you have St. Priscilla students do assignments that the Scorpions then turn in as their own work. They need only two or three weeks' worth of papers, just enough to satisfy the instructors until their Title IV funds are released. The Scorpions go to the Business Office to collect their checks and give you your share—and then they disappear. A month or two later, they use other people's names and Social Security numbers to sign up for the next group of classes—I hear they're quite adept at hacking and identity theft. In some cases, they might even talk their friends and relatives into letting them use their identities in return for a share of the funds. Did I get that all right, Brent?"

Brent's smirk changed to a look of astonishment. "Amanda, I knew you had a knack for detective work, but I have to say, watching you in action is a real pleasure."

The rest of the pieces tumbled into place quickly. "The list of students I found on the Tomb floor the day Sherry was murdered—16 of them are dead. You've been registering deceased students and collecting financial aid for them, too." *Students like Samantha Baranski.*

He clapped his hands in mock applause. "Well done, Amanda."

"Laverne Hutchins is helping you, I'm thinking. She must have overheard Mike and Sherry talking about their suspicions and told you about it. The day after Sherry was murdered, I saw Mike letting himself into the Tomb. I found it odd, but now it dawns on me that he was looking for the files Sherry told him about—the 16 files that belonged to the latest group of dead students you'd registered. But he never found them, because they weren't there. You followed Sherry down to the Tomb and—and—" I couldn't finish the sentence.

Brent smirked. "Now don't go accusing me of murder, Amanda. That's not my style. Angel, here, took care of Sherry, and Jesse handled Kraemer. These guys have to earn their keep somehow." He laughed and stared into the brown haze of the room as if he were recalling a fond memory. "I was there to watch the whole thing, though. It was quite fascinating."

"Angel," I said, "I found your ring at the scene of the murder. The sheriff has it now. All he has to do is put it on your finger, just like Prince Charming put that shoe on Cinderella's foot. Only this time, a DNA test and a perfect fit will get you life in prison or worse."

Angel laughed. "Perfect fit? My old lady's got me on a diet, and I been losin' a lotta weight...the ring slipped off my finger 'cause it don't fit me no more." He scowled at Brent. "I don't have to worry 'bout that ring, now, do I? You gonna take care of this?"

"You don't have a thing to worry about, Angel. No one will ever repeat what they've heard here today. I'll make sure of that."

Stall for time, Amanda. Think! "You had it all figured out, didn't you, Brent? If there was ever a slip-up—say, for instance, a bill accidentally went out to a deceased student and was intercepted by their family—Laverne would take care of that, wouldn't she?"

"Love that girl," said Brent. "That night she dropped me off in the parking lot, she mentioned seeing you and Terry. But you never saw her, did you?"

"Oh, I saw her, all right. But I didn't recognize her with her hair down—she looks a lot younger without the French twist. I thought she was a student. I have to ask you this, Brent. Are you the monster who locked my Aunt Sally in the Tomb?"

Jesse stepped forward. "I gotta take the credit for that one." He nodded toward Brent. "With a little bit of help. Someone needed to teach the old bat a lesson."

Brent laughed. "I couldn't give Jesse the Tomb key belonging to the Registrar's Office that Saturday because Patty had it, so I had to borrow Carole Ann's. That morning I strolled right into the English Department and took it while you and your aunt were back in your office talking some nonsense about Chinese food. By the way, it takes about two minutes to disconnect the security cameras around here, and another minute to reconnect them—easy peasy."

I repressed the urge to run at him full throttle—I knew I wouldn't stand a chance, not with his tight grip on the gun. I tried desperately to think of how I could stall for more time, but my brain had apparently gone to sleep.

Brent walked over to where Cory sat half-slumped on the sofa and gave his leg a hard kick. "Hey, guy, you still hurting?" He rubbed the muzzle of the gun across his chin. "Now here's the immediate problem. What do I do with the two of you?"

"Three, boss," said Angel. "Don't forget the guy in the bedroom."

"There's a guy in the bedroom?" I asked.

"Zach," said Cory. "He was unconscious when they put him in there."

A high-pitched voice outside the apartment announced, "Amanda, I gotta use the little girls' room."

Aunt Sally!

"You've got to be kidding me!" Jesse shouted. "What's *she* doing here?!"

Aunt Sally entered the apartment, wrinkled her nose and waved a hand through the air. "Someone's been smoking cigarettes in here, and they're definitely not Salem Lights."

Angel lumbered toward Aunt Sally, who by this time had seen Cory on the sofa, his face bloodied, and realized that she'd stumbled into a bad situation. Eyes wide, she turned and headed back to the hallway stairs, with Angel right behind her. The next sound I heard was a horrible clamor punctuated by screams.

Aunt Sally popped back into sight at the apartment door. "I'm all right, Amanda! The big galoot doesn't look so good, though. My foot somehow got in his way." She pointed to the bottom of the stairs. "I think he might need an ambulance."

I took advantage of the distraction to barrel head-first into Brent. The gun fell from his hand and slid across the floor.

As I hurried toward the gun, Dinah appeared in the doorway and put a protective arm around Aunt Sally. Her eyes first went to Brent, then to Jesse, and finally to Cory. "Amanda, are you all right? What's going on?!"

"Brent just confessed to arranging Sherry's and Mike's murders." I knelt to retrieve the gun from under the sofa. "He got these two Scorpions to do the dirty work for him."

Brent turned toward me, his face twisted in anger. "Who else did you invite to your little party, Amanda?"

The blare of sirens and the flashing of lights filled the apartment as multiple squads screeched to a halt in front of the building.

"I believe the other guests are just now arriving," I
said.

Epilogue

At Liam's Irish Pub in downtown Chandler, ten of us were gathered for dinner at one of the long tables running parallel to the bar: Terry and I, Jeff and Megan, Aunt Sally, Cory, Zach and Alana Christopoulos, Dinah, and Roy. It was the first time we'd gathered together in one place since Brent Redmond, Laverne Hutchins, and their Scorpion accomplices had been arrested.

When our server brought the champagne Terry had ordered, Aunt Sally said, "There have been a few times, lately, when I didn't think I'd ever taste this again." She raised her glass, and the rest of us followed suit. "Now here's an Irish toast I'd like to pass on to you from my sainted German mother: 'May the Good Lord take a liking to each and every one of you…but not too much, and not too soon.'"

We all cheered and drank to that. After the server took our food orders, the conversation turned to serious matters.

Dinah asked, "How much damage did Redmond do, anyway? Aside from the murders, I mean."

"Over a million dollars' worth," said Roy.

There was a collective gasp.

Jeff laughed and shook his head in disbelief. "Who thought financial aid fraud could be so rewarding?"

"Jeff!" Megan elbowed him, but it was a gentle nudge that made him laugh rather than cry out in pain. How I liked that girl.

"Well, I can tell you this," said Roy. "His final reward won't be anything like the one he had in mind."

"And here I thought the guy was about to get jumped in the parking lot that night I saw him with the Spiders—"

"Scorpions," I said.

"Whatever—when all the time he was in cahoots with them. They were probably mapping out their next move." She raised her glass in another impromptu toast. "Here's to Redmond—may they toss him in the slammer and throw away the key."

There was another hearty cheer.

Jeff asked, "How did he do it? How did Redmond get away with stealing more than a million dollars from the federal government?"

"He enrolled Scorpions for online business classes," said Roy. "The gangbangers were what the FBI calls 'straw students.' They had no intention of completing the courses they were registered for. When their checks came in, Laverne Hutchins cashed them, and she and Redmond took their shares—five-hundred to fifteen hundred dollars each—before giving the rest to whichever Scorpion's name was on the check."

"He also used the identities of deceased students," I said. "Since the tabs on those files are coded red, it was a simple matter for him to go down to the Tomb and pull the information he needed. It was even easier for him to persuade Laverne to help him. In exchange for a cut of the profits, she agreed to handle any communications from the government and to capture the funds when they came in. They split the money fifty-fifty."

"Wouldn't the Feds know not to give money to dead people?" asked Aunt Sally.

I shook my head. "They have no way of knowing they're dead. Financial aid is granted based only on need—not on how good or bad your credit is. Social Security numbers are never checked, because the credit bureaus aren't involved."

"How did you figure it out, Mrs. Winters?" asked Cory.

"The day after Sherry's murder, I took a call from the sister of one of the deceased students whose name Brent had used to apply for financial aid. A statement was generated and mailed to the student by mistake. I started to get suspicious when I found out that Laverne had lied about mailing a letter of rescindment to the student's mother."

"Both Sherry and Mike put two and two together," said Roy, "and that's what got them killed."

"I asked Redmond why we were getting cash instead of elective credit for our work," said Cory, "but he just got mad and told me not to worry about it and not to mention it to anyone. That was the first red flag."

"And the assignments Redmond was having us do were from BUS 101, a class that both Cory and I took years ago," said Zach, whose bruises from the beating he'd taken from Angel were healing almost as well as Cory's. "We couldn't understand why we were redoing old assignments for a beta test. It didn't make sense."

"I finally decided to go to Miss Davenport to see if she could explain the cash payments and the weird assignments Redmond was giving us." His voice broke when he added, "She was always willing to listen, you know? I never thought that she and Mr. Kraemer would end up dead because of what I told her."

Alana placed a hand on Cory's shoulder. "The murders weren't your fault. None of it was your fault."

"Alana is absolutely right," I said. "If you hadn't brought your concerns to Miss Davenport's attention, Brent's fraud operation might still be going on, and who knows what other havoc the Scorpions would be wreaking at St. Priscilla's."

"Detective Staatz," said Zach, "I just want to thank you again for giving me a break—I mean, six months' probation is no picnic, but it's a heck of a lot better than I deserve."

"Just don't forget our weekly meetings, Zach. They're a part of the deal." He raised his glass of champagne. "Now, to change the subject to something a bit more pleasant—Dinah and I have some good news."

"Ha!" exclaimed Aunt Sally. "I knew it! You two are gonna get hitched!"

I gave her a gentle scolding. "It isn't your news to tell, Aunt Sally."

Dinah laughed and said, "That's okay, Amanda." She took Roy's hand. "Yes, we're engaged. She held out her hand and proudly displayed a beautiful sapphire ring encircled with small diamonds.

"When's the big day?" asked Terry.

"We haven't set a date yet," said Dinah, "but we're thinking that a spring wedding in Sedona would be nice."

"Wow, Sedona!" exclaimed Aunt Sally. "Am I gonna be invited?"

"Of course," laughed Roy. "You're practically family."

While congratulations and blessings were being heaped on the couple, Terry got up from the table and went over to speak to the bartender.

"I hope he's not ordering more champagne," I said. "We all have to drive home."

I was leaning over the table to get a closer look at Dinah's ring, when I felt something cold and wet on the back of my neck. "Terry, really, this isn't the time or place—" But I could see that Terry was standing behind me, and that his lips were nowhere near my neck.

"What on earth?" I turned around to gaze into the most beautiful pair of brown eyes I'd ever seen. The dog, a miniature schnauzer puppy, lapped my cheek with his tongue and wagged his tail with excitement. His black button nose was set above a tiny white moustache, and his coat was black with streaks of silver.

"Amanda, meet Schnapps," said Terry with a grin that nearly covered the bottom half of his face. "The two of you are going to watch out for each other."

I happily swept the puppy into my lap. "Oh, he's gorgeous, Terry. Thank you!"

"To get him certified as a service dog, though, you'll need a doctor's prescription. And he'll need some training, which is going to cost me an arm and a leg, but we can talk about that later."

"Hmmm." Aunt Sally took a sip of champagne. "A real service dog—I guess that lets me off the hook."

I handed Schnapps back to Terry and got up from the table to give my aunt a hug. "No such luck, Aunt Sally—you're not getting off that easy. I have a feeling that Roy will have enough work to keep all of us busy for a very long time."

THE END

ABOUT THE AUTHOR

Carmen Will is a freelance writer and editor whose novel, *A Practicum for Murder*, was a finalist in Poisoned Pen Press' 2013 Discover Mystery contest.

Will, who earned a B.A. in Professional Communication with a specialization in writing and editing, lives in Sun Lakes, Arizona with her husband Wayne. Her first Amanda Winters' mystery is *Doubly Departed.*

www.ingramcontent.com/pod-product-compliance
Lightning Source LLC
Chambersburg PA
CBHW050416260626
47156CB00003B/1030